LOST RELICS

A SHARK KEY ADVENTURE

CHRIS NILES

Lost Relics is a work of fiction. Names, characters, places, and incidents are a product of the author's imagination or are used fictitiously, and any resemblance to actual persons, living or dead, business establishments, events, or locales is entirely coincidental.

Visit the author's website at chrisnilesbooks.com

The author appreciates your time to read this work. Please consider leaving a review wherever you bought this book, and please tell your friends who might also like it. The best way for a reader to find new favorites is still a recommendation from a trusted friend.

Cover by Shayne Rutherford at Wicked Good Book Covers

Edited by Staci Troilo

01150826

To Ric, for never letting me relax

NOTE

IF YOU'RE a fan of Wayne Stinnett, you may spot a familiar face as you're reading. My eternal thanks to Wayne for allowing his character to help mine out and for trusting me with him.

Wayne, you're the best mentor a burgeoning author could wish for. Drinks are on me. Forever.

PROLOGUE

Hispaniola, 1508

Íhon sat at the edge of a small clearing, its dirt packed from a thousand years of worship. He cradled the wooden ceremonial bowl against his side and carefully ground three large brown seeds into powder. For the other boys, it would have been the highest honor to assist the shaman in the cohoba ceremony, but Íhon's mother was the shaman's first wife and the sister of the Cacique. Everyone expected him to be chosen. Everyone except his sister, who'd found a snake in her blankets during the last hidden moon. She'd been threatening to tell on him every day since, and he'd been praying to the gods to close the shaman's eyes to his prank.

The shaman crouched before him, inspecting his work. The boy kept his head low, focused on the beans.

The cohoba ceremony was sacred, and if Íhon made a mistake in his preparations — if he chanted the wrong words, if he allowed his thoughts to drift — the connection to Atabey, the first god of his people, would be tainted.

The shaman nodded his approval and stood, his strong, narrow body rising far above Íhon's hunched one. Then he slowly glided around the clearing. Sixteen small fires burned around the outer circle, and a larger fire burned at the head of the ring to Íhon's right. Shamans from the other four tribes knelt in the center, a servant boy crouched behind each one.

"In the days before man, Atabey created the heavens above the trees and the earth below their roots. Atabey created two sons—Yúcahu and Guacar." The shaman raised a heavy golden icon high above his head. "Yúcahu was a good son. He awoke the earth and created the light and dark, the sea and the stone, the mountains and the soft ground. Yúcahu, the god of goodness, created animals. He taught the bird to fly and the fish to swim and the snake to hunt. Then he created man, and his work was complete." He placed the statue of Yúcahu on a low pedestal in the center of the clearing.

"Yúcahu is peace and goodness. But his brother Guacar was a jealous god. He was powerless to destroy Yúcahu's work, so he escaped to hide in the heavens and plot his brother's destruction. Guacar became wind and lightning, crashing waves and shaking earth.

He became sickness and death. Yúcahu did not fear for himself, but when he thought of the difficulty Guacar's jealousy would bring to the land, Yúcahu sent four spirits to the heavens to tame Guacar's anger and protect his creation."

Each of the four visiting shamans held a smaller golden icon. Íhon watched his mother's husband move from one to the next. He bowed low before each of them, touching his forehead to the earth, then he carried them to the center of the clearing and placed them on the pedestal around the larger statue of Yúcahu.

"Together we have used these zemís to call upon the spirits when we need their guidance. In times of war, representatives from each of our tribes have been granted safe passage to seek their wisdom and council in the quest for peace among us. In times of famine, our tribes have come together to seek comfort from the gods and to share what we have. The zemís have served us as we serve them." He sunk to one knee and bowed low to the collection of statues in the center of the circle. The other shamans touched their foreheads to the ground in unison.

"Since the beginning, Yúcahu and his spirit gods have protected us from Guacar. But now, Guacar has recruited new allies and sent them in their huge sailing ships from the east. They call him God. When we refuse to worship him, they take our women and kill our children." He turned to face the four elders. "I have sought Yúcahu's help to protect our people. But he came to me with the cohoba and told me we must allow Guacar to have a season of strength." Íhon heard gasps from the men in the clearing.

"In time, his jealousy and anger will destroy him, and then, humbled, he will restore Yúcahu to his throne in peace. During this season of darkness, the five zemís of Yúcahu and his spirit gods must be spread to the four corners of the sea, and we, his shamans, must guard them throughout the generations." The men all sat taller, recognizing the great honor and responsibility that lay ahead of them.

"As we take the cohoba together for the last time, the god of your tribe will lead each of you. He will show to you alone that which you and your descendants must do to protect the zemí he has entrusted to you." He paced slowly around the circle. "After tonight, we will not worship together again, and we will never speak of this. When it is time for our spirits to move on, we will teach one young faithful shaman in the secret ways. And when his time comes, he will do the same, so the zemí is always guarded."

The men nodded in unison.

"And when the time comes, Yúcahu will send a messenger to collect the five zemís. The messenger will channel the power of Yúcahu, and Guacar will finally be defeated. Yúcahu will once more rule over his creation, and the Taíno people will be restored."

He looked back to Íhon.

The boy rose to his tiny feet and clutched the large, smooth bowl in his arms.

The high priest knelt before each shaman. One after another, they drew the seed powder into their pipes while Íhon stood close, holding a glowing rock from the fire beneath the bowl. When all the shamans had been served, he placed the bowl in a special cradle before the high priest then retrieved his own stone from the fire. The heat rose from the stone and burned his small hands, despite the protection of a thick leather sling. But those burns, which Íhon would carry the rest of his life, reminded him of the protection of the gods and gave him confidence that one day in the future, the gods would reunite the tribes of the Taíno and restore prosperity to their people.

CHAPTER ONE

Present Day

Kate Kingsbury tossed an oily rag into a bin on the aft deck of her 45-foot derelict houseboat then jumped onto the dock. *Serenity* was tied in a shallow slip at Shark Key Campground and Marina, just east of Key West.

Shark Key's owner, Chuck Miller, ambled toward her. "I scheduled her at the shipyard for a complete refit after Thanksgiving, Kate. What's to work on?"

"The water pump was making a little whistle, nothing a little oil couldn't fix. Really, Chuck, I wish you wouldn't do this. She just needs to float, which she does just fine. You don't have to put a new engine in my boat for me."

"I know I don't have to. I want to." Chuck turned

back toward the little spit of land behind them. "All of this'd be gone if it wasn't for you."

"You'd have a lot more than this if it wasn't for me."

"I got more than enough, kiddo. And you're getting a new motor whether you like it or not. November twenty-ninth. Besides, I've already got the dredging scheduled, and I need your heap out of here for that." He winked and started back up the dock. "Come have lunch and a beer. Relax a little."

"Be up in a minute." Kate adjusted the straps of her swimsuit and kicked her greasy cutoffs onto the boat's wide, flat deck. In three steps she was off the end of the dock, soaring across the water and cutting gracefully through the surface. She dolphin kicked twenty-five yards out into the channel, rolled onto her back, then floated in the warm salt water.

A second later, a huge splash exploded behind her. Her seven-year-old German Shepherd swam up, grabbed a mouthful of her swimsuit at the hip, then started pulling her back toward the dock. She tapped his nose. "Whiskey, no." The dog tightened his grip on her suit. Kate twisted to keep her head above water. "Whiskey. Release!"

He opened his jaw, and Kate quickly untangled her suit from his sharp canines. One finger poked through a tooth-sized hole near the edge on her backside. She shook her head and swam back to the dock, the dog right behind her.

Back up on the dock, Whiskey shook the water from his fur. Kate grabbed a towel from the bow railing of *Serenity* and stood over the dog. "Dude. I can swim. This trying to rescue me every time I jump in the water business has got to stop. Please, buddy."

She pulled on a clean pair of shorts to cover the fresh hole in the back of her swimsuit then started across the parking lot toward the restaurant. She planted herself on a barstool beside a trim black woman and finished toweling off her hair.

"He jump in after you again?"

Kate nodded. "I've quit trying to tell him to stay. He doesn't listen. He thinks he needs to save me. I've got a call in to his trainer, 'cuz I don't know what else to do. I haven't been able to get more than fifty yards from the dock before he pulls me back. This is the third suit he's ruined since it happened."

"Kate, we're all still working through it. Give him some time."

Two months earlier, Whiskey was aboard the sixty-foot Hatteras yacht *Tax Shelter*, guarding Kate and her group of friends as they raised millions of dollars' worth of gold and gemstones belonging to Chuck's grandfather from a shipwreck near the Marquesas Keys. There'd been a little trouble. Kate and several others in the group had been injured, the *Tax Shelter* was blown sky high, and Whiskey's post-traumatic stress had been working overtime ever since.

"How's your arm?" Kate asked.

"I just got released from physical therapy. I've still got some work to get back to full strength, but it's looking good." Michelle Jenkins rubbed the spot where she'd been shot during the melee aboard the *Tax Shelter*.

Chuck popped through the kitchen door holding two red plastic baskets. His assistant manager and best friend Babette Wilkins stretched her foot out in front of her to catch the door. She balanced three more baskets on her left arm, and gripped two squeeze bottles of tartar sauce in her right.

Chuck nudged Michelle as he passed her. "Where's your dashing husband?"

"Right here!" William's voice boomed as he swept around the corner. He kissed his wife on the forehead and led her to the picnic table where Chuck and Babette were unloading the feast.

Kate slid behind the bar and loaded a bucket with beer and ice. She dropped it on the table and planted herself in front of a basket full of Babette's legendary grouper bites. "So, did you get it?"

William's eyes twinkled. "Yep. We just got back from the airport. I almost couldn't bear to leave her tied down out there. The way she sparkles in the sun...she's almost more beautiful than my wife."

Michelle slapped him on the shoulder then kissed his cheek.

Babette licked her fingers and tilted her head. "Wha…?" Her question sounded more like a caveman's grunt through a mouthful of grouper.

William grinned. "I wanted to surprise—" He broke off and they all turned toward the steps.

"*Hola, hola, mi familia!*" A huge black woman built like a linebacker and dressed for a nightclub climbed the steps then glided toward the table on three-inch platform heels.

"Kara!" Babette ran over and hugged the newcomer. "I'll get you a basket. Grab a beer and make yourself comfortable."

"Honey, there is no comfortable in this dress, but it's always better to be fabulous!" Kara perched herself on the end of the bench and swung her knees against the trestle. "Am I interrupting?"

"No, no, not at all. I'm glad you're here. But I must ask …" William looked her up and down. "You look lovely as always, but isn't it a little early for … this?"

Kara laughed. "Honey, I just came from an audition. The club is doing great, but I still gotta make these new girls pay for themselves." She grabbed her breasts and juggled them under her tight sequined top.

William cleared his throat, and the color on his dark cheeks deepened. Michelle winked at his embarrassment.

"What'd I miss?" Chuck dropped a basket of piping hot fish in front of Kara. She popped two of the crispy fried fish bits into her mouth and waggled her shoulders back and forth.

Chuck admired her surgeon's handiwork. "They look great, Kara. Really. Nice and, uh, balanced." His cheeks were redder than the baskets.

"I'm still getting used to the extra weight. How do you girls keep your balance all the time?" Her Adam's apple bobbed as she spoke.

Babette laughed and glanced at Kate and Michelle. "As the biggest girl here, I'll field that one. It helps we grew up with them, so it's more like boiling a frog one degree at a time. But my back does a lot of work to counter the extra weight. And it's easier if you don't wear three-inch platform heels around. I'll stick with flip-flops, thank you very much. But I promise you'll get used to them."

"I can't stop looking at them!"

Everyone at the table burst out laughing.

Kate coughed, then balled up a napkin and threw it at Kara. "Just ... stop! I can't eat and laugh at the same time!"

Kara wiggled her shoulders one more time for good measure, then waved at William with a flourish. "I believe you were saying something?"

"Ahh, yes. You're all looking at the proud new owner of a six-passenger TBM 700B turbo-prop aircraft." He flipped open his tablet to display a photo of a gleaming red and white plane.

Kate applauded, and the rest of the group joined in.

"I found it about a month ago. An old friend was starting to have some health issues and lost his FAA certification. He let me have it for a steal. So here we are! I can go farther and take more people with me."

He flipped through a series of photos showing the plane from various angles, first close-ups of the instrumentation and then the luxurious tan leather and glossy wood cabin. "I thought maybe before it gets too busy around here, we could take a hop over to Little Cayman for a few dives. Who's in?"

Kate's hand shot up, with Chuck's not far behind. The other three women looked at each other, shaking their heads. Babette spoke for the group. "I think we'll stay on dry land and hold down the fort here..."

"It'll be good for Kate to do something besides fix up a boat that's about to get a full re-fit." Chuck winked at her and popped a grouper bite in his mouth.

Kara froze mid-laugh, her eyes locked on the TV behind the bar. "Babette, honey, can you turn that up, please?" On the screen, a weather map showed a category four hurricane spinning up in the Atlantic, with a forecast track heading west, then making a sharp northern turn and returning back out to the ocean.

Babette reached for the remote. "It looks like it's not coming anywhere near us. It won't even hit the mainland."

"Not us. Look, it's heading straight for Hispaniola. They're predicting it to be a Category 5 when it hits."

"That's gonna make a mess."

Kara's eyes stayed fixed on the screen. "I'm from the Dominican Republic, honey. My sister still lives up on the east side of the mountains. She's gonna take a direct hit."

CHAPTER TWO

"KARA, LOOK AT ME."

Kate rested her hand on Kara's shoulder and tried to spin the barstool around. "Please. You've been staring at that TV all day. Stand up, stretch a little bit, and come watch the sunset with me, okay?"

Kara remained glued to the television, its screen filled with image after image of waves crashing over the top of seawalls, palm trees bent horizontal under heavy winds, and sheets of rain pounding flooded streets.

Kate turned to take in the blue sky and calm shallow water all around them. "Kara, please?"

"I can't get a call through." She waved her phone in the air without taking her eyes off the screen.

"I know."

"They said it's bad up in the hills. Power lines are down everywhere, and the eye hasn't even passed over yet."

"Honey, they're saying the same things over and over again. Please just come watch sunset with us, rest your eyes a little, maybe go lie down for a bit?"

Chuck leaned across the bar. "You shouldn't be alone. Stay in my guest room tonight? We'll keep trying to call for you."

Kate wrapped her arm around Kara's waist and led her off the barstool and toward the western railing. Kara's gaze remained on the TV until her head couldn't turn that far anymore. Kate found them a spot beside William and Michelle, and Babette pressed a plastic cup filled with white Sangria into Kara's hand. Kara stared blankly at the horizon and lifted the cup to her lips.

As the sun sank toward the ocean, tourists and locals all drifted from their tables at the outdoor restaurant to watch the nightly spectacle. From the east docks came the low rumble of an engine Kate was just learning to recognize. Moments later, Steve Welch joined the group just in time to see the sun drop below the horizon, filling the western sky with a blaze of pink and orange.

"Never the same show twice." Steve drained his beer, then scratched Whiskey's head and followed Kate back to the bar. Together, they watched Chuck lead Kara into his house across the parking lot. Lights flicked on in the little concrete block Florida bungalow, and through the frosted jalousie windows they could see silhouettes as Chuck helped Kara find more comfortable clothes. "What's up with that?"

Kate pointed to the TV. "Her sister lives in the mountains in the Dominican Republic. She can't get a call through, and it's looking pretty bad. Babette already cancelled her show for tonight. Sounds like Miss Dani has been looking for a chance to emcee, so she was thrilled to get onstage, and the rest of the crew over there will pitch in to keep the place running as long as necessary." Kate hollered across the bar toward the kitchen, "Hey, Babette!"

"Whatcha need, babe?" Babette's head popped through the swinging door.

"Can you throw a double burger on the grill for Kara, please? There's no way Chuck is gonna be able to keep her in there, and she's gonna need fuel."

"Sure thing. Burgers all around."

When a group of tourists left a large table near them, Kate started to clear it off. She carried the dirty dishes into the kitchen and came back with two baskets of French fries. She tossed a fry in the air, and Whiskey jumped from his spot under the bar and caught it. Nose raised, he followed Kate to the table.

"You're hoping I drop one of these baskets, aren't you, buddy?"

The dog stared at the fries with long strands of drool dangling from his jowls. Kate wiped the table with a wet bar towel, dropped the baskets in the middle, then took the towel back to the bar. She returned with bottles of ketchup and mayo and a thick pile of napkins as Chuck came back up onto the deck by himself.

Kate glanced at her watch. "It's only six. There's no way she's gonna stay in there and sleep, is there?"

"Nope. But I did talk her into taking a shower and borrowing some sweats. She'll be back out in a few minutes."

The group settled in as the sunset cocktail crowd drifted away or began placing dinner orders. The dark evening grew cool, with a light breeze coming in off the water.

Shark Key Campground and Marina sat on a long, narrow spit of rock seven miles east of Key West, Florida. Back in 1931, Chuck's grandfather had stolen millions from Al Capone and run for the Florida Keys with his girlfriend Gigi. He bought Shark Key and built a little marina with some of the bootlegger's money, and he used more of it to build the little two-bedroom house for Chuck's parents when they got married in 1960. Chuck had lived on the island all his life. Despite almost losing it earlier in the summer, Chuck was dedicated to keeping Shark Key a home to a growing family of beach bums and Conch natives.

Kara was the newest addition, having met everyone just two months before. Recovering from breast augmentation surgery, Kara had been placed in a room with Babette, who was healing from a violent attack ordered by the developer who was trying to steal Shark Key. Kara helped save the Key and quickly became a fixture among the group. She embodied the fun-loving free spirit of Key West, but Kate didn't know too much about her beyond the surface.

Chuck chose a seat beside Steve. "How's *Hopper Too* shaping up?"

"I know I'm going to love her once I get used to her, but I sure miss the old girl." Steve tipped his empty beer into the bucket on the table. He pulled a fresh bottle from the ice and took a slow pull as his glassy gaze drifted over the hedge to the listing hull of his first charter boat, the *Island Hopper*, grounded beside Kate's houseboat.

Kate rested her hand on Steve's arm. His wife had died just two days before the *Island Hopper* was destroyed, all in the effort to save Shark Key. Having lost her own husband in a robbery two years before, Kate understood he still needed more time before he was ready to talk about Susan, but she could feel his loss every time he talked about the *Hopper*. "She took good care of you. But the *Too* will be even better."

"You're probably right. The original *Hopper* was good for big groups. I think the *Too* will be better suited for the smaller groups we run. Speaking of, I've got a couple bookings for next week if you want to lead the dives?"

"Anybody good? What sites do they want?"

Steve rested his half-empty bottle on the table. "Not really anyone interesting. They want the popular stuff, so I was thinking Joe's Tug and Sand Key for both groups, probably."

"Then let Justin take it. He could use the work, and he knows those dives well enough."

"When am I gonna get you back in the water?"

"I've been in the water plenty since ..." Kate hadn't worked for Steve, or anyone else, since the incident on the *Tax Shelter*.

"But you're the best divemaster I know."

"But nothing. I'm prepping the *Katherine K* site exclusively for you. And I'll run all the dives on that site for you. We know the history better than anyone, and you know we can sell the crap out of the treasure-and-wreck angle."

After the *Tax Shelter* explosion, most of the gold and gems Chuck's grandfather had hidden in the old wreck were strewn across several square miles of the quicksands. But Kate had managed to toss several bags and crates overboard before she cut the luxury yacht's fuel lines. She needed time to salvage as much of Chuck's legacy as she could find before they let recreational divers onto the site. The other dive operations would find it soon enough, and then it'd be crawling with amateur treasure hunters. She and Chuck had been working in secret for two months, methodically sifting through silt and sand to get as much as they could recover into Chuck's safe deposit box, and she was almost ready to open the site.

She took a sip of her drink. "In fact, you know what? Go ahead and book a group or two for after Thanksgiving. I'll take them out with you, and we'll see how it goes."

"You got a deal. I've got a couple past customers in mind who would love it."

"Love what?" Kara slid into the empty chair beside Kate.

"We're opening up the dive site on the *Katherine K* in a few weeks."

"Oh, that's ... good." Kara's gaze drifted to the TV, where a reporter stood in the whipping rain, shouting into a waterlogged microphone in front of a street lit only by headlights of emergency vehicles. The scene alternated between the weather reporter and still photos of uprooted trees, downed power lines, and road signs twisting and flapping in the wind.

"Still no word from our team stationed up the mountain. We hope to get their satellite uplink working as the storm passes and bring you news from around the areas affected by Hurricane Sara. For those of you just joining us, Hurricane Sara came aground as a Category 5 storm near the Dominican town of Nagua and is barreling west up into the island's mountains. Forecasters expect the storm to turn northward within the next two hours, passing over the eastern tip of Cuba and

the southern Bahamas before it continues out to the middle Atlantic."

As the report continued, Babette set a tray of juicy burgers in front of everyone. Kara turned back to the table. "It's gonna be a long night."

CHAPTER THREE

The evening crept by, each minute stretching uncertainty into fear. Around eight-thirty, Steve said goodnight and stumbled back to his cabin on the *Hopper Too*. Kate helped Kara to a seat at the bar, and William and Michelle joined them. Kara switched from sangria to pineapple juice and club soda, and Chuck stayed behind the bar to keep her glass full. Kara's eyes barely left the screen.

When the Weather Channel switched to coverage of the high-pressure system pushing down from Canada through the western plains, Kate got her laptop, found a Dominican weather website, and plugged the video feed into the TV's input for Kara. Kate practiced her Spanish, translating for Chuck until the reporters' words flew too fast in the heavy winds for Kate to follow them.

At ten, Babette announced last call to the few

remaining tables of tourists. One by one, the tables settled their bills and piled into their rental cars. The twinkling bulbs that canopied the deck winked out, string by string, finally leaving the deck lit only by the dim fixtures above the bar.

Kate drifted out to the far corner of the deck, leaned back in a chair with her feet propped up on a table, and gazed up into the clear sky.

Michelle pulled a chair up beside Kate. "What's bouncing around in there?"

"Look at them all." Kate stared at the stars. "We spin through space at thousands of miles an hour, but it feels like time stands still. They float out there for millions of years, and it's just a speck of time. Makes me feel small. Makes me wonder if anything we worry about is worth anything at all. When I was little, my dad used to take me out back to look at the stars. He'd point out the constellations and make me recite back the stories of how each one got its name. Ursa Major, the great bear, and her cub Ursa Minor. Cassiopeia, who thought herself more beautiful than anyone else. And there, you can just barely see it — Pisces, the two fish. We'd bundle up and go down to the shore and listen to the water lapping against the rocks."

Kate looked past the railing of the deck and back up into the cloudless night. "I never realized how much this place reminds me of home. It's entirely different, yet the same." She shivered as she continued. "I'll never forget how angry Mother got when I wrapped up in the silk throw she kept on the back of the living room sofa. I loved it because it was soft and smooth and a buttery shade of yellow. But I dragged it in the dew-soaked grass and the end of it got so muddy and stained.

"She never said a word to me, but I heard her screaming and throwing things at Daddy after I was supposed to be tucked into bed. She bought another throw, an exact replacement, the next afternoon. I found the soiled one beside the garbage, so I took it and hid it in my room, and I used to rub my face against it and look out my window at the stars. One day, it disappeared from my room. Mother never said anything, but at dinner that night, she kept talking about how Kingsburys were expected to present themselves in certain ways. How we needed to dress properly for dinner at the Club, always keep our shoes shined, and keep the house just so in case one of the other ladies happened to call on us of an afternoon. Who says that? 'Of an afternoon.'? Daddy just kind of nodded and chewed up another bite of Beef Wellington."

Kate turned to Michelle. "Did you do things like that with — Oh, I'm sorry. Did you grow up with your dad around?"

Michelle looked confused. "I'm sorry?"

"I just kind of assumed, but I know a lot of black kids don't have a dad around, and you've never really talked about your family, so..."

"My father was an intellectual property attorney,

and my mother was an emergency room physician. I actually saw more of my dad than I did my mom. He had a small office in the house, and he worked from home any time I had a day off of school. He would take me on nature hikes or to the local science museum." Michelle's voice turned soft. "I thought he walked on water. It never occurred to me that he was human until he developed cancer..."

"Oh, I'm sorry, I didn't know."

"Of course you didn't. It's okay. It's not something that comes up often."

"You know, it's kind of weird, this place. It's like, on one hand, we're all family. Chuck would give anyone the shirt off his back. And for a widow or a kid, he'd give them his house. Look at me. No matter how often I try to pay him slip rent, he won't take it. But at the same time, there's an invisible line between the natives and the transplants. Do you ever feel that?"

Michelle released a little puff of air and a slight twitch before she answered. "When I was eleven, we moved to a small town where my mom had taken a job at a new hospital. When I graduated seven years later, the kids still called me 'that new girl.' But I knew they meant 'that black girl.' My mother stitched up their cuts and set their broken arms, even though she knew most of them wouldn't meet her eye in the grocery store. So yes, maybe I've seen a little bit in my time. I think maybe that's true of any tight-knit community. Every small town has its old-timers. Its own idea of who belongs and who doesn't. Best you can do is find where you fit and do what you can to welcome everyone."

Kate glanced over toward the bar. Kara perched on the stool closest to the television, eyes glued to the repeating video clips of bent trees, flying debris, and pounding surf. Whiskey lay snoring at Kara's feet, and William sat beside her, his hand resting on her shoulder. Chuck stood at the far end of the bar, talking quietly with Babette. He caught Kate's glance and pulled away to refill Kara's glass.

CHAPTER FOUR

KATE ROLLED OVER, kicked the tangled sheets from around her legs, then looked at her phone. She'd stayed up far too late watching the Dominican weather reports.

"Nothing good happens after two a.m. Buddy, I need coffee. C'mon."

Whiskey heaved his head up, his heavy eyes torn between going outside and going back to sleep. Kate threw on a pair of shorts, a tank, and some flip flops then staggered across the crushed shell parking lot to the deck. Whiskey detoured at his regular morning bush, barked at a fish near the shore, and still beat her to the steps.

Patti, the new breakfast waitress, met her at the bar with a cup of fresh coffee.

"I love you." Kate wrapped both hands around the mug and sipped.

"You talking to me or the coffee?"

"Both." Kate laughed and took another long drink. "Is Chuck up yet?"

"Yeah, he's in the back, but he's pretty wiped out. Said you all were up watching the weather half the night?"

"Kara's sister lives up in the mountains of the DR. We couldn't pull her from the TV until she finally fell asleep on William's shoulder. It took three of us to carry her inside to bed."

"Kara?"

"Your paths probably haven't crossed yet since no one ever sees her before noon. Kara owns the drag club on Fleming downtown. Dreamgirls. She was Babette's hospital roommate a couple months ago, and she's kind of become part of the family since then. I think she was a left fielder before she left the DR. She's a solid six-foot-two, and that's before she puts on her platform heels."

Kate glanced up at the TV. The night's storm images had been replaced with early morning video of the devastation. A headline streamed across the bottom of the screen: *Electricity and cell service down throughout most of the island. Many area bridges washed out. Mudslides close major highways into mountains.*

Chuck appeared from the kitchen carrying two plates. He slid one in front of Kate, then dug into his own omelet.

"Has she heard anything more?" Kate asked before she shoved the first bite in her mouth.

"Not yet. I've got her phone. Charged it in my room last night. So far, she hasn't gotten any messages or calls. I thought it'd be best to let her get a little more sleep. Worrying and watching the same footage over and over wasn't helping anyone."

"Excuse me. Good morning." Two men in cargo shorts and bare feet crossed the deck carrying mesh dive gear bags. The taller of them said, "We're looking for Steve Welch."

Kate hopped down from her stool. "You must be his divers for today. He's..." She glanced out into the parking lot to make sure Steve's truck was still there. "He's just getting the boat ready for you. How about you make yourselves comfortable and order yourselves a big breakfast? I'll go let Steve know you're here." She seated them at a table with a view of the water, made sure they had menus, and waved Patti over.

Kate was on the bottom step when Steve weaved between the seagrape hedges that separated the sunrise docks on the east side of Shark Key from the parking lot. His face was puffy and tinged with green under the bill of an oil-stained hat. He waved weakly, folded himself into the recesses of his truck's cargo lockers, then pulled out gear. "Morning, Kate."

"Your charter's here. Two guys?"

"Great. Justin's not here yet, so just tell 'em I'll be out with their paperwork in a few minutes."

"Ha. Has that boy ever been on time for anything?"

Steve shook his head, hiked a coiled line over his shoulder, then lurched back down to the *Hopper Too*.

Kate watched him climb aboard before she returned to the divers' table. "He'll be up here in just a few minutes with all your paperwork."

"Thanks. Looks like a hell of a storm." The same man who spoke earlier — clearly the more extroverted of the two — nodded to the TV. "It's swinging up through the Bahamas today. I hope it doesn't destroy the reefs. There's so much shallow water around there."

"We've been keeping an eye on it. Looks like it's turning pretty sharp. Hopefully, it'll stick to the deeper water south of Crooked Island. So, do you know what you're gonna dive today? Do you guys prefer wrecks or reefs?"

Both men shrugged. The spokesman said, "A little of both. We're both Advanced Open Water, so we like seeing some of the out-of-the-way, deeper spots."

"If you like deep wrecks, Steve might start you on the Vandenberg — it's definitely worth seeing. But to be honest, I kind of like Joe's Tug better. It's shallower, so you get more time and the marine life is so vibrant. You can probably do both if you're out for the full day, just watch your interval. Really, no matter where you go, you'll have great diving today. Just let him know what you like best."

"Sounds like you've done some diving around here?"

"Yeah, I got my Divemaster cert not long after I got down here, and I help run charters for Steve every now and then. Today, you'll have Justin. There he is, pulling in now. He'll be a great resource for you. Make sure you get him to tell you the story of the hammerhead." Kate tapped the sides of her head with the ends of her fists to make the diver sign for a hammerhead shark, then grinned and trotted down the steps to meet Justin in the parking lot.

She pointed out the charter customers to him, then pushed him down the dock toward Steve's boat. "He had another rough one last night. Keep an eye on him."

Justin nodded without turning back.

"You really are a mother hen."

She jumped at the abrupt sound. As she turned to face Chuck, her heart slowed, and she leaned her head on his shoulder. "I just know how he feels, is all."

A wind chime sound rose from Chuck's pocket. He pulled Kara's phone out. The notification from a contact labeled *Universidad* read: *Emergency Family Notification*. "Guess I'll go wake her up."

Fifteen minutes later, Kara joined Kate, William, and Michelle at a table in the center of the deck. Her eyes were swollen and bloodshot, and her normally glowing skin was ashy and dull. Patti brought her a mug of coffee and a plate of cut fruit and sausage links.

"We still don't know much." Kara took a gulp of

coffee then wiped her eyes with her napkin. "They got an emergency radio call from Lucia. Bob was hurt badly, and she begged for them to send a helicopter. Sounds like the house took a lot of damage, but they won't know more until they can get a rescue chopper up, which might not be until this afternoon. I'm going to try to get there, but commercial flights are all cancelled."

"Don't worry at all. I can be ready to go in thirty minutes, and I'll take you to any airstrip you need to get to." William squeezed Kara's shoulder. "Did they say anything about what kinds of supplies they need most? We can load up and be down there this afternoon."

"You'd do that for me?"

"Of course. What's the point in having resources if you can't use them to help when people need it?"

"Let me see if I can get them back on the line and ..." Kara burst into tears. It took her several sobs before she could take a steady breath. "I can't thank you enough for this."

"You don't have to. Just find out where we need to go and what we can bring to help."

Two hours later, the luggage compartment of William's new TBM 700B was filled with cases of bottled water, a diesel generator, three chainsaws, and a supply of mosquito nets, portable water filters, bleach, rags, and cases of beef jerky.

William tossed their backpacks on top of the pile of

supplies then climbed forward into the captain's seat. Kara joined him in the right seat, and Kate, Chuck, and Whiskey settled into the spotless passenger cabin.

"Saddle up!" William started flipping switches, then the plane's propeller began to spin.

CHAPTER FIVE

"November-Seven-Seven-Five-Four Yankee, contact Miami Center one-two-four point seven."

"One-two-four point seven for Miami Center. Have a nice day."

Kate's headset chattered with foreign-sounding pilot language above the drone of the engine as William announced his position and speed to the air traffic control center in Miami. Whiskey lay curled in the seat beside her, his chin resting on her thigh. She peered out the window. The Florida Keys fell away, and the deep blue water shimmered in the sun, dotted with shade from a few fluffy clouds drifting in the sky below them.

William's deep voice came though their headsets. "Over to your right in the distance, you can see the coast of Cuba. We've got about three hours of flight time left. We might get a little bumpy in that last hour, and then I think we're gonna get pretty busy, so if you want to get a little nap, now's the time."

He showed Kara how to connect her phone to the plane's bluetooth, and she piped some traditional Dominican music over everyone's headsets. Kate curled across the two back seats, her body wrapped around Whiskey's, and drifted off. She woke to growing pressure in her ears as the plane began to descend.

Kara twisted in her seat, and her voice crackled in Kate's headset. "I just want to thank all of you for this. You can't know how much it means to me."

Chuck's cheeks flushed. "Of course. We're happy to help."

"No, really. It's not just the supplies or the ride, although I appreciate that more than you can imagine, too. I just ... I haven't seen my sister since I left the DR when I turned eighteen. We've traded the occasional message over the years, but it's been twenty years."

"You haven't been back in all that time?"

Kara shook her head. "I didn't leave on the best of terms. I had a baseball scholarship to play up in Tallahassee, but Mami and Lucia didn't want me to go."

The plane bounced, and Kate noticed Chuck's white knuckles.

"Kara, you're fine there, but everybody stay buckled up. We're coming into a little turbulence. It's not dangerous, but it's gonna be pretty bumpy for a bit." William's calm tone contrasted the increasing turbulence.

"You played baseball well enough for a scholarship?" Chuck asked.

"Yep. Full ride. Every Dominican kid plays, even the gay boys. I had a broomstick bat in my hand from about the time I could stand up on my own. I wasn't the best baserunner, but I got big early. I could throw, and I could hit. Hard."

"What parent wouldn't be proud of that?"

"Mami thought if I went to school in the States, I'd be 'corrupted.' Lucia argued it was too late for that. I just wanted a little space to figure things out. I mean, what eighteen-year-old kid knows anything, anyway?"

Kate interrupted. "I'm sorry, Kara, but William, do you have anything—"

"There's a little pocket under that folding table in front of you. There are a few airsick bags in there if you need one."

Chuck pulled up the table and fished out a small white sack.

"Close your eyes and breathe really deep."

He clutched the little bag and bent his head between his knees. Kate pulled a bottle of water from the cooler strapped down beside her, handed it to him, then looked back up to Kara. "So, you went anyway?"

"I did. Broke Mami's heart. She died in the spring semester of my junior year. Baseball season had just started. Coach told me to take the time, but I didn't have any money for the flight. Besides, by then, I knew a lot more about who I was, and I really didn't want to listen to everyone judging me. So, I didn't go. And if I wasn't going back for my mother's funeral, how could I go back for anything else?"

Chuck closed the mouth of the bag over his face and heaved.

Ten minutes and three airsick bags later, the ride smoothed out. Chuck nibbled on pretzels and sucked down two more bottles of water.

"All right, folks, we're starting our final approach to Cibao International Airport, Santiago. We'll clear customs, fill up the fuel tanks, and confirm the next hop about thirty-five miles south to the little airstrip at Costanza. The university is sending a Jeep to meet us there."

Kara's voice shook as she added, "If it's okay with everyone, I'd like to check the hospital first?"

William tapped the iPad mounted to the plane's yoke. "Of course. It's just across the road from the airstrip, so that's no problem at all."

"I'm a little ... I'm not really sure what to expect."

"We'll all be here with you, and we'll figure it out as we go."

"I hope it's that easy."

The Santiago airport was open and busy routing planes of all sizes filled with supplies and relief workers. Kate struggled to follow the rapid island dialect of the northern Dominicans, but she pieced together enough to follow the rumors of the destruction in the mountain area where Lucia lived. William handled the customs inspection and fuel truck, and before they knew it, the group was back in the air.

The Costanza airstrip was in worse shape. Piles of debris lined both sides of the runway, and the roof of the small hangar was peeled back like a sardine can. An older cargo plane sat on the tarmac with three white pickup trucks lined up alongside it. A teenager in baggy khaki pants and a white long-sleeved tee shirt waved the plane to a tie down spot near a small boarded-up office. William flipped a series of switches and the cabin of the plane was enveloped in silence.

"You ready for this, Kara?"

She adjusted her long, blonde wig and sighed. "Ready as I'll ever be."

William opened the cabin door then pushed down the steps to meet the hot blacktop.

CHAPTER SIX

WHISKEY LEAPT from the small cabin to the tarmac. He ran a full circle around the plane, then relieved himself on a low, scrubby bush just past the edge of the pavement. He was back at Kate's side by the time she climbed down the plane's steep steps, her small backpack slung over one shoulder.

Chuck climbed out next then headed straight for the small office building, frantically searching for a garbage dumpster. Kate glanced around at the debris littering the area and wondered if it was worth the bother to find a proper receptacle at all. But better to not add to the chaos. She scanned the tarmac and the small parking lot beyond it. As she looked north, a small white four-wheel-drive pickup truck turned off the main road then wove around concrete chunks and sheets of tin roofing as it made its way to the small plane.

Kara stood frozen beside the airplane, her eyes hidden behind mirrored aviator sunglasses. She stared off into the distance as if she didn't even notice the truck, or the driver who exited it.

He approached her. "Is this Carlos Alvaro's plane?"

When she didn't answer, Kate pulled him into the spot of shade she had found for Whiskey to sit.

"*Sí*. Yes. That's Kara Alvaro. I think she needs a minute to process all this..." She waved her hand at the devastation around them. "Perhaps you can help us start unloading some of the supplies we brought?" She led the man to the tail section of the plane.

William was opening the hatch to the cargo compartment. The three of them quickly transferred the supplies into the bed of the small pickup truck, then Chuck climbed into the rear. William guided Kara to the passenger's seat of the truck, and after she was settled, gently shut the door.

The driver pulled William aside near the truck's tailgate and motioned toward the passenger seat. "This is the brother of Lucia Alvaro?"

"*Sí*."

"And you are..."

"Her friends."

The young man shrugged and helped Kate up into the bed of the pickup as William climbed in. "I am Ronald. The hospital is just across the road. *Señora* Alvaro is there."

The quarter-mile drive took more than ten minutes, with the young man stopping several times to drag debris from the road. William and Kate jumped out to help. He parked on the side of the road outside the hospital, hopped out of the truck, and slung the strap of a small but deadly-looking rifle over his shoulder.

"I will stay here and guard the truck until you are ready to leave. Take as much time as you need, of course, but know the conditions in the mountains are bad. We were very fortunate to get a helicopter up there earlier this morning. The pilot told us people are trapped, and many roads are blocked. It will take at least two hours or more to get up into the mountains if you plan to go there today. And you won't want to leave the truck unguarded."

"Thank you. We'll be out soon." Kate ordered Whiskey to stay with Ronald. She helped Kara out of the truck, then the four of them started toward the hospital building. Kate glanced back to see Whiskey at attention next to the young driver who stood in the bed of the truck, leaning against the cab, his rifle ready to protect their supplies against looters.

The parking lot was filled with people perched on the open tailgates of pickup trucks and car bumpers. Medics in stained scrubs scrambled from group to group, patching up cuts and minor injuries and finding stretchers to get the more seriously wounded inside. In a grassy area to the west, a row of bundles covered by white sheets lay near a far door. Two men dressed in dark tan coveralls carried a body from the building, laid it at the end of the row, covered it with a sheet, then weighted down the cloth with broken pieces of concrete.

The four entered the hospital building and were immediately hit with the hot stench of blood and bile and sweat and death. Chuck clapped his hand over his mouth and ran back out toward the truck. William handed Kara a handkerchief. Kate took her elbow on the other side, and together they made their way to the small reception desk.

"Lucia Alvaro? Robert Tinsley?" William asked. The harried receptionist began to shuffle through a huge stack of paperwork strewn across the desk.

"Carlos? Is that ... can it be you?"

Kate looked down the hall. A haggard but beautiful woman staggered down the hall toward them. Kara slowly turned toward the sister she hadn't seen in twenty years. She opened her arms, and her tiny sister collapsed against Kara's massive body. Kara's arms enclosed her sister, and they stood in the middle of the hallway, crying together.

Standing five foot, three inches on her toes, the woman barely reached Kara's shoulder. Her bronze skin was covered with cuts and scrapes, some bandaged, some left exposed to the air. Jet-black curls, knotted and dirty, tumbled down to the middle of her back. A small gold band on the third finger of her left hand was the only jewelry she wore.

Kara wiped her sister's tears with William's handkerchief.

Lucia hiccupped as she tried to control her sobs. "Bob is gone."

She pulled her sister tighter and rested her cheek on Lucia's matted hair. When her sobs began to subside, Kara loosened her grip and looked into her sister's red, swollen eyes.

"I'm going to check on Chuck," William whispered in Kate's ear then slipped back outside.

Kate stood off to the side of the corridor, awkwardly watching the reunion and trying to stay out of the way of the doctors, nurses, and volunteers scrambling through the hall with stretchers and wheelchairs working to save the most severely injured.

Kara finally guided her sister outside into the fresher air.

Kate found a shaded spot near the road where the two could catch their breath.

Crouching down, Kara mopped Lucia's face and stroked her cheek. "My sister, I'm so sorry."

Lucia collapsed against Kara again. Kate left the two beneath the tree to join William and Chuck at the truck.

"I'm sorry I couldn't stay in there with you." Chuck still looked green. "My stomach still hadn't quite recovered from the flight, and ..."

"It's okay. I've got a stomach of iron, and I was having a little trouble. I didn't expect it to be quite that bad."

Ronald leaned down from the bed of the truck. "*Sí, señorita.* It is very, very bad everywhere in this region. It is good you brought a small generator and chainsaws, but it may be hard to find fuel for them. We have no electricity anywhere, and many of the roads are still blocked with wreckage."

"*Hola. Buenas tardes!*" A medium-skinned man with high cheekbones and wide-set eyes waved to them as he approached. His long braids were tied in a topknot with a leather strap, their beaded ends dangling just above his shoulders.

Ronald tightened his grip on the rifle.

"*Buenas tardes.*" William met the man a few steps away from the truck.

"I see you have water and supplies." The man's English was heavily accented but clear.

William replied in Spanish. "These supplies are for survivors up in the mountains." He pointed down the runway to where they could just see the cargo plane and several white trucks. "Water and food for the town are being unloaded now. You'll have supplies soon, brother."

"You're from America?"

William nodded.

"You have American friends here?" He glanced at

the University logo on the truck's door. "At the university?"

William took a small step toward the man, subtly herding him away from the truck. "We have family at the university, *sí*. We are here to help the people who are still trapped up in the mountains."

"I am friends with the American professor Tinsley. Are you his family?"

Just then, a scream came from behind them under the tree. Lucia pointed at the man. When he saw her, he bolted back into the crowded parking lot then around the corner of the hospital building.

William looked back at Kate and Chuck. "Maybe he was not so much of a good friend?"

Beckoning to Kara, Kate turned to Ronald in the back of the truck. "I think it might be time to move along, don't you?"

Kara helped Lucia across the lawn to join the group.

"Who was that man?" Kate opened the passenger door for the women.

Lucia's hand fluttered to her throat. "I have never seen him before."

"Then why did you react so strongly when you saw him speaking with us?"

"Just a silly old legend. He wore his hair like a Taíno shaman, and it startled me."

"The Taíno are the indigenous people on the island," Kara explained. "Most of us have at least a little Taíno blood running in our veins. Our mother used to tell us when we were little that if we died without confessing our sins, the First Shaman would come to take our souls to the underworld."

"That sounds a little jumbled," William said as he swatted a huge mosquito away from Kara's cheek.

"Thanks. Whatever works, I guess. It terrified us but sure kept us in line. Sister, did you think he was coming for Bob?"

"I don't know what I thought. I just..." She shivered and climbed into the back seat of the truck, then Kara followed behind her. Chuck pulled his passenger seat as far forward as possible to make room for Kara's huge frame. Kate and William braced themselves in the bed of the truck, and Whiskey lay down on a crate of water between them.

As Ronald opened the driver's door, William caught him by the shoulder and nodded toward the rifle.

Ronald grinned, handed over the weapon, then hopped in to start the engine.

CHAPTER SEVEN

The truck pulled up the narrow lane as the sun dropped behind the ridge of the western mountain.

Kate thought she was ready for the devastation after driving through Constanza and up the mountainside. Trees stripped of their leaves. Debris they stopped to clear from the roads. But nothing prepared her for Lucia's sobs as they approached what used to be her home.

Several villagers milled around the yard, picking up trash and debris. A fire burned in a small ring at the edge of the property. Chain saws hummed and young men hauled long, thin limbs across the clearing, leaned them against a short concrete block wall, then jumped on them to split them into pieces small enough to throw on the fire.

A wide tree trunk lay across the roof of a white Jeep and the crushed corner of a small wooden structure that looked like it had been a workshop. Chuck climbed out the passenger side of the truck, then pushed the seat forward and pulled Kara and Lucia out of the small backseat.

Lucia wailed as she ran to the woman closest to her then fell into her arms.

"Drama is in the blood of the Dominican." Kara deadpanned. They all watched as her sister moved from villager to villager, simultaneously wailing and thanking them. "Traditionally, we mourn our dead over a nine-day period. The whole village would hang around, we'd feed them all, and there'd be a mass every damn day for like a week and a half. It's a whole thing. But with the storm, I'm hoping we can talk her out of some of the less practical traditions."

"So, will the body..." Kate let the question hang unasked.

"She left instructions to have him brought up here and buried in the village cemetery as soon as possible. It's law here that a body must be buried within two days, but with the storm, I don't know if it'll happen quite that fast. When they do show up, I'm sure they'll do the whole procession to the cemetery, so you'll get that singular experience. Everyone in town joins in, whether they knew the deceased or not. Every car, every truck, every scooter and moped lines up. But if you're at the end of the line, you'll miss the ceremony, so it's all jockeying for position. If you want to be seen, you make sure you're at the front of the procession. If you are only going out of obligation, a spot near the back of the line will get you out of most of it. There's a strategy to it. If you're paying attention, it's obvious."

"It's nice they all came up here to help."

"Yeah. Honestly, our villages are a lot like what you have at Shark Key, Chuck. A group of people brought together by geography, who kind of become a family. Everyone is up in everyone else's business, for sure. But also, everyone takes care of everyone else when bad times come." She waved her hand around the small mountain clearing, filled with people.

Kate smiled at Whiskey trotting from person to person, sniffing each one and looking for ear scratches. But he scared more than a few of them. She called him to her side then ordered him to guard the lane to keep him focused.

William joined them. "The roof needs some work. The tarps we brought will hold for a few days, but we'll need more supplies for a permanent repair. It looks like I can tie the generator into the house's electric box to get the basics up and running. Chuck, can you help me get it unloaded?"

Kara raised her eyebrows at him.

"I was just thinking you might want some time to grieve with your sister?"

"Honey, I love my sister, and I'm sad for her loss. But Bob was no friend of mine, and he turned my sister even further against me than she already was. The first five years they were married? She only spoke to me once. I say good riddance. She's better off without him." Kara grabbed three stacked cases of bottled water then carried them over to her sister's porch.

Kate set another case down beside them.

Kara continued, "I don't think any of the people here realize who I am, and that's just fine—"

"Carlos! CARLOS!"

Kara's head jerked toward her sister's high-pitched shout. "Guess that cat's out of the bag now. It's been so long since anyone called me that, but I still respond to it like a reflex." She raised her head, straightened her shoulders, then joined her sister in the crowd of neighbors.

Kate, Chuck, and William unloaded the rest of the supplies. Kara came back long enough to help heave the small generator out of the back of the truck, then returned to her sister's side while William wired it up and added fuel.

Soon, the low chug of the generator hummed from behind the house. Chuck primed the water pump and restored running water, and Kate and William spread tarps over the roof just as the last light faded from the sky.

One by one, the neighbors hugged Lucia goodnight then made their way back down the mountain path to the village below, leaving Lucia and Kara sitting in plastic lawn chairs beside the fading fire.

William fed it with three more logs then pulled up a chair beside Lucia. "*Señora*, I am sorry for your loss."

He patted her hand as she stared into the flickering flames.

Kate brought over two more chairs then settled into one. Chuck opened a bag of beef jerky, offered some to everyone, then sat down in the empty chair. "Where's Whiskey?"

"Oh!" Kate whistled. "Whiskey, come!"

A second later, she saw his eyes glowing in the darkness of the narrow driveway. He nudged his nose under Kate's arm, and she ran her hand down his back. His fur felt thick, like it did when he saw a threat. She scanned the woods, then shrugged. "Good boy." She tossed him a piece of jerky. He carried it to a spot away from the fire to devour it. "Everyone seemed scared of him, so I told him to guard the driveway to keep him occupied. I kinda forgot he was down there."

Chuck laughed as he chewed his beef jerky. "Do you think we'll be able to get back down into town for supplies tomorrow?"

"I think tomorrow we'll need to empty the freezer and cook whatever we can salvage. The whole village will be up here for the wake, whether we invite them or not." Kara's voice held a tinge of annoyance.

"We can shore up the basics with what we've got now, and we can go back down in a couple days for roofing materials."

"*Gracias.* You really don't have to do all this." Lucia's soft voice barely rose above the crackling of the fire.

"It's our pleasure." William spoke for the whole group. "Kara is a member of our family, too, and when her relatives need help, we help. I'm sorry we have to meet under such difficult circumstances, but we're happy to be here for you."

"Truly, I don't deserve this. My neighbors will help, and I can find my way through."

Kara reached for her hand. "No, *hermana*. This is what family does."

CHAPTER EIGHT

THE SCENT of slowly roasting beef, smoke, and sawdust wafted across the driveway. Kate's stomach growled. She strolled toward the scent to find Kara sitting in a circle with her sister and a group of neighborhood *abuelas*. The elderly women shot the latest gossip around the circle in rapid Spanish.

Struggling to keep up, Kate pulled a lawn chair beside Kara and concentrated.

"Graciela's son moved to the city and took up with a white woman. Can you believe it?"

"I heard she was pregnant!"

"Oooh, Lucia, no." The old woman leaned in and lowered her voice. "Not anymore."

All of the women crossed themselves while they muttered a low prayer Kate thought sounded a little less merciful than a prayer should be.

After they all finished, the woman across from Kate

whispered, "Did you hear about the boy they found with his throat cut not far from Manabao?"

"*Sí. Sí.*" All the women nodded.

Lucia's eyes grew wide. "Noni's grandson said his best friend's cousin knew the boy. He said it was *Las 21 Divisiones*—the Vodou." The women all gasped and crossed themselves again. "Noni lit a candle for him at the cathedral."

Lucia's eyes darted around the group. "I think the beef and *chofan* must be done by now. Kate, maybe you can help me?"

Kate followed Lucia into the house, where they loaded plates, utensils, and cups into a basket, and Lucia grabbed several large serving spoons and trays. Out by the fire, Lucia pulled two huge roasting pans from a grate. A huge puff of steam escaped as she lifted the lid.

Kate's mouth began to water at the rich spices. "What is that?"

"It's a traditional Dominican *Barbacoa* feast. It's been on the fire all day." Lucia poked a long wooden spoon into the pan containing puffy yellow grains of rice, with chunks of corn, peas, and strips of bell peppers mixed throughout. "This is *chofan*. Bob used to call it Dominican fried rice, but I don't understand why. We do not fry it." Lucia grabbed a fork from the basket in Kate's arms. "Here. Try."

The rice melted on Kate's tongue, and her mouth exploded with the flavors of fresh vegetables and spices. Her eyes closed, and her knees felt as if they might not continue to hold her body up.

"That's delicious, Lucia."

"Of course it is. And the beef is even better. Come, let's set this on the table over there."

The two women laid out the food then called the others. Whiskey raced to Kate's side, his fur covered in debris from the forest.

"Where have you been, buddy?" Kate squatted beside him, pulling twigs and leaves from his undercoat. He shook and sent more debris flying through the air while everyone else laughed and covered their plates. "Let's do that away from the buffet line, shall we?"

Two hours later, after she helped Lucia clean up the dinner dishes, Kate stood on the front porch and surveyed the little clearing where they'd arrived a few days before to utter devastation. Where there had been toppled trees and debris, now there was stacked firewood and open spans of grass. William and Kara had repaired the solar panels that leaned into the south face of the hill and provided electric power for Lucia's property. Her rickety generator had been broken beyond repair, so William built a housing for the brand new one they'd brought to supplement her solar power.

With only a few minor cuts and scrapes, the little amateur construction crew had repaired roofing and siding and built a new railing on Lucia's front porch deck. And held a funeral.

Kate stepped into the small office shed and sat down in Bob's chair to rest. Whiskey curled under his desk at her feet. The little building had taken a tree to the southeast corner, crushing two walls, the door frame, and a part of the roof. Inside, the coffee pot was demolished, but most of Bob's work had been arranged on desks and tables on the opposite side of the shed, so most of his books and papers made it through the storm unscathed. Lucia had gratefully accepted the group's help in restoring her home and her property, but she had insisted on putting this room back together herself.

Kate ran her finger gently across the spines of Bob's small academic library. From books like *The Peoples of the Caribbean: An Encyclopedia of Archaeology and Traditional Culture* to *Human Biology of Afro-Caribbean Populations*, and *The Cambridge Encyclopedia of Human Paleopathology,* most of Bob's library seemed to set him apart from the local culture.

A collection of carved wood figurines lined a shelf near Bob's desk. Miniature dugout outrigger canoes, some holding just two figures but some carrying larger groups. The models spoke to how the indigenous people had traveled from island to island. A huge map on the wall depicted the migration of the Taíno people from the Amazon basin up through the southern Caribbean and into the Lesser Antilles. Kate was surprised to see the Taíno people's territory stretch from Guadalupe in the south all the way to the northern Bahamas, and as far west as the tip of Cuba.

Kate picked up a little figure carved from what looked like driftwood.

"He saw our people as subjects to study when he first arrived."

Kate jumped and spun toward the doorway, where Lucia stood watching her. Her face flushed and she gently set the figurine back on the shelf.

"It's okay. I'm happy you're interested."

"I was a journalist a long time ago. I guess I've never stopped being interested."

Lucia handed Kate a mug of coffee, and Whiskey wandered out onto the shed's small porch. "Not very many people here can claim 'pure' ancestry, nor do most of us care to. But despite Mami's stories, it's important to us to keep our heritage alive and remember our history. When Bob first came to study here, he treated us almost like zoo animals — a novelty to study and examine, perhaps even dissect. But as he learned more and got to know us, he learned to appreciate our culture and even became part of it. I'd like to think I had a little something to do with that."

She sat on the edge of her husband's desk and tucked her feet under her. Her swollen, tear-stained cheeks had transformed, and her smooth, bronze skin glowed from the sun and work of the past few days. But her eyes carried a hollowness that Kate recognized from her own reflection. Those hollow eyes met Kate's and held on.

"How did you do it?"

"I'm sorry, Lucia. How did I do what?"

"Go on. Live. This." She swept her thin arm around the room. Her lip quivered. "We have these traditions for times of death. We cry and wail for three days. We grieve and remember for three more. Then we get on with it. At least that's what's supposed to happen. It works when the person you've lost is old or has been sick — when you're prepared for it. But how do you go on when it wasn't his time?"

Kate stiffened.

"I'm sorry. Chuck mentioned you'd lost your husband, and I thought maybe ... I'm sorry for asking."

Kate took a deep breath and looked out over the lush mountain. "No, it's okay. If you want the truth, I didn't do it so well. You get six days. I'm not sure six years will be enough." Kate tried to laugh. "I was blind-sided. I went to the grocery store a wife. I came home a widow. I was twenty-nine. Who the hell can be ready for that?"

A single tear slipped down Lucia's cheek. "No one."

"I pushed everyone away. Danny's partner and his wife were our closest friends, but every time I saw them, I saw Danny. I couldn't bear it. They came around a lot. She had to make me shower. She washed my dishes and spoon-fed me. And when she left, I threw up. Finally, Pete told me I had to decide to live for myself. So, I put the house up for sale, adopted Whiskey, and like so many people in the Florida Keys, ran south until the road ran out." Kate looked at Lucia, recognized the pain etched in her face like she was staring at her own reflection. "Running worked for me, but I don't recommend it. You've got people in this village who love you. Keep them close. Let them help you."

"*Sí*. They were my people and my life before I met Robert, and they still will be my people and my life without him. I just ... Bob was working on something. Something important." She slipped off the desk and lifted a figurine from a cluster that sat apart from the rest of the artifacts in the room. "He was close to a discovery, and I don't want to let go." Her fingers fluttered to her throat as her stare settled on something in the distance. "I want to keep his work alive. It feels like maybe if I do that, he won't truly—"

A low growl interrupted her. Whiskey stood at attention in front of the door, the hair on his back standing on end. His ears twitched, and he stared into the woods and barked twice. Kate peered out the open window. She saw nothing in the darkness, but deep into the woods, she heard rustling leaves, and then silent stillness. Whiskey growled one more time, and his fur slowly relaxed onto his back.

Lucia looked back at the figurine in her hand and then into Kate's eyes. "I can't do this alone. I need your help."

CHAPTER NINE

THE NEXT MORNING, the whole group crowded into Bob's tiny office space.

Kara settled her ample frame on a narrow stool beside Kate, then began fidgeting with the small trinkets on a shelf beside her. Out of the corner of her eye, Kate saw Lucia stiffen, then gently excuse herself to William and turn to her sister.

"Bob picked all of these up on digs around the Caribbean."

"They're lovely."

Both sisters sounded tense, and Kate wondered if they'd always been so formal with each other. Lucia lifted a small silver figure on a leather strap.

"That's beautiful. Where is it from?"

"A museum gift shop." Lucia chuckled, turning the small charm over in her hand. "It was a special exhibit of ancient Taíno artifacts from around the islands, and they were selling these necklaces on the way out. Bob bought it, but it just wasn't me."

Lucia opened the little clasp and wrapped it around Kara's throat. "But it looks good on you. Like it belongs. It's yours."

"Oh, no. I couldn't."

"Of course you can, and you will."

Kara reached up and rubbed the little ornament between her fingers, then rested it on her chest just above the low neckline of her top. The silver charm shone against her dark skin.

Lucia shifted to the corner of the room and cleared her throat. "When it comes to the Taíno people, anthropologists fall into one of two camps. Some believe our people originated with the Yanomama people of the Amazon basin in South America, and then migrated up the islands of the Caribbean, finally settling in this area." She pointed to the northeastern section of the map Kate had been looking at the evening before. "The other group believes our ancestors migrated from the Andes mountains in what is now Colombia." She tapped another area in the lower left corner of the map.

"The legends passed down among our people, though, tell a different story altogether. For most of us, the old legends are just stories our grandparents told around the fire to entertain everyone or to scare the kids into behaving. But those stories seep into our bones, and even after we've gone to Catechism or passed university classes, on some level, they still simply feel true."

Kara nodded. "Honey, caves still spook me a little."

"Exactly. And that brings us to the legend of Yúcahu." Lucia turned to a grouping of five shiny gold-toned figurines. She picked up the largest one. "Now, we have a lot of conflicting legends. One says a god joined with a turtle and here we are. Another says that the first Taíno lived in the caves and only came out at night — a vampire story of sorts. Most of them are similarly farfetched. But the legend of Yúcahu has passed down through the ages relatively unchanged, no matter which tribe tells it."

She handed the figurine of Yúcahu to Kate, who inspected it and passed it on. "Yúcahu was our first zemí — that's what we call both the gods themselves and the sculptures that represent them. Zemís. Yúcahu was good. He represents peace. He brings abundant crops and calm seas. But his brother Guacar was evil. He brings storms and earthquakes and pestilence and death." She pointed to the statue in Chuck's hands. "We don't ever make zemís of Guacar."

Lucia pulled down two more figurines. "Yúcahu banished Guacar, and then he sent four spirits." She handed the figurines to Kate and William, then pulled the other two down from the shelf. "They were to protect creation from his evil brother."

Kara took one of the final two zemí figurines from

her sister. "I remember Mami used to tell us this when it would storm outside."

"She did." Lucia had a dreamy smile that comes with old memories. "You were always so scared by the thunder and lightning. She would bring her little plastic zemís into our room and remind you that Guacar could jump up and down all he wanted, but that Yúcahu's four spirits would protect us."

"Oh, mercy. She did, didn't she?"

"Legend has it that the shamans of the five tribes would come together at the Cave of Origin and call upon Yúcahu and his four spirits. They did this for thousands of years, and our people lived peaceful, prosperous lives. They traveled to distant islands in ocean-worthy canoes, traded with other tribes, and defended our land from invaders. Until the visitors from Spain arrived."

William raised an eyebrow. "That didn't go so well, did it?"

Lucia snickered. "Not really, no. At first, they were friendly and our Caciques traded with them and welcomed them as friends. But it didn't take long for the spirit of Guacar to show himself among them. The Spaniards brought disease, slavery, and worse. They took the gold of our land as their own, and they took the women of our tribes, too. Within one generation, our once strong people were reduced to a tiny remnant hiding deep in the mountains."

She bent in front of a low bookshelf, scanned the

spines, selected one, then turned back to the group. "Until this point, all we have are the oral history and the petroglyphs that have been found in caves all over Hispaniola."

Kara shot her a suspicious look.

"Yeah. Petroglyphs. I know the word for cave paintings. I might not have finished school, but I still got an education. Being married to a university professor has its perks." Lucia winked at her sister. "Anyway, with the arrival of the Spanish came record keeping. From that moment forward, historical documents begin to back up the stories and lend them some authenticity." She waved the book, then opened it to a page marked by a small leather strip.

"Piecing it all together, Bob thinks—" She paused, took a deep breath, then started again. "Bob thought that in the first decade of the sixteenth century, the shamans of the five tribes held a summit of sorts. They retreated to *Cueva de Origen* high in the mountains for a ceremony to seek guidance from the spirits. They believed that Guacar, through the Spaniards, was seeking to harness the power of Yúcahu to permanently destroy the last of our people.

"Bob had been researching this for the better part of his time here, and he believes — he believed — that the little zemí sets we all have, the zemís you are holding, are replicas of the original zemís: solid gold statues representing Yúcahu and the four spirits. He was convinced that at this summit, the shamans performed a cohoba ceremony and separated the zemís, with each tribe taking one to protect. Best as Bob could tell, each tribe's shaman took on the sole responsibility of protecting the zemí above all else. For believers, to have the five collected zemís is as holy and powerful as it would be to find the Holy Grail or the Ark of the Covenant."

Chuck slowly raised his hand, which still held the larger zemí of Yúcahu. "So, if someone wanted power within the Taíno community..."

"Exactly. In the past few decades, interest in our Taíno heritage has increased. More and more people are leaving the Catholic faith they were raised in and returning to the ancient beliefs of the Taíno. The five tribes are rebounding. Overall, this is a great thing. Our heritage and culture are precious, and I'm honored to call myself Taíno, even though just as much Spanish and African blood runs through my veins.

"But there are some who wish to exploit our history and prey on our beliefs. They're led by a man named Diego Guzman. He preaches a twisted, corrupt version of our history. He is trying to collect the zemís to gain power over the believers and ultimately rise up against our country. Bob told me about him just before the storm. His team thought they had found one of the zemís in the British Virgin Islands, but when they got there, it was already gone. They believe Guzman and his group — cult, really — are responsible. And when they find a zemí, they perform a ritual sacrifice.

"While the university was at first just working with the Ministry of Culture to locate and preserve the five zemís, now it's even more important to keep them out of Guzman's hands.

"But now that Bob is gone, I am afraid this will give Guzman an opportunity to gain the upper hand. He has one already. The boy who was killed, the one those women were talking about? That had to have been Guzman. And for each zemí he finds, he'll kill again. With each one, he grows stronger." As she spoke, the skin around her jaw tightened and a fire grew in her eyes.

"In the days before the storm, Bob was planning a short trip to the Bahamas. He had made contact with a shaman there who he believed was willing to turn over the zemí he was protecting. While everyone else is distracted by the storm, I know we can get that one quickly. Then maybe Guzman will see he'll never have the power he craves and stop. I just need to finish this for our people. And I can't do it alone."

CHAPTER TEN

Kate stood five and a half feet away from the edge of a high cliff, Whiskey at attention by her side. Her stomach flipped and churned. But she could still gaze out over the turquoise waters of the Bahamas and appreciate their beauty. To the east, a clear line divided the pale shallow water from the deeper ocean a few hundred yards off the coast. To the west, the bright, clear shallows extended to the horizon.

Their tiny boat bobbed at a dock in the shallows on the western shore, waiting to carry them back to the airstrip on the big island to the north where William's plane awaited them. A strong, warm wind ripped up the cliff and whipped Kate's curls into her face. She brushed them away and held her hair back so she could clearly see the short, fat man standing at the edge of the cliff.

He was speaking, but Kate couldn't hear his words

because of the wind, and she wasn't planning to get any closer to the edge. He handed helmets and flash-lights around. Finally, he turned and started down a narrow path on the leeward side of the island.

"Kate, come on." William paused a few feet down the trail and beckoned. "It's wider than it looks."

Kate shook her head and took a step backward, bumping Whiskey.

Chuck had the right idea.

Citing his need to get the campground ready for a wave of arrivals, Chuck had returned to Shark Key while William flew the rest of them to the Bahamas. Kate suspected it was either claustrophobia or an intense fear of bats, but she couldn't judge him. She just wished she'd beaten him to the excuse.

William climbed back up on the little plateau, took Kate's hand, and led her closer to the edge. She peered down the path and realized the rock sloped out a safe distance and was covered with low vegetation. She whistled to the dog, who raced on ahead, then she tentatively stepped onto the path.

Once they were below the top surface of the hill, the wind died down, and Kate could hear herself think. Nelson, their guide and the owner of the land they were on, led Kara and Lucia along the trail far ahead of them.

"I didn't realize you were afraid of heights."

"I'm not. I just didn't like the idea of getting blown over the edge, that's all."

"Mmm-hmm."

"I couldn't hear a thing up there with the wind whipping up behind me. What's the story?"

"Nelson's family has owned this part of the island for as far back as anyone knows. He's descended from a direct line of Lucayan tribal shamans. Now, he says, no one believes the ancient ways, and his role as shaman is more traditional than spiritual. But he said that through the generations, a legend has been passed down from father to son about the Taíno zemí that was entrusted to his people to protect."

Nelson waved the others ahead and hung back to meet up with William and Kate. "The legend charged each shaman with protecting the precious zemí the Taíno had entrusted to us until a righteous man came to return it to its origin. So even with as many of the old ways as we've abandoned, dis one still felt important. When I turned eighteen, my father felt I was ready to know my responsibility and brought me to dis place. My son is not ready, so for now, I am the only man on earth knowing the Taíno secret. But as I got to know Mr. Bob, I felt his goal of protecting and preserving Taíno culture and history was righteous. We had been making arrangements for him to come collect it when the storm came through."

They caught up to the rest of their group on a level spot halfway down the hill. Behind a rock outcrop, a narrow crevice opened into the cliff. Whiskey poked his nose into the darkness, whined, then slowly backed away from the rock. Kate ruffled the fur between his ears. "Such a badass dog." They donned their helmets, flipped on flashlights, and Nelson helped each one through the narrow gap.

Kate hopped a short way down to the cave's floor. Five beams of light weaved around the huge cavern, illuminating hundreds of stalactites stretching from the ceiling like rows of shark's teeth.

"My cousins and I used to play in here when we were young. The cave system extends under most of the southern end of dis island, and some of it still remains unmapped. Some other families have opened their caverns to the public, but we've never seen the need. I prefer to keep it private, although I'm happy to escort serious historians such as your husband, ma'am." As he nodded to Lucia, the light mounted to his helmet bobbed in her face.

Kate drifted deeper into the cavern toward a dark area in the back. Nelson led the rest of the group in her direction.

"This is the main passage into the system, but what we're looking for is this way." Nelson directed his light in a circle around a small niche to their left. "We have petroglyphs — cave drawings — in spots throughout our caves that span nearly a thousand years. All of them are distinct to the Lucayan tradition, except this one. It's one of the most recent petroglyphs, and its style is distinctly Taíno."

Lucia and Kara paused in front of the figure carved

into the rough cave wall. Lucia gently traced the outline with her fingers.

Nelson dropped to his belly then disappeared through a shadow a foot above the cave's floor.

Whiskey stuck his nose into the narrow passage and barked.

"Come on through." Nelson's Bahamian lilt echoed through the stone. "The tunnel is only a few yards long, and if I can get through it, you're sure to have plenty of space!"

Kara shrugged and wiggled her huge frame into the shadowy tunnel. Lucia followed behind her. Whiskey stuck his head into the hole and whimpered.

"Go on."

He twisted his ears toward Kate, still crouched in front of the hole with his eyes glued to Lucia's shoes.

"Whiskey, GO." Kate thought he sighed as he stretched his front paws into the tunnel and began to shimmy his way through.

Kate and William stood at the entrance to the narrow passage, watching Whiskey's tail disappear. William stretched out his arm. "Ladies first."

Kate shivered.

"Heights *and* tight spaces? Katherine, I thought you were a badass."

"I've got no problem kicking the crap out of someone coming at me in a parking lot or blowing a dirtbag's expensive yacht to kingdom come. But crawling through a rock coffin filled with rabid bats isn't exactly my idea of a relaxing afternoon."

"All my bats have had their shots, and dey promise not to bite. Come on through, lady!" Nelson's laugh echoed through the tunnel.

Kate rolled her eyes and crawled into the tunnel. She tried to push up to her hands and knees, but her spine scraped the top of the tunnel, forcing her back down onto her belly. The passage was just wide enough for her to stretch both elbows out for a wide-stance army crawl. She extended one arm out and tentatively pushed her body forward with the opposite foot.

The light on her helmet bobbed around the walls of the tunnel, and she focused on the voices echoing near the bright spot a few yards ahead. The tunnel curved gently to the left. Just past halfway through, the passage began to widen, opening into a smaller cavern, brightly lit by the flashlights of its inhabitants. Kate tumbled out of the tunnel and sucked in a deep breath of cool, moist cave air. Whiskey nuzzled up against her and licked her face.

Moments later, William unfolded his tall frame from the passage and shined his light around the walls of the small room. "That was a little tight, there, Nelson."

"No worries, mon. It's all easy from here on." Nelson fired up a bright lantern which threw a wide blanket of light ahead of him, and he pointed to a passage leading out of the cavern. "We'll pass through a few of these smaller caverns before we reach the item you're seeking. You'll notice each of the passages we enter has a tiny marking leading the way ... if you know what to look for. My ancestors and yours wanted to ensure that it stayed safe and wasn't accidentally discovered by someone who shouldn't find it."

He took Lucia's hand and guided it to a rough spot in the stone, tracing the carving with her fingers. Lucia gasped. "I never would have seen that."

"That's de idea, lady. Your zemí has been safe with my people for many generations."

The group proceeded through a series of tall, narrow passages and wider caverns, occasionally encountering a split. At each intersection, Nelson pointed out the little Taíno petroglyph indicating the way. Finally, they stepped into an opening barely large enough to hold the five of them. Whiskey pressed against Kate's leg in the tight space. Against the back wall, Nelson's light illuminated a series of niches and shelves holding what appeared to be ceremonial bowls and pipes.

But what stood out most was a small statue gleaming in the tallest niche.

CHAPTER ELEVEN

The Lucayan Zemí felt heavier than its small size implied. Kate ran her fingers across its smooth, polished surface and traced the shallow crevices that decorated the icon, then handed it to Kara. It was shaped like a short, plump bird, with its head tucked tight against its body and its body resting low on wide, webbed feet.

"Macocael was the god of the mountain."

"Macco-what?" Kara turned to her sister.

"Macocael. He is represented by a bird, one who could float on the breeze or on the surface of the sea. He guarded the Sacred Mountain until one day when he was distracted and the First Man left the Cave of Origin and entered the world." Lucia gently took the statue from Kara, wrapped it in a soft cotton bandana, then tucked it into a small bag she slung across her chest.

"I didn't know you knew so much about our native heritage."

"I learned most of it after you left for the States. I met Bob when he was the teaching assistant for a cultural anthropology class after I moved to Santo Domingo. He was here studying ancient Taíno culture for his PhD, and he was stunned that I only knew jumbled legends about where I'd come from. I knew we had some Taíno blood from Papa's family, but Mami only told the most common campfire stories, and after how Papa left, I don't think she really wanted any extra reminders of him, anyway."

Lucia and Kara walked together at the front of the group. "I tried to explain our priorities had been a little different. Times were different, and life was hard. I mean, without Papa to support us, we had to scrape out a living any way we could. I don't know if you remember how bad it was."

"I remember digging through dumpsters looking for bottle caps to play *vitilla* in the street, and I remember getting excited if I found a bunch of bruised plantains or a coconut that had been thrown out because it was cracked. I never thought of us as poor, though. All the other kids lived the same way, so it was just normal to me, I guess. And I remember Mami wasn't around much, but when she was ... she was my angel." Kara's voice caught. "One night, she came home really late, smelling of sweat and fish. She tried so hard to be quiet and not wake us. I was probably eleven or twelve, but it feels like I was so much younger. I pretended to be asleep so she wouldn't know she'd woken me. She pulled a dirty, torn baseball out of her pocket and tucked it under my pillow. It was the first real ball I ever had, and even though I didn't know what it had cost her to get it for me, I knew it was more than she had."

Kate watched the silhouettes of the two sisters clasp hands.

"You, Carlito, you were special. You were so good at *vitilla* that none of the other kids wanted to play against your team because they knew they'd lose. And when you got older and you started making baseball gloves out of cardboard you found in the street, we knew you had talent, so Mami and I just did everything we could to provide for you. No job was too low for Mami if it meant ..."

Lucia stopped and dropped Kara's hand. "It was hard for her when you left. She knew you were too talented to stay here, but she was so afraid for you. And, well ..."

"And I wanted nothing more than to get an education and make enough to take care of her. By then, I knew you'd find a good man to take care of you, but I thought if I could get out and either get picked up by a team or get a good job, I could send money and set her up right. I wasn't sure she'd take it from me, but I figured I'd find a way."

"But you didn't even come back for her funeral."

Kara stopped and squatted in the narrow passageway, her head in her hands. "Coach told me to go, but how could I? I didn't even have money for new socks, let alone a plane ticket back here. And," she looked down at herself, "even then, Father Roberto would never have allowed me into the church or into the consecrated cemetery. What could I do?"

Lucia reached down, lifted Kara's chin, and wiped a tear from her cheek. "You could have come. We would have figured it out."

"I'm here now." Kara heaved her mass back to her feet, then pulled her sister back up. She turned to the others standing at as discreet a distance as was possible in a narrow underground passage. She tossed her head toward the entrance then started down the passage.

When they reached the final chamber, Kara helped Lucia into the passage, then followed along behind her sister. William squeezed into the tunnel right behind her while Kate and Whiskey stalled. Just as Kate was coaxing Whiskey up into the passage, she heard a sharp scream from the outer chamber, followed by more shrill screaming and deep shouts echoing down through the tunnel. Kate shoved Whiskey into the passage then scrambled through as Nelson stashed the last of his gear and scurried through behind her.

Kate climbed out into the chamber to find Lucia curled in a ball on the floor of the cave, leaning against a wide stalagmite and clutching her shoulder. Kara's body was crammed in the narrow crevice to outside, a barrage of Spanish profanity flowing freely from her lungs.

Whiskey sniffed Lucia, then bolted past Kara. His menacing barks trailed away from the cave's entrance.

Nelson scurried to Lucia's side. He pulled her hand away from her shoulder, revealing a growing patch of blood on her jacket around a three-inch gash.

"Guzman! He ... He ..." She gasped and clutched the gaping wound. "He stole my bag! Guzman has the zemí!"

CHAPTER TWELVE

Kate squeezed out through the crevice into daylight. She looked down over the tiny ledge. A wave of dizziness and nausea passed over her, but she pushed past it. Whiskey barked, trapped on a ledge about thirty feet above the water, while the thief scrambled the final few feet down the face of sheer rock.

"Hey! Stop!" Kate screamed into the wind.

The man paused, glancing around him, then dropped to the sandy beach below him and waved at Kate. He clutched the severed strap of Lucia's tote bag and flung it into a skiff resting on the beach, then began to shove the boat out into the shallow cove.

Kate scrambled down the narrowing path to the ledge where Whiskey stopped. The cliff below looked treacherous. She put a hand on Whiskey's head to quiet him. "Stop!"

The man shrugged and turned toward Kate, leaning casually on the small boat's gunwale.

She scrambled around the ledge but couldn't find a way down that didn't require rock climbing skill.

"*Señorita*, the mountains and caves are the birthplace of my people. And the time has come for our gods to return to their origin and restore power to the rightful chief. I am the direct descendant of Hatuey, the last true Taíno Cacique. You cannot keep from me what is mine." After giving the tiny boat a final shove, he leaped over its rail as it floated free into the deeper water of the cove. Then he lowered the huge outboard motor, its grumble echoing off the cliffs of the cove. As the boat turned and sped away, the rest of the party trickled down the path.

Lucia dropped to her knees and wailed. "Guzman! It never occurred to me that he could follow us here. How would he even know?"

William crouched beside her. "You said this Guzman was planning to use the zemís to gain power. What exactly does that mean?"

"I think I can answer that." Nelson's gentle Bahamian lilt grew serious. "Most of the descendants of the ancient Awarak people — we Lucayans here in the Bahamas and the Taíno throughout the Greater Antilles — have indigenous blood mixed with European and African. Whether it was smallpox or slave labor or simply intermarriage, our heritage was nearly wiped out when the Spanish came to town. Our populations throughout the Caribbean dropped by nearly ninety percent in a fifty-year time span. Most of our tribes were reported to be extinct, and in the pure sense of the bloodlines, that might not be so far off. But in recent years, there's been an effort to rekindle interest in the history and traditions among those with any Arawak lineage at all."

Lucia released her grip on her shoulder. The blood had slowed to a trickle from the cut Guzman had left in his wake. "That's what Bob's research was focused on. Finding the remaining Taínos and trying to reconstruct, collect, and preserve their culture and traditions."

"And that's why I was so interested in turning our zemí over to him. It's not from our people. It was simply entrusted to us to protect until it could be safely returned home."

Lucia continued, "But there are a few people — a small, but intensely committed group — who believe that's not enough. They believe the Taíno people deserve to have their country restored to them. They believe the five zemís carry the actual supernatural power of their respective gods, and that by reuniting them in a ceremony at the Cave of Origin, the shaman who reunites them will be granted absolute power over a new Taíno nation. These radicals are willing to do anything to further their cause. They preach cleansing the bloodlines, using modern technology to force marriages between the purest Taíno descendants and killing or enslaving those of us whose ancestry is, shall we say, more diluted."

Nelson's hands clenched into tight balls.

"A surprising number of our people believe the power granted by the gods is absolute and must be followed. Most of us were raised in the Catholic tradition of the infallibility of our spiritual leaders, and while many are falling away from the church, the radical neo-Taíno sect is tapping into that legacy of blind adherence. They believe our people are sheep without a shepherd, and they think the zemís bring both the supernatural power and the authority to take over." Lucia bent over and rested her forehead on her knees. "I thought getting one of them to safety would be enough to stop him. But I see now I underestimated Diego Guzman."

Nelson sat on the path beside her and wiped the sweat from his forehead with a faded bandanna. "Missus Lucia, I feel for you and your people. And I will pray to my god that he protect you from dis man. But we live a simple life here, and now your zemí is no longer under my protection, I do not believe I can be of any additional service to you in your endeavor. I can return you to the airstrip on the big island and attend to your wound, but after that, I must wish you well and say goodbye."

William stood then helped Nelson and the women to their feet.

Lucia nodded to Nelson. "Of course. I'd never ask

you to put yourself at risk. I appreciate the service from you and your ancestors, and I thank you on behalf of all our people."

"Honey, I think we need to get you back home and take a closer look at Bob's notes." Kara took Lucia's hand and led her back up the narrow path to the beat-up pickup truck parked on the little plateau. Whiskey leapt into the back, and William and Kate climbed in after him.

Nelson drove them down to the small dock where he'd tied up his boat, ferried them back to the airstrip, and waved as their plane climbed away from his home.

CHAPTER THIRTEEN

Kate unclipped Whiskey's harness. The dog leapt from the truck at the end of the gravel lane and took off around the perimeter of Lucia's yard, sniffing and spiraling in toward the house and office buildings. He circled the house, then crossed the small parking area to Bob's office shed. As he rounded the corner to the new porch leading into the office, the big dog dropped to his haunches and froze.

Kate hopped from the truck's bed. "Someone's been in there."

William climbed from the truck, motioning for Kara to slide to the driver's seat. "For all we know, they could still be in there. If anything happens, get Lucia back down the mountain. Don't worry about us, just go."

He pulled a small gun from his pocket and held it low in front of him. Kate slid into a low crouch behind

William. "There's only one door, and the windows are too small to climb through. You stay here with the girls and cover the door, and I'll circle around through the woods and see if I can get a look into the window."

Kate slipped into the thick mountain jungle. She kept to a path about five yards inside the tree line, circling around Lucia's yard until she was even with the small office.

The rear of the building faced west, nestled back against the jungle, with just a few feet of vegetation cleared around it. Kate crept closer to the tree line, squinting to see past the reflections of the jungle and the glint of the setting sun in the building's new windows. As she shifted to get a good angle, she saw chaos inside the small building worse than when they'd arrived just after the storm.

She crept closer to the window. Papers and books were strewn on the desks and floor, and a potted plant was overturned near the doorway.

"It's clear!" Kate hollered across the clearing. She rounded the building toward the porch and released Whiskey with a scratch on the head. "Good boy!" He wagged his tail and took off toward the woods to relieve himself after the long ride up into the mountains.

"Obviously, someone's been here." Kate pushed open the door, it's brand new jamb splintered and lock destroyed.

"Thank you, Mrs. Obvious."

Kate jumped and spun, startled by Kara's voice

behind her. "Don't scare me like that!" She took a deep breath, then stepped into the ransacked room. "Lucia, how well do you know Bob's research? Enough to tell if anything is missing?"

Kara stepped back to let Lucia through the door. Her sister gasped. "We just cleaned..." She buried her head in her hands. "This is all just too much. I don't understand why all this is happening now."

Kara rubbed her sister's back. "I'm sorry, *hermana*. You don't deserve all this pain."

Lucia looked around the room. "We'll have to put it all back together to figure out what's gone. But I don't know if I can do it tonight."

"Every hour we wait increases the chance that he will cause more harm. We can help you, but we have to do this now, Lucia." William's voice behind the women was soft, but insistent.

Lucia bent down and picked up a splayed-open copy of *The Peoples of the Caribbean*, its laminated cover torn and dangling by a thin strip of clear plastic. She gently closed the book, smoothed its bent, ripped cover, and placed it on an empty bookshelf.

For the next hour, Kate helped her sift through the ransacked office, shelving books, refiling papers, and replacing the artifacts Bob and Lucia had collected over the years of travel throughout the Caribbean.

"Dinner is almost ready." Kara poked her head into the small building. "Looks like you guys are almost done. Can you tell if anything is missing?"

"Nothing, really. Mostly everything's just torn up." Kate placed a shallow wooden bowl on the shelf. "But if they didn't take anything, I wonder how he found us in the Bahamas?"

"It's not that difficult, really. William filed a flight plan. This whole country is a really big small town. Everyone knows everyone else's business, and all it would take is one question at the airport to pick up our trail." Kara slammed a book into place on the shelf. "Lucia, this is ridiculous. You can't live like this."

Kate helped Lucia up from the spot where she'd been sorting paperwork on the floor. "She's right. You can't be constantly looking over your shoulder. We have to pull all of Bob's research together, and as much as we can find on this Guzman character, then turn it all over to the police."

"The police can't do anything about this man."

"Sure they can. It's their job. He's broken into your home and destroyed your property. He's stolen your bag containing a priceless artifact. And injured you in the process." Kate pointed at the bandage peeking out the collar of Lucia's t-shirt. "He's stalked you and your beloved late husband, and he's threatened the people of this town."

"I agree with Kate." William appeared in the doorway. "I can install some security cameras around the perimeter for you, but I think the best thing we can do is turn all this over to the authorities, and for you to come back to the Keys with us for a little while.

Chuck's got plenty of space at Shark Key if you want some space of your own, and it'll do you good to have a change of pace for a little while."

Kara looked skeptical, but finally nodded. "Yeah, why don't you come back with us for a little while?"

"I don't want to give Guzman any opportunity to collect more of the zemís."

Kate twisted her hands together. "That's the point. He can't chase them from jail. And with everything he's done, he'll be in jail for a long, long time."

"You don't understand the Dominican justice system. He won't go to jail just on our accusation."

"Of course not. But we have plenty of evidence of his plot, and they will have to take some kind of action against him, even if it's just keeping you safe."

"Truly, Kate. I have my village here, and I will be fine. I must learn to live on my own eventually. What better time than now?" Lucia's stomach rumbled. Laughter filled the room, easing the tension that had been building all evening.

"It's a good thing dinner's ready." William held the door for the ladies. "Let's get some food. We'll pack up in the morning."

The last one out, Kate secured the broken door, called Whiskey over, and stationed him on the small office's porch.

CHAPTER FOURTEEN

DIEGO GUZMAN STOOD inside the low wide mouth of a cave. Before him sat two dozen of his most loyal worshipers adorned with face paint and hair beads, awaiting his proclamation.

Guzman's path to his current position as chief and shaman of the Taíno remnant had been circuitous. Typically, the roles of Cacique, the tribe's leader and arbiter, and Shaman, the tribe's spiritual guide, were separate and distinct. But Guzman wasn't made for sharing. He found it far more efficient to serve both roles himself for his small tribe.

He claimed the title Cacique through the lineage of his mother. Although she had no ancestral records to prove she had descended from the last Caciques before the Spanish decimated their numbers, she had found a tribal staff in her maternal grandmother's things after the old woman passed away from lung cancer thirty years before. He chose to believe it had belonged to Hatuey, the Taíno chieftain who had had fought bravely against the white invaders and was burned at the stake for his troubles.

Guzman's great-uncle on his father's side had inherited a ceremonial cohoba platter from his father. Tribal lore dictated it was his responsibility to pass along his knowledge, history, and spiritual leadership to his son. But since his great-uncle never married or had children, Guzman's mother made sure her boy became the obvious heir to the old ceremonial shaman.

For as long as Guzman could remember, his mother filled him with the old legends. She taught him about the cohoba ceremony. She taught that Atabey would require him to prove his worthiness and said the goddess would send a messenger to assist him with his quest.

She prepared him to be both a chieftain and a shaman. On his fifteenth birthday, she presented him with the staff and told him it was his destiny to lead the remnant. To reunite the Taíno people and to restore the tribe to its former glory.

It was only on her deathbed that she confessed the truth about his childhood. About how she made a living. About how she'd lost him to his father and how she'd taken him back. About how many lies she'd told to keep him safe and make him strong.

Guzman wished his mother could have lived long enough to witness this culmination of her aspirations.

His tribe was small, but an electricity surged through his body when they worshipped him. And the tribe was growing. Word had spread quickly, and with each new zemí, more people of Taíno ancestry would swear their loyalty to him. Through her lies, Guzman had found a deeper truth.

He stepped out of the shadow of the cave's mouth and raised the staff high above his head. The low murmur among the men kneeling before him quieted, and they all pressed their foreheads to the dust in front of them. Guzman slammed the base of the staff on the ground with a thud, and the men all looked up in unison.

"We are here today as the faithful Taíno. You have followed me as your chief. You have worshipped with me, participated in the holy cohoba ceremony, and guarded me on my journeys to the spirit realm. You are the core of my tribe."

The men nodded together, their eyes glued on their chief. Guzman's torso was covered with tribal tattoos, and a large gold pendant glistened from a leather strap around his neck.

"For as long as we have worshiped together, we have worked to restore the power of the original Taíno. We have sought a way to overcome the tarnished Spanish blood that mingles in our veins with the purest blood of our raped Taíno mothers. We have searched for our brethren and won them to our cause. We have sacrificed the weaker tribemates who preferred to embrace the foreigner. We have sent spies into their midst, and we have gained strength with each passing season."

Guzman paused and placed his staff in a cradle near the edge of the cave. A boy dressed in a leather loincloth brought him a small wooden bowl filled with liquid. He drank deeply from the bowl, then threw it to the ground.

The boy scrambled to catch it before it rolled into the sacred cave.

"Today, my brothers, we celebrate." He reached into a leather pouch hanging at his waist. "For I have rescued this." From the bottom of the pouch, Guzman pulled out the small golden zemí statue then thrust it high above his head.

"Brothers, behold the spirit of Macocael, son of Yúcahu, and god of the mountains." A collective gasp spread among the kneeling men, and they all quickly dropped their foreheads to the ground. "For centuries, while our people have been murdered, raped, and decimated, Macocael has been imprisoned by the Lucayans to the north. Today, he has returned to the true tribe of the Taíno, and he joins his brother Opiyelguabirán', god of the dead, whom we honored together after his return from the islands to our east. Together, they will bless our search for the remainder of Yúcahu's relics. When all five zemís containing the original spirit of the Taíno gods are reunited at the Cave of Origin, our journey will be complete. Then we can reign as a restored people."

Guzman turned his back on the group and summoned the young server.

"Boy, who is your mother?"

"Atabey, Goddess of All and Mother of the Taíno."

"And who is your father?"

"I am a child of Atabey, and only Atabey."

Guzman turned to the men before him. "This boy is the holy consecrated servant of Atabey. Today, he gives himself over to the god Macocael in thanks and celebration of his return to his homeland."

The men in the small clearing began to chant in unison.

Guzman led the boy to a low indentation in the center of the cave.

The golden late afternoon sun poured into the mouth of the cave, lighting the back walls and warming the boy's bare skin. He knelt behind a low cube in the center of the dip in the cave's floor, facing the worshipers.

Guzman stood behind him, the golden image of their god above the boy's head. He slowly lowered the spirit into the boy's outstretched hands.

The boy gently set the spirit on the cube, reluctantly released it, then returned his hands to his knees.

The men outside the cave rocked together back and forth, their chant rising in pitch and speed. It reached a frenzied pace, and the men swayed and gasped for breath.

Guzman whipped a dagger from a sheath on his thigh then sliced the boy's throat open.

His eyes froze in surprise as his blood spilled over the golden statue and onto the cave floor.

The celebration of the mountain-god Macocael lasted long into the night, with the men singing and dancing in a trance under the stars. As the eastern sky began to grow gray ahead of the rising sun, the men bathed in a cold pool fed by a stream from the mountain above, then dressed in their city clothes and made their way down the path to their cars and motorcycles.

When they had all gone, Guzman pulled the ridiculous leather costume off and tossed it in a heap near the edge of the clearing. He pulled on a pair of ripped jeans and a black t-shirt, then carefully retrieved the blood-soaked statuette and wiped the dried crust off with a rag. He dropped it into the front pocket of his backpack.

Then he pulled out a cell phone.

"*Hermano,* I got another cleanup for you. Yeah, the regular place. You here by sunup? ... *Bueno, bueno*. See you soon, brother." He dropped the phone into his pocket then climbed to the peak just above the cave to wait for the sunrise.

CHAPTER FIFTEEN

KATE STUFFED a file folder into a torn cardboard box, closed it, then patted the top. "I think that's all of it."

William hefted it across the driveway to the back of the truck.

Lucia was dusting and arranging the remaining artifacts and books to fill the empty gaps on the shelves.

"With this stuff boxed up at the police station, he's got no more reason to harass you. And the new security cameras will be here in a couple of days. William has already marked the spots for you, so they should be easy enough for you to hang when they arrive."

Lucia grasped Kate's shoulders and looked in her eyes. "I can't thank you enough for all your help. I am usually very self-sufficient, but this past week has been more than I could take. For Carlos to come, that meant something to me of course, but I never imagined you and William would be so much help in getting my home back together, not to mention helping me wrap up Bob's most important work. Thank you, and send my thanks to Chuck as well." She wrapped Kate in an embrace.

She patted Lucia's back then pulled away. "Of course. One thing I've learned in my time at Shark Key — we're all one big family, and when we can help a family member in need, that's what we do. I'm just glad you're okay and your house is back in good shape."

"Did I tell you the university is letting me stay?"

Kate cocked her head to one side.

"Yes, they own the land here. I was scared that with Bob gone, they'd ask me to leave. But no, they're letting me stay, and next spring, they're going to honor him with an award for his work with the indigenous people." She began to cry.

"Oh, Lucia, that's great news. I hope some of this can help ease your pain. You know, when I lost my husband — that sounds so weird doesn't it? Like we went to the mall and he got lost?" Kate's gaze drifted out over the valley below. "I guess I should be able to say it, right? Okay, when he died, those first few weeks were the worst for me, too. I thought I'd never breathe again. And every time I turned around, I saw memories of him. Standing at the kitchen sink washing dishes. Throwing a football in the back yard."

Kate rubbed her eye. "I'm just saying, it's okay to feel lonely and to miss him. But it's also okay to feel happy sometimes. And as time goes by, you'll start feeling the happiness more than the loneliness. So, hang on to that when you're feeling empty. You've got a lot of people in town here who care about you. Let them comfort you. Call Kara and keep that connection. Lean on the people who love you to get you through."

Lucia hugged Kate tight, and both women cried.

William's deep voice boomed from the truck. "Ladies, we need to get rolling if we're going to get this stuff into town and get up in the air early enough that I don't have to stare straight into the sun the whole way home."

Kate grabbed her backpack from the tiny porch of the office shed and whistled to Whiskey. As he leapt into the truck's bed, she and Lucia climbed into the back seat. William and Kara folded their taller frames into the small truck's cab, then they made their way down the mountain.

Forty minutes later, they pulled up in front of the small local police office. Kate grabbed her notebook, where she'd outlined the most relevant details of the story. The rest of the group followed her inside. A lanky black man in a uniform shirt met them at the desk.

"We need to report a crime."

The man glanced behind Kate to Lucia, his eyebrow raised. Lucia shrugged and rattled in rapid Spanish an edited version of Guzman's theft of the zemí and the mess left in Bob's office.

The officer glanced at the Americans, and then

addressed Lucia. "Do you know this man, Diego Guzman?"

Lucia's shoulders tensed. "I know who he is. He had been threatening my husband for several weeks."

"And this white girl is...?"

Lucia pointed to the group of Americans behind her. "This is my bro— my sister, Kara, who lives in the States now, and the white girl is her friend. They came to help after my husband's death in the storm."

The sheriff nodded. "And they all witnessed the assault?"

William spoke, his Spanish clear and correct. "We were nearby. We heard *Señora* Alvaro scream, and we saw the man running away with her bag. Before he escaped in a small boat, he taunted her and claimed to be the chief destined by the gods to reunite the Taíno people."

"Mmm-hmm." The man jotted some notes on a form.

Kate straightened her shoulders. "Officer, this is more than just a theft and an assault. The artifact he stole is of great value and importance, and we believe he's trying to collect more of them to gain power and influence over the indigenous people in this area."

The officer raised his head from his form and stared at Kate, his eyebrows raised. "The item was taken in the Bahamas, no?" He stared for several seconds, then softly asked, "And he is one of the indigenous, yes?"

"I ... I ... I guess so." Kate stammered.

"Then perhaps the item is with its rightful owner now. The Taíno who remain in this area have struggled to keep their identity alive through centuries of slaughter and oppression, first from your white European ancestors who enslaved our men and raped our women, and later from historians and archaeologists who stole Taíno artifacts and put their people and traditions on display like animals at a zoo. Perhaps it's time for a leader to unite them."

"But—"

He raised his hand, cutting Kate off. "Our office will, of course, investigate the accusations you've made. And any injury *Señora* Alvaro here may have suffered will, of course, be taken seriously. But I am not Indiana Jones. And I recommend you not pretend to be, either." The man snapped his notebook closed, nodded to Lucia, then left them standing in the small front office, stunned into silence.

Kate looked at each member of her group. William's eyes were wide, but Kara and Lucia both had a more resigned expression on their faces.

Kara broke the silence. "Well, at least we made the effort."

CHAPTER SIXTEEN

The group sat around a table encrusted with a mosaic of bright ceramic shards, and Whiskey curled on the shaded tile. A soft breeze flowed through the wide windows lining two walls of the small corner restaurant. The only place in Constanza that served burgers and fries, the bar was popular with Americans at the university. A crowd of students had pushed heavy tables together near the entrance.

Kate was the first to bring up the morning's visit to the police station. "I still can't believe that sheriff. It was like he didn't even care that you'd been assaulted, Lucia! Damn corrupt third-world dogs. I bet he would have taken it more seriously if we'd tucked a couple Benjamins in Bob's journal..."

Kara grabbed Kate's hand. "Honey, breathe. In through the nose, out through the mouth. He's understaffed, still overwhelmed with storm victims and damage, and busy trying to keep the city clear of looters and the people in shelters from rioting. But doesn't mean he's corrupt, and he's certainly not a dog. He's just got to prioritize, and right now, we've got Lucia safe so the situation isn't urgent."

"But—"

"But nothing. He's right. Guzman came after Lucia in a different country. We can't prove he broke into Bob's office. We've got all the notes and research right behind you, so that's all safe. Really, there's nothing the police can do right now that we can't. In fact, maybe we're in a better position to take care of Lucia right now than they are."

"*Sí*. My friend down the hill will watch the house. I'm sure Guzman will come back when he hears I'm out of the country, and when he finds all the research material gone, he'll back off."

"Lucia, *hermana*, you're neither stupid nor naive. You know he won't back off. People like him never do."

Lucia sighed. "I guess you're right, but at least we have a little time to—"

A thin woman with long, flame-red hair threw a padded vinyl chair away from the students' table then leaned into the middle of the group, wagging her finger. "It's parasitic and racist!"

A tattooed man with his hair in a bun shouted back, "It's our responsibility to human history!"

Lucia glanced at them and chuckled. "Every semester, a new group of anthropology students arrives and debates the same thing as if they're the first ones to discuss it. They're adorable, aren't they?"

"Oh, to be nineteen and know everything." William sipped an El Presidente and watched the students.

"Y'all, look." Kate whispered, pointing to the TV hanging above the bar. The screen displayed a photo of a light-skinned, dark haired boy superimposed over a satellite map of the area where they were sitting.

A reporter said, "In the wake of the freak late-season Hurricane Sara, a new threat is reported out of the mountains of central Dominican Republic. Earlier today, federal park authorities discovered evidence of the murder of a runaway who had been missing since before the hurricane devastated the island a week ago. Sister Maria Consuela at the Good Hope shelter for orphaned children in the mountain town of Constanza had reported fourteen-year-old Jose Martinez missing three days before the storm ravaged the coastal areas and dumped over a foot of rain on the island in under eight hours. Martinez's disappearance continued to be investigated, even through disaster relief efforts, until this morning, when clothing believed to have been worn by Martinez at the time he went missing was discovered near a small cave by a narrow park access road. Evidence indicates the presence of up to two dozen people in an area believed to be considered holy by the tribes living there prior to the island's discovery by Spanish explorers in 1492. Authorities indicate significant quantities of drying blood matching the boy's blood type were found on the scene. Martinez is the second teenager to go missing from the area in the past two months, but authorities say it's too early to determine whether the cases are connected. We will continue to follow this grisly story as further information is released."

"*Dios mío.*" Lucia grabbed her chest and gasped.

"What?"

"This boy. I know him. He used to sit near the market and would run to the shops and vendors for the *abuelas*. I did not know he was missing. Not long before the storm, I saw him talking to Guzman in front of a cafe near the shelter where he stayed."

"Wait, what?" Kate's eyes bulged. "This kid knew Guzman, Guzman got the zemí he believes gives him spiritual power, and now this kid is missing and probably dead?"

Lucia began twisting her wedding ring.

"Sister, what is it?" Kara's eyes looked like they might bore a hole through Lucia's skull.

Lucia's fingers fidgeted as if they were counting the beads on an imaginary rosary. She finally looked up at her sister. "I never put any stock in the stories. They only showed up in a few obscure lineages, and we only found one complete account in all the interviews Bob conducted throughout the years. Without any corroborating evidence, we didn't think there was any chance the story could be a true part of the shamanic tradition."

"What, Lucia? What is the story?" Kara demanded.

She picked at the cuticle on her left ring finger. "One family deep in the mountains told us a story about the zemís that matched the tradition in all ways except one. That family claimed to have ties through the maternal line to a powerful shaman — the family's maternal ancestor was sister and confidante to the shaman — and they reported that as each zemí returned to their mountain home, its power could only be restored through the spilling of blood of the Spaniards who had caused them to be separated and spread throughout the Caribbean."

"Spilling of blood?"

"*Sí*. As we talked to the old woman, she made it sound like it was a ceremonial thing. That the shaman would bring a person of Spanish descent to the ceremony, prick his finger, smear a drop of blood on the zemí, and that would fulfill the prophesy. But if the rumors are to be believed, Guzman is not a man of restraint. If he has heard this part of the legend, he would interpret it as requiring the sacrifice of a life. Almost certainly."

"We have to tell the authorities."

"Kate, you saw how they responded to us this morning."

"But this is different. This is murder. And what if

there's another? Does that mean he has a second zemí? That he's killed two kids in pursuit of … of …."

Kara stared at the bright mosaic tiles. "It means with each additional zemí he gets his hands on, there will be another death."

Kate took a deep breath and slowly released it. "It means we have no choice. William, cancel that flight plan. We have to find the rest of those statues before he does. And we have to keep them safe at all costs."

CHAPTER SEVENTEEN

KATE ROLLED off of Lucia's couch just before dawn, donned her running shoes, then took off down the mountain lane into the sunrise, Whiskey at her side. When the sun crested the horizon, Kate patted the top of her head. No sunglasses. She turned around and fought her way back up the hill. With every step, she missed the long flat runs back in the Keys a little more.

At the house, she grabbed a hose from the porch to fill a deep bowl. Whiskey stuck his head under the stream, greedily lapping up the water as Kate stretched her hamstrings from running the difficult incline. While Whiskey cooled off, Kate lay on a towel in the damp grass. She stared up at the brightening purple sky and watched a small gossamer cloud drift by.

When she was rested, she whistled for Whiskey then went to work. He curled up on the cool tile in the corner of Lucia's front parlor while Kate surveyed the boxes stacked against the wall on either side of the wide picture window.

The open space of Lucia's front room offered the most space to spread out the research material on the Taíno zemís. Kate set up a folding table she'd found in Bob's workshop and pulled the top off the first box. Two hours later, she had notecards and pictures from Bob's files taped to the window, linked in an intricate web by colored fishing line. Piles of research notes lined Lucia's couch, chairs, and tables.

"Ahoy, the living room!" William's laugh made Kate jump. He leaned through the doorway.

Kate waved him in. "I think I've got something."

William stretched behind a chair to scratch Whiskey's ears. The dog's tail thumped against the wood paneling. Then he straightened, surveyed her efforts, and whistled. "You've been busy."

"I guess I'm getting the old journalism bug back a little bit. I knew if I could just get a little quiet time with this stuff, I'd be able to find some kind of pattern. That a story would somehow reveal itself." She led William to the window, where she'd used a dry-erase marker to draw a crude map of the north-eastern Caribbean Sea across the glass panel. A notecard with a drawing of the five zemís, marked "1500" was taped on top of the glob that represented the island of Hispaniola. Thick braids of fishing line led off in a starburst to surrounding areas. The line leading to the Bahamas was neon green.

"This is the one we found that Guzman stole from us." A single green filament led back to the eastern side of the island in the center of the map. A small photograph of the missing teen was taped up beside the drawing of the zemí that had been taken just a few days earlier.

"Bob's research dug deep into the ancient trade alliances and friendly tribes outside of the Taínos' home territory. He measured each tribe's spiritual tradition around the time of the Spaniards' arrival, as well as any evidence he had of trading relationships between the nations in the three generations before Columbus landed. With this, he developed a short list of the tribes who most likely would have been trusted by the Taíno and willing to guard one of their zemís."

Another line, braided with green and orange filament, led to a notecard taped to the east side of the makeshift map, with a single orange strand leading back to the photo of the other missing boy in the center. "The Lucayans in the Bahamas fit that measure, as did a small tribe of indigenous people in the Virgin Islands. While that group were in close proximity to the enemy Caribe people group, there's some evidence that the tribe had a secret meeting cave near an extinct volcano that the Caribes feared, so the zemí was believed to be safe there. After going through all of Bob's notes, it seems one had been found before any of us even knew what the zemís were. And I think Bob suspected Diego Guzman as well. Look at this."

Kate picked up a simple black and white composition notebook and flipped to a page she had marked near the middle. A crudely drawn sketch filled the page showing a man with similar features, his hair tied with the same beaded leather strap.

William traced the fishing line back to the center of the map and the photos of the two murdered boys. "I don't understand how anyone could do this."

Kate soaked in the gravity of William's comment. "The good news, though, is I think we are closer to the next one than we ever dreamed. Look at this." She pointed to another notecard, linked to Hispaniola with a single strand of orange fishing line, taped to the east coast of the Florida mainland. "The Calusa tribe inhabited the southwest coast of Florida during the same time. They were overrun by the Spanish several years later than the Taíno, and they strongly resisted Spanish assimilation efforts. They had the type of culture the Taíno would trust to guard their most precious artifacts."

"And they're right in our own backyard. Let's wake the others."

CHAPTER EIGHTEEN

Guzman dropped his smartphone into his pocket and sauntered across the carefully manicured lawn, nodding at the professors and winking at the young female students as he carried a pair of hedge clippers across the university's main city campus in Santo Domingo.

The groundskeeper uniform had come into Guzman's possession at the perfect time — no one paid attention to the service workers on campus. He had known Professor Bob Tinsley, the American, had been researching his people's deepest secret. Being invisible anywhere on campus allowed him to keep a close watch on Tinsley's movements, overhear conversations, and get glimpses at his research.

As he approached the equipment shed, the phone in his pocket vibrated again. He opened the doors then hung the clippers on a hook near the window. When he exited, he locked the door and pulled his phone from his pocket. "*Hola.*"

"You see the news, brother?"

"*Sí*. I saw it. I am not worried. In fact, I am more hopeful than ever."

"How can you say that? They've connected—"

"They have nothing. And now we know what they are looking for. So we know what not to do for the next ceremony, don't we?"

"The next—"

"*Sí*, brother. The Americans have a lead. They think the next zemí was sent to a tribe of people in Florida."

"Florida?"

"The indigenous people there were able to defend themselves longer, so at the time when the zemís were sent to safety, the tribe in Florida was still strong and independent. It seemed that they could protect themselves and keep the spirit safe."

"Getting it back out of the States will be complicated."

"Mmm-hmm. That's why I think we should let them get it for us."

"Let them find it? Let them have it?"

"Just long enough for them to bring it back to us. Those do-gooders won't be able to resist bringing it back to the university. After they bring it here, we will take it from them and restore its spirit to its homeland."

"You say that like it will be easy."

"Because it will, my friend. Easy as joining a game of street ball. You find us a nice place. I'll take care of the rest."

Guzman tapped the end button and strolled across campus. He wound through the city's streets, passing through neighborhoods that grew less affluent the farther he walked from campus. After twenty minutes, he turned a corner to a wide, dead-end street lined with ramshackle storefronts with fading paint, where iron bars were bolted to chipping concrete, providing the illusion of security, while, in truth, even the scrawniest of street urchins could pull them from the crumbling walls. But they never did, mainly because there was nothing inside valuable enough to bother with.

Guzman approached a group of young teenage boys playing *vitilla* at the end of the street. He remembered his first game in the old neighborhood in Santiago. He had begged the older boys to let him play until they finally gave in, under one condition. If he didn't get at least a base hit in the first game, he couldn't play with them again. On his first at-bat, he was startled by the erratic path the small bottle cap whizzed past, and he was nearly hit by it on the third pitch. But Guzman learned quickly, and he made contact with his narrow broomstick bat on his second turn. He didn't even wait to see where the cap flew, he just ran for first base as fast as he could.

He credited his time playing *vitilla* with teaching

him to move quickly and decisively, and he still enjoyed mixing in with the younger boys when he could to keep his skills sharp. He waved to the pitcher and pulled a cap from his pocket. The pitcher nodded and pointed to the end of the batting lineup for the opposing team. Guzman stepped to the back of the queue and joined in the kids' banter.

Within minutes, he spotted a younger boy who kept trying to join the conversation but who the older boys shut out at every try. When the boy came up to bat, the pitcher intentionally hurled a fastball high and to the inside, nearly clipping the boy's chest as it zipped by. The boy still swung his narrow stick, striking out and sending his team into the street. The captain of the team pointed the kid to a doorway behind the first baseline, then waved Guzman to take his place at third base.

Guzman played out the inning, and during their next at-bat, he sidled up next to the younger boy.

"I'm sorry, kid. I didn't know he'd bench you. How 'bout after this, we can go to the next street over for some batting practice? I can show you some tricks that'll have you hitting over their heads every time."

"You'd do that? Really?"

"Sure. I remember what it was like to play with the older guys at your age. I was skinnier than you, and the only thing that got their attention was beating them."

"That'd be great. Thanks!"

During the next inning break, Guzman pulled out his phone. He tapped out a quick text, "Got one," then hit send.

CHAPTER NINETEEN

After William landed in Key West, Kara went straight to the club to check in, pay a few bills, and make sure her staff had everything they needed to keep it running while she took some time off.

William retreated to the *Knot Dead Yet* to catch a well-deserved nap.

But Kate needed to clear her head. She grabbed her kayak for a long paddle across the inlet. As she was settling into the seat, Whiskey hopped down from the dock onto the small cargo platform on the back of the low little craft. The kayak swayed precariously.

"Whiskey! Lie DOWN!"

The dog quickly dropped to his belly and the little boat stabilized. Kate dug her paddle deep into the water to her left, then quickly pulled an equally strong stroke on the right. The little boat glided out into the channel.

Kate steered it up past the row of boats docked against the west shore of Shark Key. She waved to a couple of newcomers who'd arrived while she was in the Dominican Republic, and she made a mental note to welcome them and introduce herself once she got back.

As she cleared the dock and drifted past the steps leading up to the restaurant deck, Chuck waved her over. She paddled back up to a small landing at the bottom of the steps, then Whiskey jumped ashore. The force of his leap pushed the small kayak back out into the inlet. Kate laughed and paddled the boat back toward Chuck.

"Seminoles?"

Kate nodded. "It's our best guess. Most logical place to start, at least, since they've got tribal structure and the best historical records. William is going to make a couple calls, but I think we'll get a lot further if we just drive up and turn on the charm."

"You think Kara's charm is going to open doors on the reservation?"

"They run a bunch of casinos. I'm pretty sure she'll fit right in." Kate grinned. "And if not, well, we can always sic Whiskey on them."

As if on cue, a sparking black convertible Mustang with the top down slid to a stop in the parking lot behind them. Kara folded herself out of the driver's seat, and Whiskey bounded up the steps to greet her.

"Hey, hey, *mi familia*! Kate, I got us a toy for our little road trip in the morning!"

Kate popped up the steps and surveyed the showy car. "My Civic would have gotten us there just fine."

"Girl, your Civic can't make it to Higgs Beach and back."

Kate clutched her chest. "Take that back! Take it back now!"

"Your air conditioning hasn't worked since I've known you."

"It's November. It doesn't need to work."

"It drips water on your feet while you drive."

"That makes it easier to deal with the AC not working."

"It makes the car smell like a musty old shoe. I don't even want to know what kind of fungus is growing under your carpet."

Kate rolled her eyes. "I spray Lysol down there every now and then to kill anything that might be growing! That little car gets me around just fine."

"And this big boy here will get us up to the casino in comfort and style." Kara patted the hood of the modern muscle car.

Kate sighed. "Okay, you have a point. And thank you."

"Just be sure to bring a blanket so the furbag here doesn't cost me an extra cleaning fee for shedding all over the back." Kara winked and scratched Whiskey's ears. "Now, who's ready for a drink?"

Kate paddled her kayak back to her slip then pulled it up onto the dock. She paused a moment to soak in the sun before joining her friends up on the deck where Chuck set a cold bottle of Bud Light Lime in front of her.

"It's good to be home." She took a long pull on the bottle. "You know, the fresh fruit in the Dominican Republic is amazing, but damned if I didn't miss these grouper bites." Kate dunked a bite-sized piece of the crisp deep-fried fish into Babette's secret island tartar sauce and closed her eyes, savoring the cool sauce against the hot, fresh-from-the-fryer batter encasing a thick chunk of meaty fish. She swallowed and breathed deeply the familiar salt air. A soft breeze tousled her freshly washed hair.

Whiskey sat beside her hip, waiting patiently for his own grouper bite. The table was covered with paper-lined red plastic baskets filled with French fry remnants, grouper crumbs, and wadded napkins. Kate was the only one left eating, and she vowed to keep eating until the kitchen was out of fish.

Chuck collected a tall stack of empty baskets and leaned to whisper in Kate's ear. "One more, then I'm cutting you off, little lady!" He winked at her, then carried the trash back into the kitchen.

The calm water surrounding the deck sparkled in the evening sun, the horizon dotted with the many tiny islands making up the Conch Republic. For the two years Kate had lived in the Keys, she'd tried to keep her distance and, like many of the temporary folks who showed up in the Keys running from one thing or another, prepared to move on when trouble caught up with her. But Shark Key was a community within a community. A family, even. The events earlier that summer had forced her to choose — run or fight for the family. She'd chosen the family, and now that family was stuck with the responsibility of righting another messy situation.

Tomorrow, she'd start digging around and following leads — jobs Kate thought she'd left behind her. But tonight was all about the grouper bites.

CHAPTER TWENTY

Kate tugged at the scarf wrapped around her left ear. It was supposed to keep her short curls in place and out of her face, but the whole point of a convertible was to feel the wind in a girl's hair. She pulled the scarf down around her neck and let her locks fly.

"You look like Marilyn Monroe."

Kate adjusted her big round sunglasses. "I prefer to think of myself more like Audrey Hepburn."

"Maybe if she'd joined the Army..." Kara pulled on the strap of the utilitarian black ribbed tank top Kate wore. "Or maybe you're more Geena Davis."

Kate slapped Kara on the shoulder. "Don't even say that. This is not a Thelma and Louise type trip. We have a mission."

"Okay. Lois Lane. But, oh damn, does that make me ... Superman?" The drag queen laughed until the next stoplight.

Kate found a playlist of eighties tunes on Kara's phone and they turned the volume up and sang all the way to Florida City.

Once they reached the mainland, they wound their way through western Miami traffic to the headquarters for the Seminole Tribe of Florida. They passed through a gated entry and followed the driveway past a long, shallow pool. In the middle of the pristine water stood a tall statue of a proud Seminole in traditional clothing, leaning on a rifle. Like their distant Taíno relatives, the Seminole tribe in Florida had withstood much and fought many enemies, beginning with the Spaniards in the early 1500s. Unlike the Taíno, the Seminoles had found a way to survive. Kate hoped their survival included some kind of documentation about the Taíno zemí entrusted to them hundreds of years earlier.

The morning was cool and breezy, the sky clear blue. Kate ordered Whiskey to guard the car, and he popped to attention in the back seat. Kara rubbed the little silver charm resting on her chest and whispered, "For luck."

Kate and Kara made their way to the reception desk in the modern four-story office building. A young Seminole woman in a perfectly tailored linen business suit sat behind the reception desk.

"Can I help you?"

"I sure hope so," Kate began. "We have what's probably an unusual request. I'm a journalist, and I'm researching some artifacts that belonged to the indigenous Taíno in Hispaniola before the Spanish conquest. There's some historical evidence that one of these artifacts may have been sent north to the Calusa people for safekeeping, and I'm just looking for someone who might—"

"I'm sorry. I'm going to stop you right there. We're up to our ears with gaming commission audits this week, so unless you know exactly who you need and have an appointment..." She shrugged and turned back to her computer.

"I don't know exactly, but we suspect the item would have been entrusted to a shaman or medicine man to be protected throughout the generations." Kate thought she saw the woman flinch at the term *medicine man*.

"I'm sorry, ma'am, I can't really direct you to what you're seeking. Maybe you should Google Abiaka. Now if you don't mind, I'm in a bit of a hurry here."

Kara glanced down at the woman, raised her eyebrows, and spun on her heel. Kate scrambled to catch up to her friend, reaching her just in time to hear Kara mutter, "Hurry to win that solitaire game..." before she flung open the clear glass door leading to the parking lot.

"Wait."

Kate spun around. The receptionist was tentatively leaning out of her chair across the mahogany reception desk. Kate tugged at Kara's sleeve and pulled her back into the lobby. The receptionist met them in the center of the tall lobby.

"Look, I meant what I said. We've got the gaming commission in here, and we're all pretty stressed. I'm sorry if I was rude to you. It's just that our traditions, especially the spiritual ones, are sacred to us, and we get pretty suspicious when white people, or any outsider" — she nodded toward Kara — "start poking around."

Kara glared at the girl. "I'm not an outsider. I am Taíno, and this artifact—"

"With all respect, you're an outsider to us, and you don't exactly look like a member of another indigenous group."

Kara straightened to her full six-foot-two-inch height and hiked her shoulders back. "The Spanish overran my people before they knew yours existed. They slaughtered, enslaved, or raped everyone in a single generation. When they killed all our men, they imported men from Africa and worked them to the bone, too. Because of them, there are no pure Taíno remaining, but those of us who can still claim the lineage are proud of it. My friend here may be an outsider, but she is trying to help restore this important part of our history and tell our story so white people can know about our people and understand the sanctity of *our* tradition."

Kate stifled a snicker as Kara turned on the indigenous pride.

Halfway through the proclamation, the girl's posture began to soften. She started back toward her desk and beckoned the two women to follow her.

"Look, we have a Cultural Liaison that I'm supposed to direct reporters to. He's here in Miami and, just between us, I've never seen anyone spin answers to his purpose quite so artfully. I'll give you his contact info because that's what I'm supposed to do. It's up to you whether you waste your time with him." She handed them a card and lowered her voice. "But if you're really who you say you are, the person you're looking for is up near the Immokalee Reservation out west. He doesn't live on the reservation, and he's gotten sideways with nearly every tribal official by opposing each casino development project the tribe has proposed. His mama was half-Seminole, half-Calusa, and his daddy was the son of the last Calusa chieftain. If anyone can help you with what you're looking for, he can. But he'll see through any bull you try. So you better keep it real with him."

She pulled a sticky note off a pad and scribbled a name on it, then slipped the note into Kara's palm as if she was sneaking a tip to a maître d' at a fading restaurant. The young woman nodded to Kara then returned to her computer, ignoring Kate completely.

Kara strode out of the lobby, her head held high. Kate scurried behind her.

Out in the car, Kara glanced at the name on the sticky note — Billy Rainwater.

CHAPTER TWENTY-ONE

KATE TYPED Immokalee into her maps app while Kara pulled out of the parking lot into the late morning traffic. They turned north on State Road 7 and the Seminole Tribe's flagship casino — the Hard Rock — loomed on their left. A massive guitar-shaped skyscraper dominated the landscape.

"I saw this in the paper a few weeks ago. There's no limit to what money can buy, is there?" Kara pointed as they drove toward the monstrosity.

"Looks like the tribe is doing just fine."

Kara waggled her eyebrows at Kate. "Wanna stop for some blackjack?"

"If this Rainwater guy is anything close to what that girl said, he'd smell the casino stink on us as soon as we cross into his county. Maybe on the way back?"

Kara drove past the entrance to the massive casino's campus then wove her way through a spaghetti bowl of highway toward Alligator Alley.

As they crossed Interstate 75, the city abruptly fell away, replaced by the flat, lush beauty of the Florida Everglades. Kara downshifted and slowed as she approached the toll booth marking the entry to Alligator Alley. After passing through the SunPass lane, a wide grin spread across her face. Alligator Alley was ninety miles of flat, straight highway, cutting directly through the Florida Everglades.

"Let's see what this baby can do!" Kara shouted into the wind and revved the engine of the muscle car.

Kate swallowed hard and twisted toward the backseat. "Whiskey, lie down. All the way. Down, boy!"

Whiskey wiggled around to find a spot where he could lie low enough to please Kate, but still rest his head up on the window ledge to feel the wind in his tall ears. But as Kara passed ninety miles per hour, he tucked his head down into the footwell behind Kara's seat. Kate reached back and gently rubbed his fur as they flew down the long, straight highway.

Thirty minutes later, Kate jumped when the computerized voice from Kara's phone announced their exit was just two miles away.

"I thought it took a couple hours to get across the state."

"Not the way I drive, honey." Kara tapped a button on the steering wheel and the car began to slow. She turned off the highway and drove north at what felt like a crawl.

Kate glanced over at the speedometer and saw they were still driving sixty-five up the narrow two-lane state road. A high chain link fence topped with coils of barbed wire bordered both sides of the road. Who needed the protection more — the humans or the wildlife?

Kate pulled out her phone to look up Billy Rainwater. The "No Service" indicator appeared in the top left corner. She sighed.

Kara looked hopeful. "We can stop and check the phone book when we get to town."

"Do they even have those anymore?"

"What? Phone books?"

"Yeah? I don't think I've ever used one. I wouldn't even know where to look for one."

"I'd say at a pay phone, but there aren't too many of those left, either. But this is still rural Everglades. Time doesn't pass quite as quickly here as it does in the outside world."

They approached the town of Immokalee, and the empty green landscape began to change. First, they came to a commercial farm with row after row of white plastic grow houses. A couple miles later, they drove by a farm implement dealership, a Circle-K, and a string of warehouse buildings. After getting through what was probably the town's only traffic light, they spotted a little orange cafe on the left. Kara whipped into the parking lot.

The two women climbed out of the car and stretched. Kate tapped her leg, then Whiskey bounced from the back seat and stood on the warm concrete beside her. She threaded a harness labeled "Working Dog" around his chest and snapped a leash onto it.

Whiskey had been working for two years as a police K9 when he and his handler were attacked by an assailant with a knife. Whiskey survived, but his handler didn't. The department retired him about the same time Kate's husband Danny was killed by an intruder, and the two had bonded instantly. Whiskey could follow Kate through a crowd off-lead and never leave her side. But the general public seemed irrationally scared by the huge dog, so Kate found it easier to keep him on the leash. And the working dog harness reduced the resistance whenever she took him into public places with her.

The two women chose a table in the tiny café, and Whiskey curled up beneath it at Kate's feet. A short, elderly woman hobbled toward the table carrying a small spiral notebook. As she got close, she looked at Kara and began to back away.

"No, no. *Diablo*. You go. Go now." The woman crossed herself and scurried back into the kitchen. Kara shrugged and started to heave herself out of the tiny booth.

"Kara, you sit back down!" Kate's voice carried

through the cafe and a man seated across the room glanced up at them.

"Sit or stand, makes no difference. She won't be back out here until your friend leaves. I'm not sayin' it's right, but it's how it is around here. There's Subway down the road a little ways if you need a bite. Kids working there will be cool with y'all." The man nodded and returned his focus to his plate, his piece spoken.

"It's okay, Kate. I don't want to be where I'm not wanted."

"It's not okay. You have every right—"

"Kate, stop. I know better than anyone what my rights are. But I also know when to choose to fight, and when to walk away. This is one of those walk-away moments. Like the man said, that woman isn't interested in changing her mind, and it'd be a waste of breath for me to try. Let's just go."

"But—"

"Kate, I mean it. Let's go."

Kate stood, and Whiskey scrambled out from under the table. They started toward the door, then Kate turned to the man across the room. "Excuse me."

The man scooped a pile of eggs into his mouth.

"Excuse me. I'm sorry to bother you, but, obviously, we're not from around here ..."

The man looked up at Kate. "Obviously."

"You wouldn't happen to know of a man named Billy Rainwater, would you?"

"Who's asking?"

Kate glanced around the room. "Uh, me?"

"Too bad. I might have an answer for your two-spirit friend. But a white girl isn't going to find what she's looking for in this town."

Kate looked back at Kara, her eyes big.

The man burst out laughing. "Relax, white girl. I'm just messin' with you."

She released a breath.

The man held his hand up to his mouth and swallowed the rest of his eggs. "Oh, the look on your face was the best I've seen in weeks. You people are so serious all the time, I never get tired of it." He stood and extended his hand to Kate and then to Kara, his eyes drifting down to the little charm nestled above her cleavage. "Today is your lucky day. Billy Rainwater, at your service."

CHAPTER TWENTY-TWO

"What are the chances? You're looking for me, and here I am."

Kate surveyed the man sitting in front of a newly empty plate. He was thin, with smooth caramel skin stretched across high cheekbones and a wide forehead. He looked young, but a few flecks of gray in his black hair confessed his secret. His eyes laughed, but Kate saw something else behind the joke at her expense. This man had seen some shit.

Kate rested her hand on the back of an empty chair. "May we?"

Rainwater shook his head. "No." He pulled a ten-dollar bill from his wallet and dropped it on the table beside his empty plate. He paused, his gaze resting on the small silver pendant that hung around Kara's neck, then turned toward the door. "Let's walk."

Outside on the sidewalk, Kate caught up with him. "What was that? Why did you ..."

"Ain't very many places in this town I can eat, so I'm not excited about getting on her bad side." He led the women up a sidewalk to the north. "There's a nice little park a couple blocks this way. How about we start with why you're looking for me?"

"Well, we started with the tribal headquarters in Miami, but we couldn't get past the receptionist there." Kara's long stride matched the tall, thin Native American's. At almost a full head shorter, Kate practically had to jog to keep up.

"Ah, yes. Melanie Osceola. Good kid. Means well, but those... Never mind. She does what she's asked, and she's a good gatekeeper for them."

"She is. But when I told her my story, she slipped us your name. So, I'm hoping you'll hear me out." As they walked up the next block, Kara told Billy Rainwater about growing up in the Dominican slums. About being raised Catholic but hearing some of the old Taíno legends. About feeling out of place everywhere, and never really knowing where she belonged.

Billy seemed to be hanging on her every word.

The trio reached the small city park and found a picnic table under a thick southern live oak tree dripping with Spanish moss.

Kara said, "After the hurricane, my sister finally told me everything, including a great deal about a man named Diego Guzman, who is trying to collect the five spirit figures of the goddess Atabey to give him power over the Taíno who remain."

Billy nodded slowly, his eyes flicking from Kara to the treetops, then back to her again. "I don't know why or how, but I know my ancestors put me in that diner for a reason." He met Kate's eyes and held her gaze until she blinked. Then he repeated it with Kara, except Kara held his stare until he blinked. "When I turned fifteen, my dad loaded a canoe and took me deep into the slough."

Kate stopped him. "Sorry, the slough? Spelled S-L-O-O?"

Billy laughed. "White girl, for that little notebook in your pocket, it's spelled S-L-O-U-G-H, and it's a kind of swamp. The Okaloacoochee Slough is a huge swamp between here and LaBelle. Fifteen miles, north to south. Close to the same east to west. Most of this part of Florida and on south is pretty much continuous swamp, and it's easy for a man to disappear into the marsh and never be heard from again. But this land is in my blood. I'm as comfortable in Okaloacoochee as I am on that road out there."

Kate nodded for him to continue.

"William 'Leaping Panther' Rainwater was the last full-blooded Calusa chieftain. His ancestors lived in harmony with the Everglades for more than a thousand years before the white man came. Our people resisted. For a hundred years, we fought and made peace. We formed alliances and broke them. But in the end, it only took a generation to kill an entire culture. While the white men fought amongst themselves for land we'd lived on for a millennium, the few Calusa survivors settled into the swamps in this area, some of them marrying with the nearby Seminole.

"Many in this area still have Calusa blood, but when Leaping Panther fell in love..." He rested his hands on the picnic table and paused. Finally, he lifted his head.

"My mama was half Seminole, part of the tribe you got a taste of down in Miami. Now, the Seminole, they've endured a lot, starting with the Spanish and their diseases and their Catholicism. They've been handed off from the Spanish to the English and back again. They were driven from their homes and hid from the white man in the same swampland where I played with my white friends. But the Seminoles always tried to find a way to compromise and carve out their place here in harmony with whoever was in charge. Sometimes it worked, sometimes it didn't. Right now, it's working to the tune of a few billion dollars a year in casino money." His fists tensed. Then he took a deep breath, stretched his fingers, and nodded toward Kate's notebook.

"Dad took supplies for a few days. I had no idea where he was taking me or why. But I loved the back country, and I knew that time with my dad was important. The first evening, we made camp. Hung our hammocks high up in the trees. I thought Dad was an old relic, even though he was younger then than I am now. I was stunned at how he shimmied right up the tree and that he still remembered how to build a fire, catch fish, and grill it for dinner." Billy looked off at the horizon.

"That weekend, my father treated me like an adult, and I learned he was a man. I remember every minute of it like it was yesterday. That weekend, though, my dad taught me about his people. The Calusa."

Billy tapped a little rhythm on the worn picnic table with his fingertips. "Like I said, the Calusa weren't interested in compromise. We never made alliances with the Spanish or allowed their missionaries to corrupt our spiritual beliefs. Our ancestors paid a heavy price for their resistance, but it was a fundamental part of their tribal identity. These are the things my father taught me that weekend in the slough."

Kara started to speak, but Billy held up his hand. "Patience, two-spirit. I'll get to your answers." He dropped his hand back on the table and resumed his tapping.

"Wait, why do you call me two-spirit?"

Billy chuckled. "In the days before the white man conquered our spirit world and spread their white God and his moral laws around, sometimes a man would be born to our people with a special link to the female spirits or a woman born with a link to the male spirits. These people were revered in our culture because they had a deep understanding of both genders and possessed the strengths of both. Those people were called two-spirit as a term of respect and reverence. I feel both those spirits in you. And your Adam's apple is a bit of a giveaway, too." Billy winked at Kara. "I hope you can take the name in the spirit I intend. But I'm getting off-topic."

"Sorry, go on." Kara twirled her hand in a flourish, urging Billy to continue his story.

"In ancient times, the Calusa, like most other tribes, kept church and state separate. Each tribe had a chieftain who led the people, negotiated disputes, and generally kept the peace. Each tribe also had a medicine man or woman who was the spiritual leader. After the Spanish brought their diseases and wiped most of us out, those roles merged, and a single person in each generation was charged with learning and passing on the history of the Calusa people."

The corners of his mouth twitched into a soft smile. "My father was that person of his generation. And that weekend in the slough was his time to pass the history on to me."

The beat of his fingers was the only sound for a moment. Then he sighed. "One of the stories he told me was about an emissary from a people far to the south. The Calusa had already heard rumors of the Spaniards, mostly from Cuba. There were some Calusa as far south as the keys, and while it wasn't instantaneous like the Internet, news still traveled fast among our people. A few harvests after the first word of the Spanish, an emissary from the south shows up at our border, alone, desperately begging for sanctuary and protection. The chieftain quarantined the visitor, allowing the medicine man to pass him water and food and to see to him after a period of time had passed."

Whiskey's tail thumped on the ground, and Billy reached down to stroke his shoulder.

"Over time, the man told stories of the Spanish invaders that by this time sounded painfully familiar. He was desperate to return to his people to fight, but he told the medicine man that he'd been chosen for an important mission — more important than fighting the Spanish. He'd been among our people for nearly a year when he pulled a small, bright gold statue from an animal skin he'd worn tied around his neck on a braided leather strap. This statue, he said, held the spirit of one of their gods. That night, he entrusted their most sacred spirit to a tribe of strangers, based only on the reputation of the Calusa as resistors and the word of the medicine man who'd taken him in.

"I like to think this trust, and that spirit, were what solidified the Calusa's resolve to resist. Maybe that's true, and maybe not. But the legend has been passed down from generation to generation. And so has the figurine."

"Do you know where it is?" Kate practically bounced on the narrow wooden bench.

Billy grinned. "I do."

CHAPTER TWENTY-THREE

"THIS BETTER NOT BE A WILD goose chase." Kate pointed at Billy Rainwater's pickup truck a few car lengths in front of them.

"So what if it is? It's an adventure, and this is a part of Florida I've never seen before. Have you?"

"No, but..."

"'No, but' what? Sure, it's important for us to find the zemís. I'd even agree that the faster we find them, the better. But it's the only lead we have, and if it's a dead end, I can guarantee Diego Guzman doesn't have any better ones. So, there's no point in being all fussy about it. Enjoy the ride. Besides, I like this guy. I feel like I can trust him."

"You feel like you could feel his abs."

"Girl!" Kara playfully slapped Kate's arm, "You are so bad!"

"Tell me it's not true. You didn't look? Not once?"

"Well, maybe once. But I'm sure I'm not his type. Damn shame, that." Kara shook her head and gunned the engine to keep up with the white truck headed north on State Road 29.

"You know where we're going?"

Kara nodded. "Yes, love. I got the deets while you were primping in the little park potty." Kara waited for Kate to laugh at her turn of phrase before she continued. "The first place we need to go is to meet Chief Rainwater."

"Wait, who? I thought..."

"Billy's father. He was in an accident many years ago, and his wife — Billy's mom — was killed. His dad hasn't spoken since, but he's still formally the chief. Billy wants to take us there as a sign of respect. Then we need to go by Billy's to pick up ... something. It seems like protecting the zemí is kind of serious business to these folks, and I, for one, appreciate that."

Small businesses and side streets had replaced the wide, flat farm fields as they entered the small town of LaBelle. Kate pointed to the truck ahead. "He's turning."

Kara followed him down a narrow side street and into the parking lot of a low-slung, stucco building with a white high-topped van parked out front. As they exited their vehicles, Kate ordered Whiskey to stay in the back seat.

"Bring him," Billy said. "The residents here will love him."

"You sure it's not against some kind of code or something?"

He scoffed. "This isn't the city. Out here, we run mostly on common sense and handshakes."

Kate snapped on the dog's leash, then he bounded out of the car.

"Hi, Billy!" The woman at the front desk was old enough to be a resident. "Your dad is out on the back porch. Who're your friends?"

"Miss Kara Alvaro, ma'am. Nice to meet you." Kara held out her hand and shook the woman's hand gently.

"Kate Kingsbury, ma'am."

"Nice to meet you both. Any friend of Billy's is welcome here. Especially if they bring such a beautiful dog along. What's his name?"

"Whiskey. He's a retired police K9."

The woman rolled her chair around the small desk to give Whiskey a pat on the head. He leaned against her and his hind leg thumped against the tile floor as she scratched down his back.

Billy led them through a common room where two elderly women sat at a table playing cards. They stopped their game to pet Whiskey.

After the dog received a generous dose of ear scratches, the small group went out onto a wide screened-in porch. A man sat in a white rocking chair staring across a sandy lawn spotted with clumps of St. Augustine grass and short sand pines.

"Wait here for just a second."

They stood near the door while Billy squatted beside his father's chair, resting his hand on the older man's shoulder. Billy spoke in a low murmur, but Chief Rainwater's stare remained fixed on a point far beyond the facility's back fence. Billy twisted back toward Kate. "Can Whiskey come here for a minute?"

Kate nodded, dropped his leash, and nudged the dog forward. "Whiskey, go see the Chief."

Whiskey trotted up and sat beside the chair. He tilted his head backward at the chief, then fixed his gaze toward the yard. The two sat together, staring at the same point far past the horizon. When Billy rose from the floor and joined the women near the door, his father lifted his hand from his lap and rested it on Whiskey's shoulder without looking down.

Billy smiled, waiting a few moments before leading the women over to the end of the porch. He lowered himself to one knee in front of his father and spoke quietly, even though the porch was empty except for their small group.

"Chief Rainwater, I present to you Kate Kingsbury and Kara Alvaro. Ms. Alvaro is descended from the Taíno people who entrusted us with their most sacred possession many generations ago. Her people are returning and a false prophet with evil in his heart seeks to gain power over them. Ms. Alvaro will protect the zemí from the false prophet and will use it to unite her people in peace."

Kara and Kate stood awkwardly behind Billy. A slow, rhythmic tick drifted from the clock on the wall. Finally, the old chief nodded almost imperceptibly, and lifted his hand from Whiskey's shoulder and placed it back in his lap. Whiskey looked up at the man once more, then trotted back to the door, wagging his tail. Kate and Kara followed the dog.

Billy pushed himself to his feet, leaned over and whispered something in his father's ear, then joined the women. They followed him as he led Whiskey through the small facility to visit the rest of the residents. As they left, the woman at the front door waved to them. "Thank you, Billy. And ma'am, you have a lovely dog. Bring him back here anytime. Y'all have a nice afternoon, now."

Kate waved behind her as the trio stepped out onto the warm pavement. "She's so nice. It feels more like we're in the Deep South than coastal Florida."

Billy laughed. "Yeah, you don't have to get too far inland to find the state's southern roots. The snowbirds rarely stray this far away from their precious condo complexes and strip malls. But this is the real Florida, the one worth protecting from all of you transplants. No offense intended, of course."

"None taken," Kate glanced at Kara. "Even though the culture is a little less down-home and a little more quirky, we see the same thing in the Keys. Rich developers running the locals out, squeezing families who've been on the islands for generations. We had a problem with a developer trying to take Shark Key out from under our friend earlier this fall. It didn't end well for him."

"Wait, I think I heard something about that from a buddy of mine down in Marathon. The guy's brand new yacht blew sky high somewhere out in the Dry Totugas?"

Kate laughed. "Yeah. Something like that. They said it was a fuel leak in the engine room." She winked at Kara and opened the door of the Mustang to let Whiskey in the back seat.

"So, you live on Shark Key?"

"I do, yeah. Got a forty-five-foot houseboat with no motor. *Serenity.* Kara here owns a club in town and lives in the loft above it."

Billy nodded and opened the door to his truck. "Well, landlubber, you're about to get your feet wet."

CHAPTER TWENTY-FOUR

KATE STRAPPED a fiberglass kayak down in the truck bed alongside Billy's wooden canoe. Whiskey perched beside the boats, his tongue lolling at the promise of a ride.

Noting the speed of the dropping afternoon sun, Billy promised their trip was a short but necessary one. Kara put up the Mustang's top and left it parked in front of Billy's shop. Then the three of them crowded into the cab of his truck.

Billy drove them back down the arrow-straight highway, then turned down a series of back roads that narrowed to barely a trail. The trees thickened and the ground softened the closer they got to the slough. Finally, he parked on a small dry rise then opened his door. When they all piled out, he shook his head. "Kara, those shoes won't last five seconds out there."

Kate looked at Billy's bare feet and her own Teva sandals. Then she raised her eyebrows at Kara.

With a shrug, she kicked her high-heeled platform sandals into the footwell of the truck then stood barefoot in the dirt, wiggling her toes.

They unloaded the boats and paddles, and Billy handed each of them a bottle of water. Kate pushed the little vessel halfway into the water, slipped into the seat, then shoved off with the long, double-ended paddle. After steering the tiny boat into the creek, she spun herself around against a mangrove to wait.

Billy settled Whiskey into the center of the canoe, then helped Kara get situated in the bow. He waded ankle deep into the creek, guiding the boat into deeper water before climbing into the stern and paddling into the center of the waterway.

Billy steered the canoe against a gentle current, and Kate followed, paddling the kayak on alternate sides to stay on a straight path behind the longer, sturdier boat.

"Don't worry, we're not against the current for long before we turn a little deeper in. Just means the last leg of the trip back out will be easier, right?"

Kate resisted the temptation to splash Billy with her paddle. The man clearly had a sense of humor, but she hadn't known him long enough to know quite how playful he could be, and he was the only one who knew the way back out of the slough. "I'm good. I missed my workout this morning, anyway."

They paddled deeper into the thickly wooded swamp, Billy leading the way through a maze of streams and channels. Kate's kayak easily navigated even the shallowest passages, but Billy and Kara had to climb out of the canoe and carry it across the shallower portages, Whiskey following behind them through the soft ground and tangled roots. After nearly an hour of paddling, Billy spun the canoe down a narrow stream and ran it aground on a small, muddy shore.

"Kara, you'll want to watch your step. That mud will suck you down faster'n you can take a breath. And the gators over there on the opposite bank are hoping for a big dinner."

Kara's breath quickened and her eyes grew huge as she scanned the other side of the creek.

Billy howled. "I'm kidding about the gators. Mostly. But do be careful. Use the bigger exposed roots to step on and pull yourself up, and then I'll tie off and meet you on that little dry rise."

Kate sat in the center of the stream watching Kara and Whiskey climb ashore, then she and Billy secured the boats before joining them on the small clearing.

"So, do you two think you could find your way out?"

Kate shook her head. Kara answered a little more strongly. "Honey, I was lost before we even got in the boats!"

"Good. Only a very few people know about this place, and only one of them could find it on his own.

You met him, and he ain't comin' out here any time soon. My point is, this place is both secret and sacred, and bringing you here is a huge sign of trust."

"Thank you. We appreciate it and promise to honor that trust." Kate bowed her head in respect.

"Wait here." Billy glanced around the clearing, then shimmied up a tree faster than Kate would have thought a man of his age could climb. Twenty feet up the tree, Kate noticed a small box, its wooden frame tucked perfectly into the niche where the tree's trunk split and branched out into a wide canopy. Billy propped himself against a vertical branch, his feet pushing against the opposite limb. He reached in and retrieved a small metal case. He fiddled with it for a moment, opened it, then tucked something into a deep cargo pocket. He locked the box before securing it back in its spot high in the tree, then quickly lowered himself back to the ground.

Kara stared, wide-eyed. "You hid a thousand-year old priceless artifact up in a tree?"

Billy laughed and shook his head. "Of course not. Your priceless artifact is in a safe deposit box at a bank down in Marathon. This is just the key." He pulled out a small marine float keychain. He tossed it up in the air, caught it, then dropped it back in his pocket.

CHAPTER TWENTY-FIVE

THE SUN WAS SETTING behind the sweeping groves as the group drove back toward LaBelle.

Kate's stomach rumbled. "I'm hungry enough to have eaten that gator back there. I think all I've had all day is a candy bar I picked up at the Circle K."

"I'm sorry." Billy glanced across to the two women. "You missed lunch. I've been so focused, I didn't even stop and eat. I'll stop at the market and pick up some steaks. We can throw them on the grill when we get to my place."

"Thanks, Billy, but I think we'd probably rather get back on the road. We're still four hours from home. We can hit a drive-through somewhere and eat on the run."

"About that. I have a deal for you ... I've got a buddy from down in Marathon who had to leave his boat up here last week. I need to run it back down there for him, anyway, and was gonna stay a few days and do some fishing. How about we return your rental here, and you all can ride down there with me tonight? It's got two staterooms if you want sleep, or you can hang out up on deck and keep watch with me. When we get in, we can tie up, get some breakfast, then we can all run into the bank together in the morning."

"That's too kind of you."

Billy shrugged. "Hey, I have to be at the bank to open the safety deposit box anyway, so it'll kill a few birds with the same stone. Besides, the crossing down to the Keys always feels faster with some company."

"All right, then. We have a plan."

Billy made a couple phone calls, first leaving a message for his friend and then catching the dock-master to make sure the boat was fueled up. Finally, he called his buddy who ran the service station that also served as the local car rental agency and asked him to stick around a few extra minutes so the girls could drop off the Mustang. They could hear his excitement through the tiny speaker in Billy's phone.

"Sweet! I won't have a problem getting that back to Key West. Hell, I might take it down there myself this weekend! See you in a little bit, Billy!"

On the way back, while Kara called her sister, Kate and Billy stopped at the supermarket and picked up a huge pack of New York Strip steaks and some lettuce. "I'd offer you homegrown, but we're a little out of synch. I've got home grown tomatoes and cucumbers, but the first winter lettuce just got planted last week."

Thirty minutes later, they sat on a concrete pad behind Billy's shop on the edge of town, devouring medium-rare steaks and nearly home-grown salad.

"This is the best steak I've eaten since I moved south," Kate said as she chewed a full hunk of meat.

"Our market only sells locally grown, grass-grazed beef. None of that commercial crap around here."

"Well, it's delicious. What seasoning do you use?"

"I could tell you, but then I'd have to—"

"Hey!" Kate turned to Kara. "He trusts us with his tribe's biggest secret, but not his steak seasoning?"

"A man's gotta draw a line somewhere." Billy popped the last bite of steak into his mouth and tossed his leftover chunks of fat to Whiskey. "Y'all about ready to set sail?"

Kate whistled for Whiskey as she and Kara grabbed their overnight bags from a pile at the corner of the building. Billy slung a backpack over his shoulder and grabbed a cooler and his fishing pole. They walked three short blocks to a small marina on the river where a big dark blue Rampage sportfishing boat floated near the end of the dock.

Kara whistled. "Nice friend you've got."

"We grew up together, and now he runs charters out of Marathon when the spirit moves him. Mostly he just hangs out at his place in the Content Keys. He has a nice little setup with solar power, a little aquaponic system for vegetables and crawfish, and all the fish he can catch."

"That sounds like bliss." Kate set her bag down on the u-shaped banquette in the boat's roomy salon. Whiskey curled up under the table and immediately began to snore. "I wouldn't trade Shark Key for anything, but it does start to get a little bit crowded this time of year."

"It's always nice to visit for a weekend, but I like my modern conveniences a little too much to live that way full-time." Billy climbed the ladder to the flying bridge. A few moments later, the engines rumbled to life. After Kate helped untie the lines, Billy gently nudged the big boat out of the slip and down the river toward the Gulf of Mexico.

It was after three in the morning when they crossed under the Seven Mile Bridge and approached the small harbor. The tiny sliver of moon shone like a slash in the dark night sky as the Rampage idled up the center of a narrow channel. Kate spotted as Billy carefully piloted past smaller boats tied up on both sides. He eased into a wide turning basin at the end of the channel and deftly spun it around and against an open spot near the back of the basin. Kate hopped ashore to tie the lines, and Billy killed the engines. The low chug was replaced with the hollow sound of silence, pierced by a solitary cricket somewhere near the low hedge at the border of the nearby deck. A loud snore drifted from the dark cabin, its door flung open to catch the cross-breeze.

"Let's just let her sleep."

Billy nodded and grabbed his pack. "I'll give you ladies some privacy."

"Oh, no, Billy, please. I can't run you off a boat that's not mine. Please, you take the other stateroom, and I'll sleep out here on deck."

"The couch in the salon pulls out. I can sleep there."

"No, really. I prefer the open sky. Please, take the real bed."

Billy shook his head. "You've known me all of fifteen hours."

"And you've invited us into your swamp. I should start calling you Shrek."

"Does that make you Donkey?" Billy stifled a laugh.

"Oh, just go to sleep!"

Billy dropped down into the boat's cabin, and Kate grabbed two towels and climbed out onto the long foredeck of the boat, with Whiskey on her heels. On clear, cool nights, she loved to sleep up on the top deck of *Serenity* in the open air. She spread the towels one on top of the other for a little soft cushion and lay down. Whiskey curled up against her and she rested her head on his coarse fur. She fell asleep counting the stars in the wide black sky.

CHAPTER TWENTY-SIX

KATE AWOKE to bright morning sun warming her skin. Between her and the dock, Whiskey sat at attention. Muted footsteps sounded on the sole below, and the boat rocked gently. Kara's heavy snores rose through the open hatch on the foredeck.

"Hey, Billy?"

"G'morning." His voice echoed off the still water.

"Does your friend keep any coffee on board?"

"Meet me in the cockpit."

Kate pushed herself up and stretched. The fresh salt air smelled like home. She draped a towel over the boat's sparkling rails and wiped them dry of the morning dew, then made her way forward along the starboard gunwale, Whiskey close behind her.

Billy helped her up onto the dock then led her across the deck into the small tavern. A short, stocky man in an orange Rusty Anchor t-shirt ambled from behind the bar, then wrapped Billy in a bear hug. When he finally let go, Billy took a step back.

"Rusty, this is Kate. She and her friend have a little business to conduct in Marathon, so they helped me bring the *Revenge* back last night."

"And who is this gorgeous animal?" Rusty held out his hand out for a friend-making sniff.

"This is Whiskey. He—"

Whiskey licked Rusty's fingers then ducked his head to demand a scratch. Rusty obliged, then slipped back behind the bar. After washing his hands, he set a steaming mug of coffee in front of Kate.

She took a sip and her eyes rolled back into her head. "This is the best coffee I've tasted in ... I don't know how long."

Rusty smiled. "I get that a lot. It's from a little spot in Costa Rica, and if I tell one more person where to get it, I might just run through their annual supply. Enjoy." He drifted from table to table, checking on his other guests.

Billy checked his watch. "The bank opens in about thirty minutes. I think we should wake Kara then start on up there. It's just a short walk to the main road from here."

Kate pulled her phone from her pocket. She called Chuck and asked him to grab her keys and bring her Civic up to meet them at the bank in Marathon. She downed the rest of the coffee in a single, joyful gulp, then went back out to the big blue boat to wake Kara.

At nine on the dot, they stood at the door to the bank. The manager unlocked the door and opened it wide. "Hi, Billy. What brings you down here?"

"Just need to open my box."

"Sure thing. Let me get my keys."

Whiskey stayed at the front door as the manager led them through the small lobby to a tiny room, the far wall lined with small boxes. She checked the computer, asked Billy for his ID, then removed a key from her ring. After they retrieved his box, she left them alone in the room.

"You know, I expected that someday I'd take my son for a weekend in the slough. We'd camp. We'd fish. I'd show him the box where the key was hidden and teach him the combination to the lock. Then, thirty years later, he'd do the same with his son. I'm not sure I ever thought I'd be using the key to return this to anyone, but I feel it. It belongs with you." Billy reached toward Kara's shoulder, then hesitated. "May I?"

Kara nodded.

Billy gently lifted the leather strand away from Kara's neck and rested the little silver charm on his fingers. Then he turned to the box. After lifting the lid, he pulled out a small gold figure shaped like a man. It was engraved with delicate stylized tattoos and wrapped in a faded cloth. He gently placed it in Kara's hands.

"On behalf of countless generations of Calusa

people who have guarded this item, I return it to its Taíno home." Billy bowed low in front of Kara.

"Thank you. On behalf of the generations of Taíno since this was entrusted to you, I am grateful for the help of the Calusa people." She touched Billy's shoulder, and he straightened to his full height. He returned the box to its slot in the wall, removed his key, then dropped it back into his pocket.

As they exited the lobby, Kate's Civic pulled into the parking lot. Kate and Kara turned to say goodbye to Billy, but the quiet man had already disappeared. Their only clue was in the rustling leaves beyond the wide hedge at the edge of the parking lot.

CHAPTER TWENTY-SEVEN

Diego Guzman smiled, feeling the boy's grip around his waist tighten. He pulled the motorcycle out of the sharp turn and dodged holes and large stones as it climbed the narrow mountain lane, the mid-morning sun on their backs. The boy had clung to him up the mountain the same way he'd clung to Guzman since they'd met.

The small bike sputtered to a halt at the top of the lane. Guzman lowered down the kickstand and nudged the boy off with his elbow. They pulled off their scuffed helmets and hung them by the chinstraps from the handlebars. Guzman was only ten years older than the boy, but it felt like generations. He looked deep into the boy's eyes.

"Look at you, a strong Taíno warrior, chosen by Atabey herself to help me in her most important work."

He dipped his thumb in a little jar of red paint, rubbed it in a wide stroke across the boy's cheek, then repeated the movement on the opposite side. "Atabey is your spirit mother. Your true mother. That whore who leaves you at home night after night is not worthy of you."

The boy's eyes gleamed. Guzman glanced up at the house. Bright, lush flowers hung above the porch railings, and fresh paint spoke of the recent repairs to the little wooden home in the mountains.

"We are here to serve Atabey. The man who lived in this house was an enemy of our people. He sought to cage Atabey. To put her spirits on display and to study her like a fossil your teachers would talk about in school. We can't allow that to happen, can we?"

"No!" The boy's enthusiasm pleased Guzman. He was perfect. He devoured the little attention Guzman flung his way, and he stayed hungry for more. His allegiance was unwavering. And today would be his first test.

"Inside, we will find that man's notes. We will take back what belongs to Atabey, then destroy the rest as punishment for his crimes against her." Guzman released two thick straps around a small canister on the back of the motorcycle. "You are here to protect me as I do Atabey's work. I need you to stand inside the door and watch this lane. Call out to me if anyone tries to come near the house. Can you do that?"

The boy nodded.

They started in the smaller shed. The tiny room stank of new wood and sawdust. The boy stood in the doorway of the shed while Guzman rifled through the file cabinets and bookshelves. He selected a few folders, and took two small artifacts off the shelves behind the desk, but he was surprised at how little he found in the office about the Taíno zemís. When he was satisfied he'd collected everything of use, he took the canister from the boy and poured some of its pungent contents on the floor of the shed. He flung a match in then shut the door behind them.

Guzman led the boy up the steps of the main house. He started to charge the door, but the boy simply turned the knob and the door opened into the main living area.

Inside, Guzman gasped. The dining table had been dragged into the center of the room, and papers and books were scattered everywhere. Notecards and photos were taped to the big glass window. The sound of the diesel generator outside the window chugged, and wisps of gray smoke drifted away from the house on the mountain breeze.

Guzman stacked all the papers and notes in order, tucking them into a sturdy box. He began with the research on the two zemís that were still missing, ignoring the materials connected to the two zemís he already possessed and finishing with the one he knew the Americans were hunting down in Florida. He was stuffing a book into the box when the sound of the generator died. The boy looked over at him, and he froze, listening in the eerie silence.

He heard a clatter from the back of the house, followed by a long string of Spanish profanity from a musical female voice.

Guzman stuffed the final items he needed into his box and waved to the boy to spread the remaining gasoline around the room. The boy did as instructed then tossed the empty can after the fuel. Guzman shoved the loaded box into the boy's arms as the two scurried to the front door.

Guzman pulled a matchbook from his pocket, ripped out one of the thin cardboard strips, and tried to strike it. He pulled the tip of the match across the rough strip three times, but the red tip just crumbled. Guzman tore out another match, folded the cardboard cover backward over the match and the striking strip, and tried again. He squeezed too tightly and again, the match refused to light. Finally, he was able to produce a flame with the third match. He lit the sulfur tips of the remaining matches in the book, tossed it near a small puddle of gasoline on the living room rug, then ran down the steps past the flaming shed toward the motorbike.

Guzman quickly strapped the box to the back of the bike, then jumped on the seat in front of his young accomplice. After punching the ignition of the bike, he revved the engine then sped down the rutted lane as the house behind them burst into flames.

Halfway down the mountain, Guzman pulled the bike off the road and down a wooded lane. He told the boy to wait with the bike and guard the box, then he pulled his phone from his pocket and stalked further into the woods, punching at the phone's lighted screen.

"You told me the house would be empty."

The woman on the other end of the phone was silent.

"Who was in the house?"

Finally, the woman answered. "It must have been Consuela from the village. She's been helping to cook and clean, but she was not to come until Monday. Did she see you?"

"I don't think she did, but she may have heard us. The generator was loud and I thought we were alone, so I wasn't trying to be quiet. Unless there's a back door, it won't matter anyway."

The woman swore. "You said no one would die."

"You said no one would be there."

The low hiss of the connection filled the silence until the woman finally spoke. "They have the third zemí."

"You're sure?"

"Certain."

"How long until you can get it from them?"

"Of that, I'm still unsure. You just focus on finding

the others, and I'll keep you informed of their progress."

The line went dead and the screen on Guzman's phone showed the call ended. He stuffed the phone back into his pocket. When he reached the boy, he climbed back onto the bike then drove them back to town.

CHAPTER TWENTY-EIGHT

The little Civic chugged west past the low-slung shops and sweeping trailer courts of Marathon and onto the long causeway. Kate dropped it into fourth gear as it slowed on the climb up to the peak of the Seven Mile Bridge.

"You could have brought my Mercedes, Chuck." In the back seat, Kara's knees were squeezed together and folded up against the center console, her feet wedged in the opposite footwell.

"I could have brought my truck and put you in the bed." Chuck twisted toward the back seat and blew her a kiss. She laughed, mimed catching it, then planted it on her ample rear end.

"You two. What am I gonna do with you both?"

"Drive our asses back home. I'm sure Chuck has work to do, and I could use a nap. I'm not used to sleeping on a boat like you are."

Kate yawned. "I could use one, too, but I think maybe I'll take the kayak over to Horseshoe and back to loosen up my shoulders. Going against that current yesterday was a hard paddle, even for me."

"Much as I'd like that nap, I'm probably going to spend the afternoon arranging a flight back to Santiago so I can get this thing a little closer to home, where it belongs." Kara patted the small bag that lay on the back seat between her and Whiskey.

"Don't be ridiculous. William's got his plane already fueled up and ready to go. He was talking about it at breakfast this morning. He wants to give you a little more time alone with your sister, so he's taking Michelle up to one of the beach resorts for a few days."

"He doesn't have to do that."

"Of course he doesn't have to, but he's a boy with a new toy. It's fun for him. Besides, what are the chances you'd get through security and customs at a commercial airport with that thing in your bag? And are you gonna put it in your checked luggage? It'll end up in Chile."

"Okay, okay, you win." Kara fished her phone out of the bottom of her purse.

An elderly woman answered on the first ring. "Oh, thank God, Carlos." She was out of breath and her voice trembled. "There's been a fire."

"A fire?"

Chuck twisted in his seat, tapped his ear, and mouthed, "Put it on speaker."

Kara tapped the screen.

The woman's voice resonated through the small car. "Your sister's house, *mi amigo*. It is gone."

"Gone? Wait, who is this?"

"*Sí*. Gone. I am *Señora* Gutierrez. I live in the village. She came down to the market to buy fruit and vegetables, and she stopped to have a coffee with me. As we sat on my porch, she saw smoke rising up on the mountain. I said, 'No, no, nothing like that could happen after everything you've been through...' We called for the fire trucks, but..."

"Can I please speak with Lucia?"

"*Sí*, just one moment."

Sounds of shuffling came through the phone, and Lucia's sobs grew louder as the old woman activated the speaker.

"Car ..." Lucia hiccupped, and finally composed herself enough to speak. "It's all gone. All gone. When I got there, everything was ash. It's all gone."

"Oh, honey, I'm sorry. Are you okay? Where are you right now?"

Lucia's sobs grew more violent, so the old woman answered for her. "She is not hurt, and the firemen brought her back to my house. They said a corner of the back bedroom still stands, but everything else is burned. Even her husband's office, God rest his soul."

"The office? That's all the way across the clearing from the house. There's no way..."

"It was not an accident." Lucia's tear-laced words burst from the small speaker.

"Guzman?"

"Who else could it be?"

While the women talked, Chuck frantically typed on his phone. He held up a message from William between the seats for Kara to see.

"Honey, you just sit tight, okay? William is getting the plane ready, and we'll be there as fast as he can fly. We're coming to get you."

Kate drove as fast as she dared through the small towns and over the bridges that led back to Shark Key. When they pulled in, William was waiting for them on the dock beside Kate's boat.

"Kara, let's take my car," he said. "You can drop me at the airport, and then run by your place to get whatever you need while I fuel the plane and file the flight plan. Kate, are you ready to go?"

"I could really use a shower. I can meet you over at the airport in about twenty minutes?"

"Kara, you don't have room at your place, and I think Lucia might feel a little safer out here. I'll get my guest room ready." Chuck caught William's eye. "How late do you think you'll be back?"

"I want to go up and check out the damage and see if we can salvage anything for her, and with stops in Santiago to get fuel and clear customs, we'll definitely be after midnight. I'll call you once we're in the air and give you an arrival time."

"I'll be ready. Then you all can finally sleep."

Kara looked at her friends in the little crushed-shell parking lot, a fat tear on her cheek. "Thank you." She climbed into the driver's seat of William's MDX. "Let's go rescue my sister. Again."

CHAPTER TWENTY-NINE

KATE CLIMBED down the small plane's steps into the sweltering late afternoon heat, then Whiskey bolted across the tarmac to the nearest bush. A string of dark storm clouds hovered slightly north of them. Debris still lined the fields to either side of the runway, and the wide hangar's roof still lay curled back, leaving its contents at the mercy of the elements.

Lucia waited in the front seat of a small extended cab pickup truck parked near the airport's one-room office. Kate waved to her as she pulled the truck around and backed it up to the plane's cargo hatch.

Kara hugged her sister. "Your eyes are still swollen and red. You didn't have to come get us. We could have found our way up to the village."

"It gave me something to do. Better than sitting up there staring at the charred remains of my life."

"Can anything be salvaged?"

The smaller woman shrugged. "I didn't stay very long. It was ..." She took a long, deep breath.

Kate wrapped her arm around Lucia's shoulder as Kara began unloading supplies for residents of the village who still had no power or running water. "It's okay. You've been through too much already. We'll drive you back to *Señora* Gutierrez's house, you can help hand out water and supplies to your friends in the village while we go and see what's left, okay?"

Lucia nodded, her eyes focused on the storm clouds in the distance. Kate helped her into the back seat while William and Kara loaded three small gas-powered generators into the truck's bed.

"William, I think if we unbox those and drop Kara off with Lucia, the two of us can get up to her place, box anything that's left, and get back down within an hour or so, can't we?"

"Yeah, but we need to hurry if we're going to beat that storm."

"Okay. We can stop by the university to drop off the zemí on the way back down. They'll make sure it gets catalogued and returned to the Ministry of Indigenous Affairs."

Kate tossed the last few cases of water into the back of the truck and piled into the back with Lucia. The truck's gears made a loud grinding sound as William shifted it into first.

"Helps if you use the clutch."

"I am using the clutch, Katherine. I've been driving a stick since before you were born, young lady."

Kate flicked her finger at his graying temples. "I'm sure you have, old man. But those gears are still grinding."

Lucia tried to laugh. "This old truck has seen a thing or two. Sometimes it needs time to get used to a new driver."

They drove up into the mountains and quickly unloaded the water and generators in the center of town, leaving Kara and Lucia to help distribute the supplies to the villagers. Kate jumped into the driver's seat as William unloaded the last of the supplies, then he climbed into the passenger seat.

"Maybe it'll like me a little better." She popped the truck into gear then zipped up the mountain to Lucia's place.

They gasped as they drove into the clearing. The house was nothing but a blackened pile of rubble, with one wall still standing near the back. Debris covered the area they'd just repaired. Charred beams and paneling lay amidst the dead stems of flowers they'd planted days before.

Kate looked across the clearing to where the small office building had once been. Trampled grass lay between the two burned buildings, and the scent of gasoline still lingered in the heavy, humid air.

William walked around to the back of the

remaining wall. "It wasn't the generator. That's got the least damage of anything here."

"No, this was no accident." Kate climbed up into the rubble of the main house, and lightly hopped across the debris to the unburned floor joists of Lucia's bedroom. "The front room and most of the kitchen are completely gone. It had to have started right where all the notes and research were. There's no way to tell what burned up and what he took. And I'm sure that was his intention."

"Is there anything up there that we can salvage?"

Kate pulled at the filthy, drenched curtain that had hung in Lucia's closet and picked through the dresses and shoes that remained. "There's no cleaning any of this." She pushed further back into the closet and found a heavy plastic tub. It was sagging but still intact. She stripped back the lid, then sat on a burned chunk of wood. "Look at this. It was just far enough back not to burn. The tub is a little melted, but everything inside still looks okay. It's full of photo albums." Kate rifled deeper in the container. "And here's a report card. Carlos Alvaro."

William put the box of keepsakes in the back seat of the truck while Kate continued through the bedroom. She flipped a charred mattress out of the way and gasped. "William, there's a fire safe down here!"

He ran back to her. Together, they carried the small, heavy box to an open spot in the lawn. The paint on the outside of the safe was bubbled and blackened from the heat, but it had done its job. The door was securely latched.

"Lucia had to have known this was under the bed. Do you think she has the combination?"

William grabbed the handle and pulled. "Looks like she doesn't need to." The handle slid up, then the door to the small safe popped open.

Kate gaped at the little box. "Who the hell hides a safe under their bed and doesn't lock it?"

William began to pull documents from the charred safe. "Passports, birth certificates, and ... Kate, look at this." William handed her a small leather-bound journal as fat raindrops began to fall. They gathered the contents of the safe then ran to the truck. The sky opened above them.

In the safety of the cab, Kate flipped through the pages of the leather journal.

"This is filled with drawings of the zemís, and names and phone numbers of contacts all over the Caribbean. William, if we'd had this, we wouldn't ... Oh, my God. He knew how to get all of them. It's all right here."

"Why would Lucia leave this?"

"A better question is why would Guzman leave it?" Kate continued to flip through the pages. "Looks like our next stop is Jamaica."

CHAPTER THIRTY

KATE WHISTLED TO WHISKEY, slung her backpack over one shoulder, then followed William out of the small private terminal at Norman Manley in Kingston.

A lanky man with ink-black skin and long dreadlocks leaned against a four-wheel drive. "Mistah Jenkins? I be Anthony Jackson. Mistah Martin Thompson, he say you a good friend, and I take good care of you today and tomorrow until you be going home to Miami."

William laughed as he took Anthony's hand. "Yes, Martin spoke very highly of you, as well." He introduced Kate and the Alvaro sisters. Anthony looked Kara up and down as he shook her hand.

"You a mighty woman, Miss Alvaro. I be careful wit you, I do." He turned to Lucia and raised her hand to his lips. "And you. You small, but perhaps be even mightier."

He hopped back to the open tailgate. "I take your tings?"

William nodded and handed off his duffel bag then Kara and Lucia's bags.

Kate pulled her small backpack against her side. "I'll keep mine, thanks."

"No problem, mon." Anthony opened the door for her and waved her in with a flourish. Kate patted the bottom of her bag and felt for the small lump of the Calusa zemí in the corner. She tucked the bag between her feet as Lucia and Kara settled in on either side of her. Whiskey climbed into the back and draped his head over Kara's shoulder.

William pulled the front seat forward and twisted back to the ladies. "I probably should have asked for a larger car."

"No worries, we're just getting closer and closer, aren't we, girls?" Kara nudged Kate's shoulder and laughed, then picked a dog hair off her sleeve.

Anthony dropped into the driver's seat and handed them each a sweaty bottle of ice-cold water. He scratched the dog's ear. "Got more in da cooler. Ya just tell Anthony you want."

Kate cracked the seal on hers and drank half the bottle in a single gulp.

The SUV hopped forward and the driver guided it onto the causeway that led from the airport into downtown Kingston. They passed a vendor selling cold drinks and potted plants out of the back of an airbrushed van. Around them, the flat waters of the harbor stretched out to their left and huge boulders rose up to form a seawall shielding them from the open ocean to their right.

At the end of the causeway, the truck whipped around a tight roundabout. Lucia and Kara both grabbed at the plastic handles on the ceiling, but Kate's body bounced between the sisters before she dropped her water and grabbed the two front seats to steady herself. As abruptly as it entered, it whipped back out of the roundabout then down a wide, divided highway.

Kate picked her water bottle off the floor, thankful she'd screwed the cap back on. The small SUV sped toward Kingston past container ships docked in the harbor awaiting their cargo from the industrial sites across the highway, then past a large walled facility.

"Dis be our jail. Mi bredren be dere for dis las tree year for da ganja." Anthony waved at the high brick wall topped with looped razor wire as they passed.

"I'm sorry, Anthony. Your ... bredren?"

"Oh. Mi ... uh, friend? He live down de road when we kids. I watch after his woman and dey kids now."

"I'm sorry. Three years seems a little extreme."

"Yah, mon. He got no money for da lawyer. He shoulda run faster, I say. But what you gwan do?" He shrugged and made a quick left into a maze of streets. "Dis Downtown Kingston. But I think you wan know 'bout de old ways, yah? And I be takin' you to Trench Town. Best stay close to old Anthony dere. Trench Town ain't good for no farin lady." He looked over at William, barely missing an old woman in a crosswalk. "You neither, my man. You no walk in Trench Town, you like dat watch."

William wrapped his hand around his wristwatch out of reflex. "I appreciate your warning, Anthony. Yes, we do want to learn about some of the old ways as you call it. *Señora* Alvaro here is researching her ancient ancestors, and we just want to talk with anyone who might be able to help."

"Yah yah yah. Den we start in Trench Town. Right round here, now." Anthony squeezed the truck against the curb between a beat-up delivery truck and a small motorcycle. He helped Lucia out of the passenger door on the street side. Kate joined Whiskey on the sidewalk with her small backpack slung over one shoulder. Anthony tapped it and waggled his finger at her. "Lady, don' bring that wit you. Da sufferas here, dey take what dey want."

Kate pulled the bag closer. "Well I'd rather see them try to take it from me than have them break your window."

"No problem, mon." Anthony led them up the block, past crumbling concrete walls, faded paint, and rickety fences. A sea breeze blew across the fisheries and blended with the smell of three-day-old scraps baking on the curb and jerk chicken smoking on people's stoops.

Whiskey trotted at Kate's heel, his head twisting in

all directions. Food, spices, humans, ocean, garbage ... the dog's nose twitched as he took it all in. Scrubby bushes collected scraps of trash in every corner and alcove, and a group of barefoot children chased a white goat through a vacant lot.

Finally, the group stopped, and Anthony opened a gate in a brightly painted garden wall. An elderly man with high, wide cheekbones sat in a rocking chair on the front porch.

Their guide bowed low before the old man then presented Lucia. The old man looked past her into the middle of his yard where Whiskey stood beside Kate. A grin spread across his face, revealing his two remaining teeth.

"Come here, boy."

Whiskey looked up at Kate. When she nodded, he trotted up to the man and tucked his head under the gnarled hand.

"Oh, you're a good one, aren't you?" The man bent down, and Whiskey licked his face. The man giggled as he nuzzled the dog, seeming to forget the humans were there to talk.

William finally cleared his throat.

"Oh. Right. I am terribly sorry. I see nothing but goats walk by in the street. It's been too long. Too long." The man spoke with an almost perfect British accent. "Please, do sit down. May I offer you some tea? Anthony. Get your guests some tea."

"Oh. No, thank you, sir. We wouldn't want to be any trouble."

"Not any trouble at all for him to help an old man. Not any trouble at all."

Anthony scurried through the front door, and Kate heard him clattering through the kitchen. She looked to the old man. "May I help him?"

When he nodded, she slipped into the spotless little kitchen. "Anthony, please, I'd feel terrible taking anything from him."

"Oh, no worries. I bring da fresh fruits and meats and plenty a tea and beer to him. My gift to you." He filled a kettle from a five-gallon water jug and put it on to boil. Kate helped him arrange the teacups on a wooden tray, and when the aromatic tea was steeped, she carried it back out to the front porch. Lucia and the old man were speaking in rapid Spanish, with Kara adding a little now and then. The man's hand dangled over the armrest of his chair and stroked Whiskey's fur as they spoke.

William pulled Kate off to the side. "The bad news is that he doesn't know anything about a Taíno zemí that may or may not have been entrusted to any of the tribes in Jamaica. The good news is that he's suggested a couple places to dig a little deeper. There's a Taíno exhibit at the national museum which, while the zemí most certainly won't be there, might be interesting to stop at while we're here. There's a medicine man in Old Harbour, which is a little further west of here, and he says there's also a pocket of traditional Taíno high up the mountain to the east, but he doesn't know exactly where. So, we've got a little more digging to do."

"I gotta ask. What's with the British accent in the middle of the slums of Kingston? And where did he learn Spanish?"

"I asked, too. His parents were groundskeepers on the estate of a British family, and he was educated with their children. The family was fond of him, and when he was a teenager, they sent him to university in England. He travelled all around Europe, which is where he learned Spanish. When he learned Lucia was a native Spanish speaker, he refused to speak another word of English. Anyway, when he returned to Jamaica after he got his degree, the family appointed him the manager of the estate. It was all well until the family went bankrupt in the late eighties and left him with nothing but his tea set."

"Well, then, I guess it's tea time." Kate sat on the end of a concrete block, stuck out her pinky, then sipped her cup of Earl Gray.

CHAPTER THIRTY-ONE

The dense city gave way to green pastures and farm fields as the SUV drove west out of Kingston. They left the highway, passed through the city of Old Harbour, then wound through a series of smaller villages in the rising hills. As the road twisted and turned, Kate sucked down another bottle of water and closed her eyes to fend off her rising motion sickness.

Finally, the truck lurched to a stop in front of a half-built cement block home. Colorful floral curtains billowed out the open windows of the one-story, unpainted building. Thin rods of reinforcing steel bars extended up from the concrete walls, reminding Kate of a witch's straw broom standing on end, and a dog barked from the open roof.

Whiskey bounded over the backseat and out into the dirt yard. His body quivered and his hair stood on end, but he held his bark, waiting for Kate's direction. "Whiskey, sit. Relax, buddy, it's okay. It's his house. He gets to bark at you." She scratched his neck and he planted his backside in the dust.

"Shut up, you!" a thin, high voice shouted from around the corner. The dog's barks quieted and they heard shuffling and the rattle of falling metal.

Anthony peered around the corner. "Ay. Him in Trench Town say you's a medicine man, yah?"

"I be no tourist sight, mon. Just take your white folk and go."

Anthony waved Lucia forward. "She no white woman, here."

"I am Taíno, from the Dominican Republic." Lucia joined Anthony near the corner, her palm telling the others to stay back. Another crash sounded, and Anthony ran forward. A moment later, he reappeared leading a stooped old man with cloudy white eyes, wearing only a long swatch of fabric wrapped around his waist. The man's scalp was scarred and mostly bald. The few hairs that remained were braided and beaded, and wrapped together with a scrap of leather. His lips curled in beneath hollow cheeks, his teeth long gone.

"Some medicine man..." Kate whispered to William.

"I hear a white woman. I tell you, I be no sight to see. Take her and go."

"Kate, you wait in da car." Anthony tossed the keys across the yard toward her.

Whiskey jumped up and barked once.

The old medicine man spun around toward the sound. "Wait. That dog sounds mighty. Bring him to me."

Kate tensed and shot Anthony a questioning look.

He nodded and waved for Whiskey. The dog stayed on his feet at Kate's side.

"He belong to da white woman. He only stay by her."

"Fine. She come, too." The old man shook his head, appearing resigned to the fact that Kate came with the dog.

Kate led Whiskey up to the man. "Sit," she whispered, and the dog dropped to his haunches.

"Mmm. Him good. Obey da woman." The man reached his hand out in the general direction of the dog. Anthony guided it to the dog's head, and as soon as the man touched Whiskey's fur, he shuffled a step closer, patting the dog's head, then feeling his shoulders and chest. "Yah, mon. Him good. Him bark strong. How much, lady?"

"Oh, no, I'm sorry, he's not for sale, sir."

"Den why Old Edmund send you here if'n not for da new dog? Everyting got a price, mon. Everyting. So how much?"

Anthony buried his face in his hands and shook his head. Kate shot a bewildered look to William.

Finally, Lucia gently touched the man's elbow and spoke softly as she guided him to a rusted table and chairs on the edge of his yard. "Cousin, my name is Lucia Alvaro, and I am descended from the Taíno people, just as you are. We are one blood. For many generations, my people have passed down the story of how our gods, our zemís, scattered to protect their legacy when the Spaniards arrived. Now, I'm looking for others who have received the same stories. I'm looking for my cousins like you."

The man settled into a chair. He leaned his elbows on his splayed knees and blindly stared at a point a few feet to Lucia's right.

"One blood. Yah, times, they change. In dem long time 'go, medicine man be a man. Now, dey go and be dis woman. Hmph." The man snorted, and then fell into a fit of coughs that ended when he spit a huge wad of mucus into the dirt between his feet. "So, you be dis medicine man now?"

Lucia shot a look at Anthony, whose eyes grew big as he nodded. "*Sí*. Something like that, yes."

He frowned and his head bobbed as he tried to fix his gaze on her. "Tell me da story of your god, den."

Lucia sucked in a deep breath and began the tale of the zemís. He let her talk for three sentences before he broke in. "No. No. No. Da medicine man, he be a man. Dis story not for da woman."

Lucia looked at Kara, her eyes wide with panic. Kara's eyes, though, sparkled, and a tiny grin began to form. She fluffed the hair on her blonde wig and stepped forward. As she passed Kate, she whispered in her ear, "Let's find out how blind he really is."

"*Señor*. My name is Carlos Alvaro. I am Lucia's brother, of her same blood. I am your cousin, too." Kara dropped her voice lower than Kate had ever heard it. The man sat straighter and held his hand out in the direction of Kara's voice. Kara took his hand and shook it firmly.

The man grinned, and settled back down on his elbows. "Yah, cousin. Him more true." He nodded in Kara's direction. Kate's hand flew to her face to stifle a laugh.

"Cousin, I tell you the truth," Kara winked back at Kate and William, "My sister has the blessing of our ancestors. She speaks for them and for our people."

The old man slowly nodded. "Fine, den. She speak."

Lucia continued the short story of Atabey and Yúcahu and the four spirits until the old man interrupted again. "Mmm ... dis Yúcahu, him come out da cave, and he make god to my people. I know none de gods spread to de four corners you say. But I know who be god to me many many generations, and he be god to my children and da children beyond. Him hide up in da mountain where da coffee grow and stay dere always and always." The man nodded once, spit another glob into the dust, and reached over to pet Whiskey. "So true be true. Him dog not for me?"

Kate laughed. "I'm sorry, no. Him dog not for you."

Anthony left a small box of food and a case of bottled water on the porch, then the group piled back into the SUV and made their way back toward town.

CHAPTER THIRTY-TWO

"Well, that was a waste of time." Kate's stomach rolled.

"I don't know," Kara fluffed her wig. "It was almost fun being Carlos for a hot second."

Kate leaned forward between the two front seats. "Any chance we could find some food soon?"

"True be true, lady. You ask. I answer." Anthony pointed to a brightly painted van parked near a small, makeshift lean-to and a smoker made from a rusty barrel. "Dis me cousin, Teddy. Freshest jerk chicken on de island. Kill dem dis morning."

Kate raised an eyebrow. "That doesn't look like something the health inspector would approve."

"Some of the best meals I've eaten all over the Caribbean are from stands like this," William reassured her.

They sat at a rickety picnic table under the shade

of a sprawling guango tree. By the time Kate sat down with a paper plate filled with a half chicken, peas and rice, and a mysterious but delicious-smelling pile of greens, she decided her objection might have been a little premature. She squeezed the air out of her bottle then tossed it over Whiskey's shoulder into a barrel at the edge of the dirt lot. After cracking open another water, she took a huge bite.

"What are these greens, Anthony?" came out more like a muffled string of vowels through her full mouth.

Anthony laughed. "I tell you true. Dems callaloo. Dey be greens, cook wit de onion and garlic and spicy spices. Dis one good, but not good as my Mama's." He said it loud, and the proprietor heaved himself up from his webbed lawn chair and whacked Anthony on the head with an empty water bottle, laughing and showing off two silver teeth. Anthony balled up a napkin and threw it back at the man, and they teased each other back and forth in full Jamaican patois. Kate heard "mama" several times and assumed the argument was over whose mother made the best food. Boys were the same everywhere.

But Anthony was right, the chicken did not disappoint. Fresh and tender, it was soaked in a blend of spices that was both sweet and savory, both spicy hot and soothing, all at once.

"It wasn't a waste." Lucia's nose was buried in her phone.

"What?"

"The time with the old blind man. Not a waste. Look." She swiped and scrolled on the tiny screen, then showed it to William beside her. His mouth full of chicken, his eyes grew wide. He nodded to Anthony. Lucia turned to the driver and showed him her phone. "He said that their god hid up in the mountain where they grow coffee. When he first said it, I thought it was figurative. But 'where the coffee grows' is a pretty specific detail."

Anthony expanded the map on her phone and zoomed in on a different area. "No, here. Coffee grow many places on de island, but the coffee anybody talk about grow here." He tapped the screen.

Kara leaned over. "Blue Mountain. I've heard of that. One of my distributors has been trying to get me to order it for the club, but the only people who order coffee at my place are already drunk. They can't tell it from Folger's."

"Ya, mon. Da Blue Mountain, she has da oldest coffee estates on de island." He leaned back, his eyes scanning the horizon. His expression grew grave. "And many man and woman follow de old ways up da mountain. Many."

"Is that good or bad, Anthony?"

His shoulders shivered, and he picked up a chicken leg. "It neither, lady. For dem? Dey happy 'nuff, I be guessin'. Makin' spells and cursin' dey enemies. Dey make tiny dolls wit de people hairs, and..." He shrugged. "I don' want no trouble with dem. Dat's all.

But you wan go dere, I take you. No problem, mon. No problem."

He finished his chicken and pushed himself up from the table. "You stay. Eat. I be back." He pulled his phone from his pocket and wandered off behind the roadside chef's van. A few minutes later, he returned, grinning to show every one of his perfectly straight, white teeth. "I and I gon' sleep in da mountains tonight. Me cousin got herself a guesthouse wit four big bedroom, perfect for everyone. She even say good to the dog because I tell her him good dog."

"Do you have a cousin for everything?"

Anthony doubled over. "True be true, lady. Anyting you need, I got a cousin can take care of you. And I mean anyting." He waggled his eyebrows.

Kate blanched.

"That's fantastic, Anthony. Thank you." William closed the travel app on his phone then slipped it back into his pocket.

"Yeah, yeah. So, eat up. Tomorrow, we climb to da mountaintop and find you god."

CHAPTER THIRTY-THREE

Kate's shoulders and back ached. Hours in the middle seat over winding, rutted roads couldn't be erased by one night's sleep.

After climbing out from under a heavy pile of soft comforters, she reached her arms high, then bent, flat back and strong legs, into a forward fold. She planted her palms on the bare wood floor and extended her feet behind her into a downward-facing dog pose.

Blood rushed to her head and she suddenly felt both perfectly relaxed and completely alive.

She lowered her hips into a plank and held it for five breaths. Her triceps trembled as she slowly flattened down to the floor then pulled her chest high, stretching her back and shoulders.

Kate pushed back to her hands and knees then flowed through three sets of cat-cow poses, dropping her head low, arching her back up, taking a full exhale to drop her back and stretch her neck high and backward.

Finally, she leaned back with her hips on her heels, pressed her forehead to the floor, and emptied her mind. No thoughts of the whirlwind of the past several days. No thoughts of the search for little golden statues. No thoughts of the lives that had been cut short in the name of an ancient religion or a future power. Kate was perfectly in the moment, just her and the clear, cool mountain air. Then Whiskey padded over and licked her face.

She giggled and grabbed a t-shirt from her bag to wipe the slobber from her face. Then she pulled herself back up and stepped to the window. The sun was just above the horizon, and the air was dry and clear. She could see all the way down the lush green mountain to the sparkling Caribbean Sea, its bright turquoise waters dotted with tiny whitecaps and a few miniature ships.

The world is full of such beauty. Such peace.

She gave Whiskey a scratch under the chin, and he bounded to the door.

Downstairs, the group gathered in the large dining room. Anthony's cousin had laid out a huge buffet of what looked like scrambled eggs, fried bananas, and moist, dark muffins.

"This all smells delicious, Anthony. What is it?"

Anthony beamed. "Dis," pointing to the dish of eggs, "Is ackee and saltfish. Traditional breakfast here in da islands. What look like egg? Dat ackee. Da fruit grow everyplace. My cousin, she boil da ackee and den put da peppers and da spices what taste good. Da ackee give energy, and saltfish — it make da body strong. And dis here be plantains. Dey like bananas. But better."

"Sounds like a great breakfast before a long day in the mountains." She glanced around the table at the group of friends. "Carb up, y'all!"

The friends passed bowls and platters around the table, filling their plates and devouring the delicious and hearty breakfast. Kate slipped a few chunks of saltfish to Whiskey, who gobbled them up, then crawled under the table, popping his head into laps at random, hoping to find some suckers to share their breakfast with him. When the platters were empty and the bowls scraped clean, the team turned conversation to the task at hand.

"Anthony and I walked into the village last night after you all went to bed." Lucia began. "He helped me make a few, uh, discreet inquiries."

"True be true. Obeah — de voodoo — it be bad stuff, mon. Nuttin scare me, no. But de obeah, de bad way? Dat scare me. Dat scare everybody."

"Voodoo is illegal, and most people claim they don't believe in it, but they're all scared by it, and it's one of those things you can't talk about. But the practice is one of the oldest in the country, so I thought it might give us a lead."

"And did it?"

Lucia grinned. "Did it ever." After Anthony cleared the dishes away, Lucia spread a map of south-eastern Jamaica on the table. She slipped on a pair of reading glasses and pointed to a landmass. "We are right here. The woman we talked to told us about a place, the home of an ancient god named Boinayel, who'd been cast out of his home far across the water by the Spanish slaveholders. Even though they had a common enemy, the islanders saw his power as a threat. He landed at Morant Point, here, on the eastern end of the island."

"Great! How far is it to drive from here?"

"It not quite dat simple, Miss Kate. De Obeah legend claim de islanders drove him west along the coast. He escaped up de Yallahs River here, into de mountains where man cannot follow. Dey feared he try to dominate dem just as the Spanish did. So strongest spell casters in de island, dey all come together and cast a curse on his people. After, dey catch every disease. And those who did not die were made slaves, or dey hide in de mountains and die."

"Which is exactly what happened to the Taíno people." Lucia added bitterly. "But it's also exactly what happened to everyone in the islands as the Spanish rolled through. She told us they also cursed the valley where he was hiding. The curse says Boinayel can never escape the valley, and any human who tries to enter the valley will meet a violent end."

"A violent end?"

"The Taíno in the area were certainly at odds with the other tribes. While they had a common enemy in the Spanish, their roots were different. The Obeah religion was brought with the enslaved Africans imported by the Spanish conquistadores. It's largely godless and a bit anarchistic. Every person channels the power of the spirits, and there's no authority figure or god or common morality beyond the dark spirits or light spirits. The organizational structure of the Taíno and their submission to gods, good or bad, was a power that offended the Obeah sense of independence. So, despite their common enemy in Spain, they simply couldn't find common ground and each saw the other as an existential threat."

Lucia pushed back from the table and removed her glasses. "The legend definitely correlates with what we know. The Taíno zemí has to be hidden in the 'cursed valley.' There's nowhere else that makes sense. The good news is, everyone knows where the cursed valley is. The bad news? No guide in the area is willing to even approach it. So, we're on our own, friends."

CHAPTER THIRTY-FOUR

When the breakfast dishes were all cleared away, Anthony stood on the porch handing the hikers bottles of water, jerky, and dense moist bars wrapped in foil. Then he dragged a large backpack from his cousin's barn to load it with large bladders of fresh water, ropes, webbing, and carabiners.

While everyone else was occupied, Kate spotted him tucking three handguns into an outside pocket of the pack.

"What do you think we're going to run into out there?"

Anthony jumped, then forced a smile. "It da mountain. Best every mon be ready."

His attempt didn't fool Kate. Instead of calling him on it, she pretended, too. "I feel safe in your hands, Anthony. I have a backpack for Whiskey. Can he carry a few additional supplies for us?"

"Yah, yah. Here." He handed her two coils of rope and a tattered bag filled with carabiners. She raised her eyebrows and glanced toward the pack where Anthony had hidden the handguns. "Got a couple more of those?"

Anthony hesitated, and Kate took a step forward. She reached into the pack and pulled out a sheathed knife and a heavy 1911 pistol with a black plastic grip. With one fluid motion, Kate ejected the magazine and racked the slide back. A heavy .45 round dropped into her hand. She held it up, waggled it in front of Anthony, then dropped it into her pocket. She peered down the barrel through the gun's empty chamber, then tapped the slide release. The slide snapped back into place with a heavy crack.

"Yeah, this'll do." She snapped the magazine back into place, racked a round into the chamber, then dropped the magazine to replace the empty slot with the bullet from her pocket. When she was done, she jammed the magazine back into the gun, then tucked the heavy weapon into the back of her waistband.

Anthony stared at her, slack-jawed, eyes wide.

Kate winked at him as she strapped the knife to her leg. After slinging the ropes over her shoulder, she picked up the canvas bag then trotted back toward her friends on the porch. "You guys ready to rock this mountain?"

Anthony draped a whistle around Lucia's neck.

"We stay close, I see you. You see trouble, you blow dis. We too far up, you blow dis."

"I get it. If anything goes wrong, I blow the whistle."

The group set off up a narrow trail. Anthony took the lead, with Kate and Whiskey following right behind him. William and Kara walked together just in front of Lucia, who struggled to keep up. The trail was steep, switching back on itself as they climbed deeper into the jungle.

An hour into their hike, Anthony raised his hand in a fist. Ten feet behind him, Kate's fist popped up and Whiskey froze in place. The others went silent and stopped in their tracks. To the left, a few feet from the path, a low, flat boulder lay in a patch of sun. Coiled in the center, Kate spotted a thick yellow and black snake. Its narrow, tapered head lay across its coils, pointing directly toward the path. Very slowly, Kate reached her left hand down and pulled her knife from its sheath.

"Wait. Put de knife 'way. She safe. Just move slow on by." Anthony waved his charges past the clearing, and took up the rear with Lucia. Several minutes passed in silence before he hollered up the trail, "Whoooo! She a beauty, no? Miss Kate, you just follow de trail and watch for more dem snakes. Jes no kill 'em, okay?"

"No promises," Kate hollered from the front of the line, then let the group catch up. "If it's me or the snake, I'm telling you now, I'm gonna win."

Kara shivered. "I know we're kind of in his home turf, but I'm not a big fan of snakes unless they're a new pair of shoes."

Lucia nudged her sister. "That's not very environmentally conscious of you. You know snakes manage the rodent and insect population and keep the ecosystems up here balanced, right? None of the island snakes are poisonous, and back in my village, it's considered good luck to have a snake in the forest near your house. It pretty much guarantees you won't have rats."

"But you better watch out for your pet cats, eh? No thank you."

"Carlo— Sorry, Kara, have I ever had a cat?"

"Uhhh, not that I know of."

"And there you go. I don't want to get attached to snake food."

Kate laughed at the sisters' banter. "Note to self — don't let Lucia pet-sit."

"I think Whiskey could hold his own against that thing."

The group continued up the mountain, laughing and joking as they climbed. Two hours later, Kate stopped beside a small clearing, dappled in late morning sunlight. "Let's stop for minute. I need a bite, and Whiskey could use a little break." She pulled a folded tarp from the pack on Whiskey's back and spread it in the sun. Whiskey lay down flat on a corner and stretched his legs out straight behind him.

Kate poured water into a canvas bowl, and he slurped it up.

She bit into a stick of homemade jerky and laughed. "This is awesome. Jerk jerky." She nudged Kara, who sat next to Anthony. "Have you tried this yet? The seasoning is to die for. Almost as good as the chicken we had last night."

"Yah. When de jerky dry, it grow strong. Gotta watch you don' cover da flavor of da goat."

"Wait, what? This is goat?"

"True be true."

Kate shrugged and tore another bite of jerky from the stick.

"How much farther do we have to go, Anthony?"

The Jamaican grabbed his phone and pulled up a satellite map of the mountain. He pinched in toward the blue dot that showed their current position. "Maybe half hour. Maybe more." He pointed at Whiskey flattened out in the sun. "Depend how fast da dog he climb."

About twenty minutes later, Kate's skin warmed as the tree cover thinned where the path neared another hairpin switchback. She gasped at the view of the deep gulch dropping off to their left. A thick tree stood between the segments of the trail, narrow planks were nailed to its trunk to form a rough ladder. "What's—" Kate looked up the tree. Six feet up, a tiny platform curled around the tree's trunk, and a thick steel cable wrapped around the tree and extended across the wide ravine, disappearing into the forest on the other side near what looked like a small house.

"It be da jungle elevator. Workers hang da coffee bags and send dem down da mountain wit dis zip line. Den when dey done for de night, dey ride it down, too."

"People zip line on this thing?"

"Ya, mon. E'ery day. Best part o' de day, dey say. Wind in dey braids, fly tru de sky...what better?"

Kate shivered. "Glad that's not me. I'd rather hike the two hours back out."

"We gotta move, else we never get back out." Anthony adjusted his shorts and marched around the switchback up into the thinning forest.

CHAPTER THIRTY-FIVE

As Kate crested a ridge, her heart slammed in her chest. She held her right hand up at shoulder level in a fist and extended her left to help her balance. She loosened her knees and shifted her weight low. Very slowly, she took one step back. Then another. Her eyes remained glued to the ground. Or more accurately, to the spot where the ground disappeared.

Kate clutched the first tree she reached, a squat, sprawling lignum vitae tree, and trembled there until William crested the tiny ridge with Whiskey right beside him.

"Jamaica's motto might be 'No Problem,' but we have a problem." Kate tried to cover her shaking voice with a weak laugh.

William looked over the drop-off. He returned to the edge of the ridge and helped Kara over, guiding her to a safe spot away from the precipice. Behind them, the ground had become rocky and the forest had thinned out. The only trees near the edge were low and narrow. The ground rising above them was covered in low brush.

They heard a rustle in the trees behind them. Lucia appeared, followed by Anthony. "We take da long way. Good good. We be here." Anthony bounded right up to the edge of the drop-off and peered down the cliff's face.

"Yeah, yeah. Da story be true, just like me cousin say it be. Cave where your god be hidin'? It be right down below." He hopped up and began pulling rope and webbing from his pack. Whiskey stood away from the ledge facing into the woods, his ears turned forward. Anthony patted the animal and tied a rope off to a small tree.

"Miss Kate, come off dat tree and come to me."

Kate shot a panicked look at William, then back to Anthony.

"Kate, look around. None of the trees up here are strong enough to support me or Kara. You and Lucia are the only ones light enough to make the climb."

"The climb?"

Anthony began to wrap webbing around Kate's waist and thighs into a makeshift climbing harness. Kate's feet remained rooted to the rocky ground.

"Kate." Kara's voice reverberated behind her, but Kate's eyes stayed fixed on her fingers wrapped around the tree. "Kate, honey. You are half my size.

Literally. What do you think would happen if I tried to go down there? What would happen if you were trying to hold the rope for me? We'd both go flying down that mountainside and get impaled on some tree down there. But what happens if you go down, and I hold the rope? You get to the cave, you find the zemí, I pull you back up, and we are all home in time to enjoy some of the island's best ganja before we make our way back to civilization. Your choice, Kate. Dead at the bottom of a ravine or floating on the Jamaican clouds?"

"I'll take option three — clinging to this tree."

"That one's not on the list, honey."

Anthony rigged another harness up for Lucia, then showed William and Kara how to wrap the ropes around the trees to raise and lower the climbers. Then he slung a gear bag across his back, clipped himself to another rope, dropped over the edge, and scrambled down the cliff face.

A minute later, Anthony's voice echoed up the rock. "No problem, lady! Come on down. Da view is to die for!"

Kate sighed. "Couldn't he have chosen his words a little better?"

"Come on, Kate. We're almost there." William bent down to meet Kate's eyes. "Anthony is a good guide. My friend recommended him. But we don't really know him. Do you want to send Lucia in there with him alone?"

Kate's pulse quickened, and her hand shot to the weapon in her waistband.

"Exactly, Kate. He doesn't truly know what he's leading us to. The zemí could be a hell of a temptation once he sees it. She's not armed. I can guarantee he is. She needs a guardian, and neither of us can do that. We have to be up here to hold the ropes and get you back here."

One by one, Kate released her fingers from the tree's small trunk. She checked the strap of the bag slung across her chest, then patted the knife on her ankle.

"Okay. But you have to lower me down there. I'm not opening my eyes until my feet are on solid rock."

She hugged Whiskey, then lowered herself to her hands and knees and crawled sideways to the ledge. Kara wound the end of the thick rope around two trees and anchored it. William donned a thick pair of leather gloves and helped Kate over the edge. The two friends gently lowered Kate down twenty feet to a small outcrop where Anthony waited to catch her.

When she felt solid rock under her feet, and Anthony's hands on her shoulders, Kate opened her eyes and scrambled deeper into the cool shadow of the opening. She watched as Lucia lithely bounced down the rock then swung into the little cave.

The Dominican woman grinned as she unclipped herself from the rope, then she pulled a small flashlight from her pocket and shone the beam into the darkest recess of the small cave. "Kate, look. Petroglyphs."

Beside a jagged crevice, a figure was carved into the brown rock.

Kate stepped farther into the cave. The deep cuts felt rough compared to the smoother stone face. "This looks just like the one in the Bahamas. This must be it."

Anthony retrieved a lantern from his gear bag. When he flipped the switch, the entire cavern lit up in a flood of light. Kate grinned and bounded down the damp passage.

"I wonder—" Kate's voice caught in her throat. The floor of the narrow passage was wet and slippery. Her foot landed on an uneven rock and slid out from under her. The weight of the pack on her back pulled her down, so she thrust her weight forward to compensate. Arms reached ahead, her right palm caught a hold of a rock just as her knee slammed into the wet stone. She yelped, rolled onto her hip, then cradled her bent leg in her arms.

Anthony scrambled to her side, his lantern held high.

Kate pulled a bandana from her forehead and wiped her knee clean. "That's gonna leave a mark." Blood oozed out of the scrape. She probed her kneecap. "I don't think anything's broken. Give me a second. Anthony, do you have any water?"

He handed her a bottle. It felt warm. She poured a little over her cut, then wet the bandana with it and handed the bottle back to her guide. She tied the bandana around her knee and carefully pulled herself back up to her feet. She tested the knee, starting with just a little weight and progressively leaning more onto it until she was hopping on it like a pogo stick, wincing with each bounce. "It'll hold. Let's get in and find this thing so we can get back out."

Kate limped through the cave for another five minutes. She felt the cool air change as the passage widened then opened into a huge chamber.

Anthony came out behind her, his lantern lighting the area in front of them. The light barely reached the stalactites at the top of the cavern.

They stood near the edge of a massive underground lake. The light from their lanterns stretched far enough across the water to see something reflecting the light in the center.

"Is that ..." Lucia's voice drifted off as she began to explore the shore of the lake to the left. Her flashlight bounced in the darkness. She stopped just beyond the reach of the lantern and scanned the water with her flashlight. "The water goes all the way around. Whatever that is in the center, it's surrounded by water. Unless you've got an inflatable boat in that pack, Anthony, we're gonna have to swim."

Her flashlight began its journey back toward them. As she came back into the light, her eyes sparkled. "It's a little closer to the edge over there. And that's definitely the zemí in the middle."

CHAPTER THIRTY-SIX

Kate shivered as she shined her narrow beam of light through the darkness. "Whoever put this here had to have had a way to get back and forth. Look for some kind of... There. Look!" Kate pointed her light at a small pile of rotting boards that could have once been a little raft. It leaned against the wall of the cavern near a pile of rocks. Anthony climbed up onto the rocks and grasped the end of one of the boards. The raft collapsed on itself into a pile of rotten splinters. He jumped backwards as several small, dark shadows scurried from the heap and into the rock pile.

"Dem beetles be death. I go many places. I do many tings. I help you find dis place. But ..." Anthony shrugged the gear pack off his back, then handed his lantern to Lucia and took her flashlight. He retreated. They listened as the sounds of his feet scrambling down the passage echoed, became faint, and died out.

"Well, I guess it's up to us girls." Kate shrugged, rubbed her knee, then began to dig in the gear bag for something that could help them, pulling everything out and spreading it on the floor.

"Kate?"

Kate looked up at Lucia, whose face was contorted, her eyes filled with terror. "What is it?"

"I can't swim."

She stood and wrapped Lucia in a hug. "I can." After stepping back, she pointed to a jagged rock sticking out from the wall. "Hang your lantern there."

While Lucia stood on her toes to hang the light, Kate shrugged off her bag, set it on the ground against the cavern wall, then pulled two plastic garbage bags from her gear. She fumbled through the pile until she found the scuba regulator, then she attached it to one of the small pony tanks Anthony had packed. Next, she used the regulator to inflate the garbage bags. After she'd tied the mouths of the bags in tight knots, she coiled rope in long loops, then tied a garbage bag to each end.

She stood and nodded as she surveyed her handiwork. Then she glanced around the cavern, her eyes landing on Lucia. "I'm going to swim over there and get the zemí. While I do that, I need you to keep watch here, and pack the remaining gear up in that bag. Okay?"

Lucia nodded.

Kate looked around once more. "Do you know how to use a gun?"

Lucia shook her head.

Kate pulled the pistol from her waistband, placed it in Lucia's right hand, then wrapped her left around the grip.

"Okay, you want your right hand wrapped around it up high like this. See how this piece up here pushes in? That's the safety, so make sure you're holding it tight against that, okay?" Lucia squeezed the grip against the webbing between her thumb and her palm.

"Then you extend your right arm. All the way out."

Lucia stretched her arm away from her.

"Now, feel what's happening with your left arm. You're pushing out with it, too. Aren't you?"

Lucia nodded.

"Keep pushing out with your right, but then pull against it with your left. Can you do that? It'll keep it steady. Push with your right, pull with your left. Got it? Push. Pull."

Kate watched the shaking gun stabilize in Lucia's outstretched arms.

"Now, look down the barrel. Concentrate on these two dots at the end of this sight, and line up this little dot here close to you in the slot between them. Don't look at the near one. Use only the ones at the end of the barrel. When everything's aligned and you're ready to shoot, just gently pull back on it."

Lucia's muscles began to tense under Kate's hands.

"Wait, Lucia. Not NOW!"

Lucia let go of the trigger then lowered the gun.

Kate released a breath and took it from her.

"Only put your finger on the trigger if you're ready to pull it. Only pull it if you have no other choice and know exactly what it's going to hit. You shoot it in here, and it could bounce off that rock and go anywhere."

Lucia slowly nodded. She held her hand out and took the gun back. Kate showed her how to grip the gun with her finger extended beside the trigger. Lucia raised the weapon up in front of her and practiced holding and aiming it.

"Okay, I think you've got it. You shouldn't need to use that. Just listen carefully while I get the gear packed back up."

Kate took a flashlight down to the edge of the water and shined her light across the surface. It looked clear and still. She reached into the water and scooped some up in her palm and held it near her face. She sniffed the water, then touched her tongue to her palm. It tasted fresh and cool.

She stood, stepped away from the shore, glanced around the cavern one more time, then shrugged. "I guess it's just us girls here. No point in soaking my clothes." Kate pulled the makeshift climbing harness down over her hips, dropped it on the ground, then stripped off the rest of her things and added them to the same pile. She strapped the knife back on her bare ankle, grabbed the garbage bag float, then waded into the water.

As soon as it was thigh-deep, Kate lowered her torso, draping her arms over the rope of her makeshift flotation device. She held her flashlight out of the water in her left hand and used her right to steer as she kicked across the water to the little island in the center. As the water grew shallower, her knee struck the bottom and she swore, her curse bouncing through the chamber.

"Are you okay?" Lucia's voice echoed across the water.

"Yeah, I'm fine. Just stupid is all." Kate rolled to float on her back. She curled her knee in and rubbed it, then rolled back and climbed out of the water, dragging her float ashore behind her. She clicked on the flashlight and shined it around the tiny rock. Directly in the center, a small golden figurine sat on a little pedestal. Kate squatted beside the pedestal and lifted it. At the moment she pulled its heavy figure from the pedestal, she heard a grinding noise and the small pedestal began to rise, rubbing against the rock it was embedded in.

Lucia's voice carried across the water. "It's a trap!"

Kate clutched the figure, dropped her flashlight, and ran toward the water. She dove in and broke into a strong freestyle, kicking hard and breathing every other stroke. With the zemí clutched in her left fist, her strokes were uneven and her speed slower than usual.

Over the splashing of the water in her ears, she heard a deep rumble from the darkness at the cavern's ceiling. On her next breath she shouted to Lucia, "Get to the passageway!" Kate didn't wait for Lucia's response. She just swam.

A moment later, Kate felt the water churn as stalactites began to fall, crashing into the lake and onto the small island. She plunged deeper and dolphin kicked until her fingers hit the bottom. She tucked her legs under and launched her body up and out of the water toward Lucia's light. A hard blow glanced off her shoulder. She fought to regain her balance and run forward.

Kate focused on the opening to the passage back to the outside. Pain shot through her bare feet with every step. Falling stones glanced off her body, cutting her skin but driving her forward until, at last, she sprang from the cavern into the shelter of the narrow tunnel.

Curled in a ball, the zemí clutched against her belly, her bare skin cold against the rough stone, she watched a thick cloud of dust fill the cavern and snuff out the beam of light still lying in the center of the island.

When the haze began to clear, Lucia wrapped her arms around Kate and helped her to her feet. She led Kate further down the passageway to a spot where it widened then found a large, smooth stone for Kate to sit on. "I got your things."

As she pulled Kate's t-shirt from the bundle under

her elbow, the heavy gun clattered to their feet. Kate's hand was still shaking when she set it beside her.

Lucia tended to all the cuts and bruises on Kate's back and legs, then helped her dress. Finally, Kate loosened her grip on the small zemí and held it close to the light of the bright lantern. The small figure depicted a man sitting with his knees hugged near his chest, his teeth bared, and a small bowl balanced on his head. Like the others, it felt far heavier than its small size warranted.

"Boinayel. The god of rain." Lucia's eyes glistened.

Kate pulled the other zemí from the bottom of the bag and held them side by side. "Guzman has two, and we have two. I guess now, it's a race to the last one."

"Well, we need to get out of here first. Let me take those, and you figure out what you can carry." Lucia took the two zemís, carefully wrapped them in a cloth, and tucked them in the front pocket of her bag.

The two women adjusted their loads, then Kate slung her backpack over her shoulder. It swung around, hitting one of the deeper cuts on her back. Yelping, she dropped the bag. Then she writhed, trying to squirm away from the pain that followed her. She looked down the tunnel toward the only way out. The pain would only get worse from here. No point prolonging the inevitable.

She sucked in a deep breath, slipped her arms through the straps on her backpack, dropped into place against her chest, then gingerly tucked the gun into her waistband.

Lucia helped her back to her feet.

The two women made their way through the passage and out into the fresh air of the mountainside. The wind had whipped up in the hour they'd been deep in the cavern. Heavy black clouds threatened a deluge at any moment. The dark clouds were ominous, but the cool fresh smell of rain was a gift after the musty cavern air.

Anthony was waiting at the cave's mouth. Lucia took Kate's bag and dug Kate's harness from it, then found a small boulder along the edge of the wall for her to sit. While Kate carefully slid the contraption up her legs, Lucia and Anthony tested the dangling ropes.

"William? Kara?" Lucia shouted up the mountain, but the wind carried the sound away and howled over any returning answer.

Anthony shook his head. "No problem. De ropes, dey are secure. We climb ourselves up." He bounded around the small cave and gathered up their gear. Kate joined them, then Anthony showed them both how to use the rope to stabilize themselves and climb the short way back up to the top.

Kate glanced down, then instantly grabbed her head and dashed back into cave. Lucia wrapped an arm around her. "Kate, you're the bravest woman I know. You can do it. Just keep your eyes straight ahead or look up."

Lucia guided her back to mountain's face and pulled the rope over to her. Kate grasped the dangling line, then looped it through the carabiner clipped to her harness. Staring straight up, she wrapped the rope around her leg like she'd seen aerialists do with long strips of fabric, then she found a foothold on the steep rock face and began to climb.

CHAPTER THIRTY-SEVEN

KATE GRIPPED THE ROPE, planted her feet just below the lip of the cliff, then pushed up. Right into the barrel of a gun.

She clutched the rope, collapsing her knees and dropping tight against the face of the mountain, but the man grabbed the collar of her t-shirt in one meaty fist, jerked her over the ridge, then flung her across the tiny clearing. Her gun flew from her waistband and rattled on the stone near the ridge. She fought the instinct to catch her fall. Instead, she curled her body tight and rolled, bouncing back to her feet to face the gunman.

It only took a split second for her to scan the clearing. Near the head of the trail, William sat on the ground with his back to a tree, his wrists tied around its trunk. Kara was tied to another tree just a few feet away, struggling to scream against the gag in her mouth. Another smaller man stood nearby. In his hand, a long, narrow blade glinted in the sunlight. The underbrush rustled behind him in the wind.

Kate lifted her head and stared past the gun and directly into the assailant's face. The whites of his eyes popped against his dark skin. The smell of metal and oil filled her nostrils, and she struggled to keep her breath steady.

"Get over by da tree." As he flicked the tip of the gun toward her friends, Kate thrust her hands together and upward, grasping the barrel of the gun and forcing it up toward the sky. Simultaneously, she dipped her left knee and kicked hard into the man's groin with her right. As he crumpled, she launched forward, forcing his wrists back and pressing the gun against his ribcage. She wrestled it from his fingers then scrambled backward to put distance between them.

She spun toward the man with the knife. He circled away from her. As soon as he stepped away from the trailhead, Kate shouted, "Whiskey, attack!"

The huge dog burst from the bushes and tore at the arm of the man in the center of the clearing.

"Get him off me!"

Kate turned back to the man she'd disarmed. He was crouching, lunging for Kate's pistol, and came up with it already extended in front of him. A quick pivot, then he took aim at Whiskey.

When Kate saw his finger tense on the trigger, time slowed to a crawl. She lined up her sights on the man and squeezed. The gun bounced up, and she countered the gun's kick with her elbows, refocusing as his body twisted and fell backward. She stared at her target, pulled the sights into her line of vision, and pulled the trigger again, and again, until the man's body toppled over the cliff's edge. Then she spun on her heel and turned her attention to the other attacker.

"Whiskey, down."

The dog instantly released the man's bleeding arm and sat at attention.

Kate held her gun pointed at the man. "What do you want?" The man lunged backward and scrambled into the woods.

Kate ran over and cut William and Kara loose just as Lucia pulled up into the clearing, her face pale and her eyes wide. "What ... who..." Then she fell flat on the packed dirt of the clearing.

William dashed to the cliff's edge and helped Anthony up to the clearing. Kate's gear bag was slung across his back beside his own.

Kara rushed over and helped her sister up. "We need to get out of here!"

The five of them scooped up the loose gear, left the ropes attached to the trees, and ran. Anthony bounded into the lead and down the hill, stopping when he reached the coffee elevator. He shouted a high-pitched call that echoed through the valley, then grabbed Lucia by the shoulders.

"Here. We get to da bottom fast." He cut a length from the coil of rope over his shoulder and strung it through Lucia's harness, under her arms, and through a huge carabiner. He clipped the carabiner to the thick metal cable and tied the rope ends together. He pressed Lucia's hands around the knot. "Hang on, lady."

Before Lucia could object, Anthony pushed her out into the ravine and she flew down the line and into the trees on the other side. Kara's scream drowned out Lucia's as her sister flew across the ravine and into the trees on the opposite slope. Anthony grabbed Kate and tried to clip her to the line next. Kate flailed and fought until William grabbed her and wrapped his arms around her. "Kate. Stop. It's our only way down. Count with me ... ten ... nine—"

"NO! I'm not—"

"Eight ... seven—"

"I'm not going anywhere without Whiskey!"

William laughed. "Is that the problem? Do you trust me? If I let you go, will you quit fighting?" Kate warily nodded, unsure of where William was going, but choosing to trust him.

William grabbed a pile of webbing from the pile where Anthony had dumped the gear bag and began to weave a harness around Whiskey's body. "Kate, come here." William hefted the big dog and tied the harness over Kate's shoulders while Anthony strapped her up the same way he had Lucia. "Hold his weight by his hips." Kate's mind froze as the dog's weight settled and her body stiffened in response.

"You go fast, lady, but de leaves, dey slow you down. You be okay." Before Kate realized what was happening, she and Whiskey were flying across the ravine. She tightened her arms around him, squeezed her eyes shut, and screamed.

A few seconds later, she felt the first leaves smack against Whiskey's back. She buried her face in his side as leaves and branches scraped them and slowed their descent before they whacked into a thickly padded landing pad on the opposite slope. Lucia lay in a heap off to the side. Two Jamaican men scrambled up, unhooked Kate's carabiner, then pulled her over beside Lucia.

"Where you come from, lady?"

Kate pointed across the ravine and then collapsed, her body wrapped around the dog.

"Anoder comes!"

Kara came flying through the branches. One of the Jamaicans grabbed the cable behind her and pulled down hard to slow her. She stopped and dropped off the cable just ahead of the thick bumper. "Thanks. Two more men are coming behind me."

"No problem." The Jamaicans helped William and Anthony as they glided in while Kara helped Kate and Lucia catch their breath and untangle the webbing that had carried them across the ravine.

Anthony pulled the men aside. A moment later, he rattled a set of car keys toward the group. William looked up at him. "Maybe one of us should have come across first. Both girls hit pretty hard over here."

"Sorry, mon. Dey clip fast. Dey okay." He stuffed the pile of rope and webbing into his bag as he sauntered toward the parking lot.

William helped Lucia to her feet, picked up her bag, then followed Anthony out of the thick jungle.

"What the hell was that?" Kate slapped Kara in the chest.

Kara held her hands up and backed away. "Watch the girls..."

"Who were those men and how ... what ..." Kate was so angry she couldn't form words.

"Kate. Breathe. We're safe, but something is really wrong. I don't know where those guys came from or how they knew where to find us." Kara caught Kate's eye and forced her to take three deep breaths. "Did you get it?"

Kate nodded.

"Okay, then we need to get the hell out of here." She grabbed Kate's hand and started jogging toward the parking lot, Whiskey on their tail. Anthony held the door of a small white pickup truck.

"Straight to the airport, please, Anthony?"

Anthony peeled onto a narrow lane and bumped down the mountain to the airport.

Almost two hours later, Kate settled into the buttery leather of William's plane. She snapped the buckle of her seat belt and flopped over onto Whiskey's warm body, curled up in the next seat. Kara and Lucia snapped into the seats opposite her. William ran through his preflight checks then taxied to the end of the runway. Within minutes, the small plane soared into the sky and banked away from the thick Jamaican mountains they'd escaped just a few hours before.

Kara pulled lukewarm water bottles from the small cooler at her feet and passed them around. "Got any aspirin to go with this?"

William reached below the instrument panel and tossed a small pouch with a thick red cross symbol into the back cabin. Kara snatched it from midair and dug out a bottle of painkillers.

The headset crackled, then William's voice flowed through the speaker. "Welcome, ladies and gentle dog, to your Jenkinsair flight from Kingston to Santiago. We're all a little worse for wear this evening, so I'm going to try to keep to smooth air and get us on the ground as quickly and safely as I can. When we get a little closer, Lucia, we can call your buddies at the University to meet us at the airport, then we can hand the zemís over to them. I think at this point, we're all happier to not be carrying them around, am I right?"

Kate groaned and sat up in her seat. "Lucia, you hit pretty hard off that zipline. Do you want to lie down over here?"

Lucia shook her head. "I'm fine, thanks. You had a harder day than I did." Kate unsnapped her seatbelt, buried her face in Whiskey's fur, and closed her eyes.

CHAPTER THIRTY-EIGHT

Guzman tapped his foot on the hot pavement outside the tidy Trench Town house. His walk from the harbor had been short, and he didn't plan to stay in Jamaica any longer than he had to. Finally, a rusty white truck squeezed into a space down the block and its lanky driver ambled up the sidewalk. Guzman met him halfway.

"You got them?"

Anthony held out a small canvas sack. Guzman reached for it, and the Jamaican pulled it back against his chest.

"You got da money, mon?"

"Of course." Guzman hated doing business with Jamaicans. Damn disloyal mercenaries would work for the highest bidder. And anyone he could buy could be bought back. Guzman quietly thanked the universe that he was the highest and last bidder this time. He fished a pile of bills out of his front pocket and took a step closer.

The Jamaican snatched the cash from Guzman then handed over the small bag. As he'd noticed with the others, the bag was heavier than its size should have been. Guzman spun on his heel and disappeared down a narrow alley back toward the wharf. He tucked the bag into his jacket then hurried back to his boat.

Back on board, he nestled the two gold figures behind the false back in a galley cabinet and packed the empty space with paper towels. He returned pots and pans to the cabinet and snapped the door shut.

Opening a Red Stripe, he planted himself in a folding chair in the boat's cockpit, kicked his feet up on the transom, and watched the sun set. After dark, Guzman locked the boat then walked down the docks. He found a group of dockworkers huddled around a fire burning in a tall barrel. He waved a fat joint toward them and raised his eyebrows. The men made space for him, and he passed the ganja to the first man on his right to light. While the dockworkers shared a smoke, Guzman dropped the small canvas bag into the fire and watched it burn. Before the joint made it around the circle to him, he disappeared.

Guzman gently guided the boat from its slip, out of the harbor, and set a course due east across the Caribbean Sea.

CHAPTER THIRTY-NINE

KATE WOKE UP SCREAMING.

Her headset lay on the floor of the cabin where it had fallen as she tossed and turned on the tiny seat. She screamed over the drone of the plane's engine, but no sound came out of her mouth.

Even with her eyes wide open, even with the clear sight of Kara and Lucia in the seats across from her, of the tan leather and polished wood, of the blinding blue sky out the windshield and the blanket of cottony white clouds below them, Kate still saw, superimposed on all that, the wide eyes. The individual drops of blood splattering from the man's chest. The body jerking behind the sights of her gun, each shot jerking the man further back toward the cliff until she saw only empty space where his life had been.

Kara knelt on beside her. Kate felt her large hands around her shoulders, saw the shadow of her face fill her line of sight. But Kara was just background behind the dead man's eyes. His falling body. His splattered blood.

The drone of the engine and her silent screams were replaced by a high-pitched shriek as the headset snapped around her ears. Kara wrapped her hand around Kate's mic and pulled it away from her lips. Then her gentle voice filled the space in Kate's ears. "Honey, hush. Shh. It's okay, baby girl. Kate, honey, we're here. Look into my eyes, Kate. My eyes. Look at me. Focus on me, Kate."

Kate fought to center her focus on Kara's brown eyes, but all she could see were the wide brown eyes of the Jamaican. She let out another noiseless scream.

"Kate, honey, That screaming's just gonna make you hoarse. With these headphones on and that loud engine, ain't nobody gonna hear it. Come on honey, just breathe with me and come back to us, okay?" Kara pressed a single finger to Kate's lips. "Focus on my finger. Focus on my voice. Come on back, honey."

The words pulled Kate back to the present. She felt Kara's finger pressing her lips into her teeth, her breath backing up in her closed mouth. She saw Kara's eyes, and only Kara's eyes.

When she nodded, Kara lowered her hand.

Kate pulled air into her lungs in halting gulps, then shoved it back out against her locked chest. She repeated the effort. Kara breathed with her, matching every constricted breath with her own gentle, smooth one. Finally, Kate's breath steadied, the visions of the dead man faded, and words formed on her tongue.

"I ... he ... blood ..."

In her headset, Kate only heard a low hiss. Her heart pounded. Her breath jerked through her choked throat. Her eyes bulged.

Kara bent Kate's microphone back against her lips. "Here, take a breath and try again."

"I ... oh. There. I can hear me." Kate took another deep breath. "I couldn't hear, and I couldn't scream, and I ..."

"It's okay, baby. You were screaming just fine. We all heard it even without your mic on."

"It was, like, you know when you have one of those dreams where you try to run but your feet won't move? You try to scream, but your breath is frozen?"

Kara pulled Kate toward her and wrapped her in a tight hug. Kate's resolve crumbled, and she burst into sobs. She felt Kara nudge Whiskey off the seat with her hip, and then she was curled up in her friend's arms, her stalwart dog pressed against her leg.

When her sobs faded, she realized Kara was singing softly through the plane's comm system. She opened her eyes and fought to focus on Lucia in the seat across from her. Lucia's eyes were closed, and her body swayed to the sound of her sister's soft voice.

Kate twisted her shoulders and settled into a more comfortable niche against Kara's side. Soon, she began to hum along. When the song reached the end, Kara brushed Kate's curls back from her cheek. "It's gonna be okay, baby girl."

Kate sighed. "But will it? Can I ever be okay again?"

"You can be, and you will be." William's voice resonated with a hope Kate couldn't feel.

"How can you say that? Have you stared into some-one's eyes and then blew their heart out their back?" She sat up, her cheeks hot and raw. Lucia's eyes were open again, and Kate caught Kara throwing her sister a panicked look. Kate closed her eyes, pulled a deep breath into her lungs, then focused on the clouds below them. "It's okay. I'm ... I'm not gonna lose it again. I just..." She struggled to find the right words buried in the haze of her exhausted brain.

Lucia reached across and rested her hand on Kate's knee. "Kate, you didn't have a choice. You did what you had to do, and you saved our lives. I think I speak for all of us when I say we're thankful for what you did."

"She's right, Kate. While you two were down there with Anthony, they popped out into the little clearing and caught us by surprise. Whiskey had been really jumpy from the moment you went over the edge. We had no reason to think anything was wrong and figured he was just being that way because he couldn't follow you. He kept looking over the edge of the cliff where you'd gone, then running to the edge of the clearing and whining. We kept telling him to lie down, kept trying to call him off. Finally, he went down the trail to do his business, and I suspect they were waiting to make their move. When they came out, one had a gun pointed at us, so of course we froze. But the other had a knife. We didn't see Whiskey again until he came out of the bushes when you called him."

Kate slipped off her seat and down to the floor beside Whiskey. She stroked his fur and murmured, "Good boy. You're a good boy, buddy."

Kara chuckled and scratched the dog between his ears. "He'd have been better boy if he'd have bitten them before they got to us. But it all came out okay in the end."

Kate's shoulders fell. "Not for everyone. What if the other guy goes to the cops? What if they—"

"He's not going to the cops. He won't even go to a hospital to get those bites looked at. Kate, do you think those guys were on that mountain for their health? That they were on a jaunty little hike to see the vistas from the peak? The only reason they were there was for us. Before you and Whiskey came to our rescue, they were asking about the zemís. They followed us up the mountain. And I guarantee they had no intention of letting us go back down alive. Kate, honey, it was them or us. I'm just glad it was them."

"Why couldn't it have just been Guzman who followed us up the mountain? Why couldn't it have been him I blew away?" Kate's body began to shake. She looked out the window. The endless blanket of white clouds faded as Kate's memory played a scene from just a few months prior. Kate watched as an eerily similar scene played out in her mind. The angle was different. The location was different. But the rest was the same — the movement as a bullet slammed into a chest, as a body exploded and fell backward, as life bled from a man's eyes.

Two months ago, the bullet had come from the hand of the man's own mother. Kate had felt nothing when she sliced open the fuel lines of the fancy yacht or when she stripped every wire inside the little walkie talkie or even when she pressed a button and watched a cloud of smoke form on the horizon. But now, the two blurred together, cold white eyes in a black face and innocent brown eyes in a pale moon-shaped face.

"The developer. And that rat-nosed woman who shot her son. Now this Jamaican. Don't tell me they all got what was coming to them. Don't tell me they were up to no good." Kate looked up, her eyes glassy. "I'm a killer."

The plane's drone filled the air as Kate's statement hung heavy.

"Do you think there's some kind of support group for that?" Kate tried to laugh.

"Honey, there are support groups for everything. If you want, when we get back home, I'll help you find a Killer's Anonymous meeting. And if there isn't one, I'll let you host one at the club. Everyone can wear a disguise. I have plenty of wigs I can lend out. They can pick one—"

Williams voice buzzed through their headsets. "We're getting close to DR airspace. I'll radio and see if we can get cleared straight to Costanza to save us a stop. Either way, we'll be on the ground soon. Lucia, we're probably close enough to call now."

Lucia's bag was lying under Whiskey's feet. Kate pushed the dog aside and grabbed the strap. The bag swung easily in the empty space between the seats.

"Wait a minute. They should be in here, right?"

"What should be...?" Lucia reached toward Kate.

"This isn't heavy enough." Kate unzipped the front pocket where she'd stowed the zemí back in the Blue Mountain cave. She reached down into the pocket and pulled out an old napkin. Her forehead tightened as she stuffed her hand back down into the empty pocket. "Lucia?"

"*Sí.*"

"The zemís were in this pocket?" Kate frantically began to dig through the main compartment of the bag, rooting and shaking it.

"*Sí*. They were wrapped in a white cloth and—"

"They're both gone."

CHAPTER FORTY

"Where are the zemís?"

The contents of every bag were strewn across the floor between the seats of William's plane. Kate frantically dug into the bottom of each empty bag. Hers, Lucia's, and Kara's. Even the bag Whiskey had been carrying. Everything they'd had with them in Jamaica was there except for the two golden zemís.

"Lucia, think. I put them in the pocket of your bag after we escaped the cavern. What happened after that? You had them when I climbed up to the clearing."

"I had it...wait. Anthony carried my bag so I didn't get it tangled as I climbed up. But he gave it right back to me as soon as he got to the top with the rest of the gear."

Kara did a double-take. "Wait, what? He had your bag, he was all by himself, and the zemís — the priceless artifacts that people are dying over — were in your bag, and now they are not. What the actual—"

"Kara." William's voice cracked over the headset. "Do you think Anthony took the zemís?"

"Well, when faced with a number of possibilities, the simplest one is usually the right one. He had the opportunity. It would have been easy, and that was the only time they were out of our hands. So, it begs the next question. Why?"

"Maybe he means to sell them?" Lucia suggested. "The gold alone would be worth thousands, and he was taking care of three families. He had the old medicine man, his own family, and his friend's family, right?"

"He knew what we were looking for. And he surely knew they were worth a lot more than the melt value of the gold."

Kate stretched between the front seats. "William, can you call your friend who recommended him?"

"Already ahead of you. I just sent him a text."

She winced as she flopped back against the seat back.

Kara rested her elbows on her knees and hung her head. "Now what?"

Kate picked at the edge of a cut on her forearm. "Anthony could just be looking to sell them, but I think we have to assume the worst case and work from there. As I see it, the worst I can imagine is that somehow Guzman knew where we were headed and got to

Anthony. We have to work under the assumption that Guzman has the zemís. And if we're right about him, then it means he's planning to kill two more boys."

"We can't let that happen." Kara's voice sounded more defeated than determined.

"There's only one zemí left. He won't stop. So, we have to stop him."

"How, Kate? Do you want to kill him?" Lucia's voice shook.

"Is that..." Kate's fists tightened, and she counted loops in the carpet until she felt steady. "No. I'm not suggesting anyone straight up kill him, as much as he deserves it. Look, it's obvious he doesn't know where any of them are. He's following us. He's relying on us to find them, then he's puffing up his bully muscle and taking them from us. The first time it happened, shame on him. But this time? Shame on us. I don't know about you, but I'm not going to give him another chance. "

"What do you propose?" Kara asked.

"A trap, I guess. We lure him in and..."

"And what, Kate? We've already seen the authorities won't do anything about him."

Kate met Kara's glare. "That was before the missing boys. That was before anyone knew he was a murderer. Now they have to take us seriously. We can dig up evidence. Security cameras. Witnesses. If they won't investigate, we will. It shouldn't take long to come up with something. Enough that they can't ignore him, anyway."

"And then?"

"And then we bait the trap." Kate looked at Lucia.

Lucia waved her hands. "Oh, no. No, no."

"What's the one thing he wants more than anything. The one thing he'd interrupt his plans for?"

Kara answered. "The last zemí."

"Right. So, all we have to do is make it sound like we've found it. Talk about it in town. At the bar. You know he'll show up. He won't be able to resist it."

"Kate, he sent people to kill us." Lucia clutched her throat.

"No, he didn't. He sent people to get the zemís from us. If it had just been a hit, we never would have made it off that mountain. Do I think that guy would have killed me? Or you? Or Whiskey? Sure. But I don't think Guzman meant for them to kill us all. He needs us. If he could find these things on his own, he would. We'd be nothing to him."

"Then how do we catch him?"

"Best to confront him in a public place. I don't think he'll risk exposing himself by creating a scene in public."

"I'm not so sure about that." William's deep voice in their headsets startled Kate. "He believes his mission is from the gods, and we know he's willing to kill to fulfill his so-called destiny. I think it's safer to get him alone. We can say Bob had more records stored on campus. We could pass around a rumor that we're going there."

"But he won't come alone."

"We need to give him a reason to."

"Would it be safe to catch him on campus?" Kate asked. "If we said Bob kept some important research materials locked up in his office, that would be believable. And there's enough security there that he wouldn't dream of showing up with an army."

"Not at the university. But he had an office at the Ministry of Culture in Santo Domingo."

"Okay. William, can we reroute to Santo Domingo?"

"Absolutely."

"Great. Lucia, you'll need to call around. Get the word out that we're going to Bob's office in the morning to check some research about the location of the last zemí. With any luck, Guzman will show up, then we'll have him.

CHAPTER FORTY-ONE

THE GROUP LANDED in Santo Domingo, the capital of the Dominican Republic, then took a cab to the historic district. After the hell they'd been through, they deserved a treat. William booked them into a posh hotel just two blocks from the ocean. After checking in, each took a room key then disappeared behind heavy doors with security locks.

Kate's hotel room door clunked shut behind her. She snapped the security bar into place and twisted the deadbolt. With the heavy thud, her heartbeat slowed, and she felt protected for the first time in days. Whiskey rubbed against her leg and gazed up at her.

She pulled a towel from the bathroom and spread it across the foot of the king-sized bed. The dog bounced up, circled three times, then curled into a tight ball. His snores bounced against the textured wallpaper as Kate flipped on the shower to the hottest setting.

After undressing, she stepped into the tiled shower. The water beat on her neck and shoulders before spilling down her cut and bruised body, softening her skin and relaxing her aching muscles. Her eyes closed, and she rested in the peaceful, rhythmic sound. As she pulled the steam into her lungs, she smiled at Whiskey's gentle snores.

Kate fell into a deep sleep, her first since the hurricane.

The next morning, a sound like light tap dancing followed Kate as she and Whiskey crossed the terrazzo. She waved at Kara and Lucia, who sat together at a small table in the hotel's cafe. "When we get home, remind me to make him an appointment at the groomer. His nails sound like Fred Astaire." The dog curled up under the table and began to chew on his foot.

"How'd you sleep?"

"Amazing, thanks. I usually don't sleep well when I'm away from *Serenity*, but this place is so beautiful, it's impossible to not relax."

Lucia nodded. "This section was an old church." She waved at the interior courtyard. The walls were a light terra cotta stucco with arched porticos in the old Spanish Mission style. Marble tile stretched across the full breadth of the open courtyard, with a tall fountain surrounded by a colorful mosaic in the center. "Of course the hotel tower section is new. They built it maybe five years ago? Bob and I spoke on Taíno history at an anthropology conference here not too long ago." At the memory of her husband's name, Lucia's voice slowed and softened. She looked down at her hands gripping her coffee cup.

Kate reached up and rubbed Lucia's shoulder. "That'll happen a lot. He'll come out of nowhere and hijack what you thought was a perfectly normal conversation. People say you'll get used to it, but you don't. You just learn to cover it better. First, you'll learn how to keep the hitch out of your voice, then maybe you'll try keeping eye contact with whoever you're talking to. But what I can promise is that eventually, when he pops up, you'll smile when you think of the twinkle in his eye, or that cute dimple ..." the corners of Kate's mouth turned up just a little, as she stared off into the colorful plaza, its colors blurring through her tears. She wiped her eyes, shook her head, and turned back to Lucia. "And sometimes, even after a few years, that'll happen."

"You loved your husband very much, didn't you?"

Kate closed her eyes. "Yeah."

Lucia wrapped her tiny hand around Kate's.

"I'll go find William." Kara whispered and gently pushed her chair back from the table.

"It doesn't really get easier. They say it does, but it's not easier. It's just different. You haven't asked for my advice, so I won't tell you what to do. But I will say that I kind of wish I had let people help me a little more. I just didn't want to seem weak or be vulnerable, you know? So, I'm glad you're letting us help you. And as hard and frustrating and terrifying as this all is, it's good that you're focusing on finishing something that was so important to Bob."

Lucia gazed across the plaza, her eyes glassy. Then she clenched her jaw and waved to a waitress for refills. Kate and Lucia sat, shoulder to shoulder, two widows drinking coffee.

A few minutes later, Kara returned to the table, William in tow.

Lucia spoke first, her voice clearer and stronger. "William, thank you for arranging for us to stay here last night, and thank you for everything you've done for me since the storm. I could never have dreamed of the kindness you've shown. All of you, really. I appreciate your help, and I don't know how I can ever repay you."

"You don't have to repay anything. Besides, Michelle is working on another new app idea, and I think she's happy to have me out of her hair for a little while." William grinned, and then his eyes grew dark. "And on the more serious side, people like Guzman can't be left to roam free. If I can use my time and resources to help make the world a little bit safer and more just, then it's my responsibility to do just that."

"And on that note," Kate pushed her chair back. "We probably should be heading over to the Ministry."

Whiskey groaned as he pushed himself up to his

feet and followed Kate and her friends out onto the street. She clipped his leash onto his thick work vest.

As they navigated the narrow, winding streets of the Colonial Zone, Lucia pointed out landmarks. Many of the buildings dated back to the early fifteen hundreds. Finally, they crossed through an ancient gate, passing into the more modern section of the sprawling city. They walked a few blocks along the muddy waterfront where the Rio Ozama spills into the Caribbean. Just beyond a roundabout circling a tall monument, a jetty stretched into the harbor. Past it, the water cleared to the Caribbean's customary crystal turquoise. Across the street stood the Ministry building surrounded by a low stucco wall.

Lucia led the group past two rows of columns, up the wide steps, then into the building's atrium, where workers were carefully hanging lights for the upcoming holiday season.

Kate turned and looked out the building's doors across the street. The sun shone brightly down on a wide grassy boulevard and tall, thin palm trees to the sparkling Caribbean Sea beyond. It was hard to remember Christmas was just over a month away.

At the top of a wide staircase to their left, Lucia waved a small identification badge to the guard. "We're expecting another guest to help us with Bob's office. Please show him back when he arrives?"

She turned to Kate and muttered, "I hope this works."

"*Sí, señora.*" The guard turned his bored gaze back to his phone and the group proceeded down the hall.

Kate grinned at how easily they got away with their deception.

The office Bob shared with a group of anthropologists and archaeologists from the university was wide, with work tables in the center and a series of small desks scattered around the edges of the room. A lone man sat at a desk on the far wall.

"The Ministry invites all the major historical scientists to use this space to collaborate or just as a base while they're in the city to obtain permits, present at conferences, and such." Lucia explained. "You never quite know who you'll run into, but it's a great way to keep up with the various digs and projects going on, and it makes it easy for the Ministry to keep tabs on everyone and make sure none of the projects is going off course."

"How many projects are running at once?" William asked.

"We never know for sure. They keep especially close watch over anything that might involve new discoveries, and they work hard to keep religious and burial sites secret to prevent looters and grave robbers from desecrating those sites." Lucia waved as the man across the room glanced up at them, nervously scanned the room, then returned to his work. She approached a desk along a wall dotted with jalousie windows, opened to allow the light sea breeze to cool the room.

"Bob didn't come down here to work very often, but it's where he kept all his legal documents and licenses and permits." She chose a small key from a ring and unlocked his desk. "I suppose I'll keep it all here ..." She stopped then pulled a folder from the center of the file drawer. "What's—"

"I'll take that now, thank you."

Kate spun around and found herself face to face with Diego Guzman. Behind him stood two men with automatic rifles. A younger boy straddled Whiskey, wrapping his muzzle with duct tape.

CHAPTER FORTY-TWO

GUZMAN DROPPED a thin stack of cash on the desk of the man across the room then returned to his prey. The man scurried from the room, the sound of his steps echoing through the polished marble halls.

"I suppose I could have broken in, but it's so much more civilized to use a key, don't you think?" His eyes lingered over the exotic blonde American, her fiery eyes glaring at him. As he stepped up closer to her, she took a step back, bumping into the desk.

Guzman leaned in closer. She smelled of hotel shampoo and light, salty sweat. He rubbed his cheek against hers as he whispered in her ear, "You're not what I would normally choose, but I hear the gods asking for you as a special gift."

He slowly pulled away and winked at her, then deftly dipped as she swung at him. He popped up and pulled her arm around behind her, using the momentum of her swing to spin her around in front of him. "Mmm, feisty, this one."

Guzman took a roll of duct tape and taped the thin woman's wrists behind her, then he pressed his body up against her. His heart stirred at her warmth, and he could almost taste her panic. He tossed the duct tape to one of his men. They surrounded the group of friends.

Reluctantly, he pushed the woman toward the group then began to slowly pace. Patience had never been a strength of his, but over time, he'd learned people hated silence. So, he waited.

On his fourth pass in front of the group, the blonde spat at his feet.

"You're the one with the dog, no?" He tossed his head back to his man who held Whiskey by his head.

"Hurt my dog and it'll be the last thing you do."

Guzman laughed at the little blonde's snarl. "I don't think you're in a position to threaten me." He turned to the others. "You thought you could draw me into your little trap? Do you really think I'm that stupid? That I wouldn't be watching every step you make? Just because my goals and methods are different from yours doesn't mean I'm an idiot."

He circled in front of them. "Are you so naive to actually trust every person you've worked with?" He pulled out a photo of himself holding the two zemís that disappeared in Jamaica.

"When I was just a boy, my mother told me all the

stories. The townspeople started rumors and called her a whore because they were jealous."

And because most of their husbands paid for her services. Guzman shook off the truth and returned his focus to the Americans.

"They were scared of the power they knew I held. My mother's father was a direct descendant of the Taíno chieftains. My father's uncle was a direct descendant of the Taíno shamans. Their lines have converged with me. I am the Taíno destiny."

He resumed his pacing.

"I have something you do not. I have learned patience. I am willing to sacrifice for what I know the gods want. They have been patient for five hundred years. They can wait for opportunities. Because you do not possess this patience, and because you underestimate me, you brought the opportunity right to me. So, here you are. And here I am. I am standing. You are captured. I have four gods. You have zero. I am the true Cacique of the Taíno people."

He stopped and stood looming over them. "The gods have chosen me. And now, they will use you to lead me to the holy place."

"You. The professor's wife." He grabbed a small knife and cut the duct tape from Lucia's wrists. "Get that box over there and empty this desk."

The small woman hurried to follow his commands. He assessed her curves as she bent over the desk, and he reflected on her usefulness. Too old to keep around for long, but good for a time. And the blonde could be interesting.

The man and the abomination, though, he had no use for. He'd have to get rid of them quickly. And he knew just the marsh along the southern coast where a bask of crocodiles lived.

When the woman had put the last of the files into the box, Guzman motioned to his men. "Load them all up." His men began to push the group out, shoving them with the stocks of their rifles. Guzman grabbed Lucia by the arm then pushed through the door a few steps behind his men. They went down the back stairs then into the waiting van. Once his prisoners were secure, he stalked down the alley to his own car.

CHAPTER FORTY-THREE

The cargo van jostled down the narrow streets of Santo Domingo. Kate and the others sat on the metal floor, their hands taped behind their backs. Whiskey lay on the floor, his nose wrapped in tape. His eyes pleaded with Kate, but she was helpless to relieve him of the pain the tape was causing as it pulled his fur.

"If we get out of this, I'm gonna kill that skinny bastard with my bare hands."

Kate glanced up through the metal mesh separating the cargo area from the cab to see if their captors heard Kara's snarled whisper. The two men and the younger boy all stayed focused on the road ahead. "Get in line, my friend. And I think Whiskey will want to take a few pounds of flesh, too." Kate bent over and tried to comfort the dog with a nuzzle.

The van jerked to a stop, and the driver cut the engine. The three Dominicans climbed out then slammed the doors behind them. A heavy metal door clanged shut in the alley outside. Kate struggled to her feet then scurried to the front of the cargo compartment.

"We're in a narrow alley, looks like maybe the middle of a block. Graffiti and garage doors all the way to the next street."

Lucia slumped against the side of the van. "That's the whole city. Could be anywhere, really."

Kate returned to the middle of the tiny space. "Here, William, I'm gonna squat down back to back with you and try to undo your hands. Hold still, okay?" She lowered herself and fumbled against the tape around his wrists but couldn't get it to tear.

"How are we gonna get—" Kate stopped at a sound outside the door of the van. She hopped away from William, landing beside Kara near the back door just before the latched clicked.

The door swung open, then the younger boy climbed in with them, a rifle slung across his chest. The driver leaned in behind him. "Cacique will meet us up at the *loma*, and he just wants the women. We'll stop and take care of the other two and the dog on the way. Keep them still until we stop."

As the driver slammed the door shut, Kate leaned to Kara and whispered in her ear, "Does he think we don't understand Spanish?"

"I don't think he cares."

The boy glared over at them. "Silence!"

Kara shrugged.

After the men climbed into the van, the engine growled to life. The vehicle lurched up the alley then into the maze of city streets. Kate sat folded forward with her eyes closed, her feet stretched in front of her, her hands resting just below the small of her back.

When they'd traveled nearly forty minutes, stopping and starting, the transmission's gears grinding with each shift, she felt a light touch on the shoulder. She glanced up.

The boy bent toward her ear and whispered, "Don't move. Stay quiet."

She felt a subtle sawing motion between her hands and started to turn her head toward him.

His grip on her shoulder tightened. His whisper turned urgent. "I said don't move."

Kate felt the pressure of the tape release around her wrists, but the boy held her arm steady. He shifted to the other side of the van, where he caught her eye as he whispered to William across from her and began sawing at the tape on his wrists. She nodded and held her hands behind her.

"Kid, what's going on back there?" The driver's eyes were wide in the rearview mirror.

The boy yelled over the groan of the engine, "Just checking to make sure there was enough tape, *Señor*. I don't want any of them getting loose and attacking me."

"Good. We'll be there in a few minutes."

"*Sí*. I'll be ready."

He moved around the van, "checking" the tape around Lucia and Kara's wrists and whispering to them as well. He glanced at Kate, down to Whiskey, then back to her. His eyes looked pained and he gently shook his head back and forth. Kate understood why he couldn't cut the tape on the dog's nose without being caught.

She very slowly twisted her wrists to be sure the tape released from her skin all the way around, and she hoped the others were doing the same thing. They needed to be ready.

The van finally stopped. When the men got out, Kate bounced up into a crouch and Kara matched her stance

"Whiskey!" she whispered, and the dog scrambled to his feet behind her.

"Good luck," the boy whispered just as the door latch snapped.

The second the door to the van opened, Kate launched herself at the first man, knocking him off balance and toppling him to the pavement. He dropped his rifle on impact. Out of the corner of her eye, she saw Kara fly at the driver, pulling him off to the side and pounding him with her fist.

Kate somersaulted over the guard's head and bounced to her feet. As he tried to get up, she kicked him in the side of the head and knocked him back down. While he recovered, she dove for his rifle. The man rolled, getting his hands on the strap just as Kate grabbed the barrel.

She gripped it hard and twisted. The strap wrapped around the man's wrist, and the stock flipped around and slammed into the side of his head. The man's body flopped down on the ground.

Kate pulled the gun's stock up against her shoulder and checked the thumb switch. The safety was off and the gun was hot. She rested her finger alongside the trigger guard and spun around. William stood against the van with Lucia behind him. The boy was already a hundred yards down the road, running like the baseball scouts were watching.

Kate spun around and sighted the rifle on the driver. "Kara. I got him."

Kara landed one more punch on the man's bloody face, then pushed herself up and spit on him.

"William, can you bring that roll of tape, please?"

"Gladly."

William bound both men's hands and ankles with tape. Then Kara propped them up back to back and they taped the two men together.

They left them by the side of the road and drove the van to the airport.

CHAPTER FORTY-FOUR

Kate dipped her finger in a small tub of antibiotic ointment. Wincing, she stroked it onto Whiskey's nose. The dog whimpered but stayed still while Kate tended to him.

The flight home had been smooth, and Kate spent most of it sprawled on the floor of the small plane's cabin, gently cutting the tape off the dog's muzzle, hair by hair. Whiskey had looked at Kate's knife with terror, and in the end, Lucia ended up on the floor with them, stroking the dog's ears and singing softly to him. She covered his eyes while Kate patiently cut away the tape.

They'd landed just in time to watch the sunset from the roof of Kara's apartment above the club. The weather was finally cooling off, and Kara's chef had sent up a pot of thick chicken corn tortilla soup and a pitcher of weak sangria. After Lucia fell asleep on

Kara's couch, Michelle picked up Kate and William and drove them back to Shark Key.

Early the next morning, Kate gently patted her thigh and Whiskey followed her up to the deck. Chuck backed through the swinging door to the kitchen then spun around with three plates in his hands. When he saw Kate, he dropped them on the bar to run over to her, arms spread wide.

"Katie, I didn't realize y'all were back." He wrapped her in a bear hug and squeezed until she yelped.

"Easy, Chuck. I'm gonna need a day or two for the aches and pains to heal up. And I told you to never call me that!" She winked at him. "Go get those tourists their breakfast, then I can catch you up."

He grabbed the plates and dropped them at a table over near the water, then he settled in on the barstool beside Kate. He leaned over and whispered to her, "What do you say I play hooky today and we take my skiff out and go fishing?"

She whispered back, "I haven't heard anything that good in a long time."

Chuck slid off the stool. "I'll tell Babette and pack a little cooler. Get your gear. I'll meet you at the end of the east dock."

Fifteen minutes later, Kate stepped down the dock toward Chuck's skiff. He stood on the casting deck and held his hand out to her. She climbed aboard and stowed her things, then they slipped wordlessly out onto the water. They fished for two hours before Kate finally broke the silence.

"I killed a man in Jamaica."

Chuck nodded and cast his line back out across the water.

"It was him or me."

"I believe you."

"He would have killed us."

"You don't have to convince me, Katie."

"Will you please stop calling me that? It's like you think I'm twelve."

"Then stop brooding like you are."

"Did you hear me? A man is dead. Dead. Shot and fell off the side of a mountain dead."

"Sounds like he deserved it."

"How..."

"William was up early for breakfast. He told me everything, including that you're not doing so great with what happened." Chuck set his pole down and looked Kate in the eyes. "You've had a rough few days. It's okay to not be okay."

Kate flopped into a tall pedestal seat. "I don't want to go back there. I'm just a little American girl. This shouldn't be my fight. But I don't know how to let it go, either. Chuck, that guy is killing kids. Teenagers with their whole lives ahead of them. Just because they've got Spanish blood in their veins."

The shallow water glowed a pale robin's-egg blue, fading into a solid deep cerulean line where it met the horizon. Chuck sat on the casting deck and wrapped his arms around his knees. "He sounds pretty bad."

"He's a monster. And the thing is, he is always one step ahead of us. No matter where we turn up, he's there. I don't get it."

Chuck pulled a bottle of water from the cooler, cracked the cap, then handed it to Kate.

"He's got four zemís now. All he needs is one more. If he gets that, all hell breaks loose down there. His followers believe they'll be restored. They'll try to take back the island with violence, even though most of the Taíno people don't want that. But Lucia says he's got enough crazy believers to cause problems. A lot of people are going to die if this guy isn't stopped."

"Then stop him."

"I don't know how. Every time we turn around, he cuts us off."

"Then be ready for him."

"How?"

"You're a bright girl, Kate. Outsmart him."

Kate sagged in her seat. "Let's outsmart these fish first, okay?"

Chuck picked up his rod. He whipped it, and his little lure sailed through the air before gently landing in the water.

CHAPTER FORTY-FIVE

A STRONG LATE-AFTERNOON breeze blew across *Serenity's* top sundeck, ruffling the pages of Kate's notebook. An open can of El Presidente sat on the deck beside her chair, weighting down one edge of a topographical map of the mountainous center of the Dominican Republic. She ruffled through the small notebook that had been Bob's, cross-referencing it with her own research notes about early Taíno culture.

As she turned the pages, the edge of her vision caught something. She frantically flipped Bob's journal back a few pages until she saw a rough drawing of a cave entrance near the peak of a mountain, higher than any of the others. It showed the setting sun, with the cave entrance facing west behind a tall waterfall. She grabbed the map on the deck beside her and found the tallest peaks. The third-highest peak on the island also had a similar topography on its western slope.

She scooped up all the papers and journals and ran up to the deck.

William was sitting in front of his laptop at a shaded table near the water. Behind him, local guitarist Branson Tillman was setting up his equipment near the bar.

Kate dumped her armload on the table then spread the map in front of William. She flipped pages and pointed. “Look!”

He dropped his head into her line of sight and caught her eye. “What’s got you so excited? Use your words.”

She shook her head and focused. “I think I know where the last zemí is. And if I’m right, I think we can use it to capture Diego Guzman and get all the zemís back together and to safety.”

William raised an eyebrow. “So far, that hasn’t gone well for us. What makes this time different?”

“This time, we know he’s coming for us.” Kate tapped out a message on her phone and hit send. She set it down on the table and waved at Babette, who bobbed from table to table, checking on the crowd of happy hour visitors. A minute later, Chuck appeared with a bowl of ceviche and a tray of drinks.

“Pompano Caribbean ceviche. It’s a new experiment with the fish Kate and I got this morning. I used a little rice vinegar and some mango and pineapple to bring a little island style to it. Try some.”

William scooped a spoonful onto a cracker. His

eyes closed and his brows shifted just a little closer together. "Is there some..." He trailed off, licked the corner of his lips, then chewed a little more. "Is it allspice?"

Chuck clapped. "It is. Still have the traditional lime and cilantro to balance the sweetness, but just a dash of allspice to bring out the fruit."

The sudden twang of Tillman's electric guitar made everyone jump. The musician quickly turned down his portable amp and shrugged. "Sorry, man!"

William waved behind him as he took a swig of beer and another bite of ceviche. "It works." He spooned a pile out onto an appetizer plate. "Michelle is gonna love this."

"Where is she, anyway?"

"She's working on her new app. The guest stateroom is covered in flowcharts and user stories. I won't see her for another couple of weeks when she figures out if she can build it or not."

"What's it do?"

William shook his head and twisted his fingers in front of his lips. "Top secret." He laughed. "Well, maybe not so much top secret as I completely don't understand how it works and couldn't explain it if my life depended on it, but she says it taps into the phone's GPS, Bluetooth, and wireless features to create a communications net that will help people stay connected during a natural disaster when cell and Internet services are all down."

Kara and Lucia pulled chairs to the table as Kate asked, "I thought there were apps that kind of did that already? Like a walkie-talkie app thing?"

"There are a few that are advertised as working when cell service is down or overloaded, but most of them still need an active Internet connection, and that won't happen if the power is out. She thinks she's figured out a way to work around that and is determined to build something that will work anywhere, not just in developed areas."

Lucia set her phone on the table. "That sounds promising."

William turned to her. "You're the inspiration for the idea, actually. Michelle was so heartbroken when she heard what happened to Bob. She just kept muttering, 'If only they could have called for help.' That stuck with her until the thought turned into how she could give people in similar situations a way to call for help. Then she ran into the guest cabin we use as an office. Within ten minutes, every surface was covered with butcher paper and she had her markers and sticky notes out. I learned a long time ago — when that happens, give her alone time to work it all out. She barely stops to eat, and she usually falls asleep in there. She'll go like that until either she figures it out or she's exhausted every possible solution and decides it won't work."

Kate nodded. "I can relate. When I was working at the paper, I was the same way with a story. I've learned to quiet my mind a little bit, but sometimes the story or the problem is worth pressing into. Which brings me to our little zemí hunt. Kara, Lucia, thanks for coming so quickly."

"Of course. We were already in the car. I was taking Lucia up to the Middle Keys to see a little more of the area, so we were close. What do you have?"

"I think I've found the last zemí."

CHAPTER FORTY-SIX

As Branson warmed up with the first two verses of "A Pirate Looks at Forty," Kate looked across the table. Kara sat beside her sister, the two whispering and grinning like they'd been close all their lives.

Kate rose from her seat, pushed a pile of clean plates and silverware off of her map, then pointed to a peak near the center. "This is on the western side of the Dominican Republic, maybe sixty miles from your house, Lucia. *Loma Gajo en Medio* is the third highest peak in the country, and there's a wide west-facing slope that drops off just beyond it." She grabbed Bob's notebook and flipped it open to the drawing. "See here, where it shows the mouth of a cave facing the setting sun? And this rock formation here? It matches this on the map." She pointed at what she'd found.

"And did you hear when we were in the van?"

Kara asked. "He said 'Cacique will meet us at the *loma.*' Kate's right. This could really be it."

Lucia didn't look as certain. "I hate to be negative here, but Guzman has been on our tail every step of this. What's to say he won't follow us here?"

"Nothing at all." Kate leaned against the back of her chair. "In fact, I'm counting on it. We just need to get there first."

"Set up an ambush?" William sounded skeptical.

"Last time we tried that," Lucia said, "it didn't go so well."

"No. Last time was a ruse. This is the real deal. We just need to slow him down." Kate paced around the table. "What if we send you to him with a peace offering? Suggest a truce. Tell him we're back because we think we know where the last zemí is but we need his help, and you will endorse him as the Cacique if he agrees to leave all five of the zemís in the mountain cave. Grant him legitimacy by offering him a position at the cultural ministry as the Taíno liaison. Tempt him with all the power and acknowledgments he craves. But tell him we won't play ball if he brings his little punk army. He comes alone and he brings all four zemís. Then you lead him up the mountain, where we'll be waiting."

Kara laid her hand on her sister's arm. "Could you get this kind of message to him?"

"Doesn't matter if she can or not." William's voice

grew strained. "It'd be easier if he just doesn't come up the mountain at all."

Kate's cheeks burned. "There's no scenario where he doesn't come up the mountain to find that zemí. None, except the one where he's dead. And while I might be willing to twist the truth, I'm not willing to murder the man to keep him off the mountain. We know he's coming up, so let's make it on our terms."

Kate pulled her tablet from a pile of books and zoomed in on a satellite map of the area. "It looks like there's a village not far from the peak. I don't see any roads, but there are some donkey paths, and there's a little open airstrip just to the north right here. William thinks he can get in there with the TBM, and then we just need to convince one of the locals to be our guide up the trail."

Kara raised an eyebrow. "That sounds too easy."

"What do the remote villages need more than anything else?"

Lucia chuckled. "They need health care. Doctors. Dentists. But solar panels and water filters will help them right away."

"All right, then. That's what we bring them." William grabbed his laptop and started typing.

"We've gotta change things up, you guys." Kate tried to sound confident. "We've been shooting first, then aiming afterward. Sure, we need to act. But we also need to get smart and think ahead. Instead of just hopping in the plane and racing off, let's visualize it. We land. What or whom do we encounter first?"

"Villagers."

"Hostile villagers."

"Goats."

Kate rolled her eyes at Chuck.

"No, really. They love to butt things with their heads."

"Not helpful, Charles. Go back to your kitchen and make up something delicious." Kate gave him a playful shove toward the swinging doors. He winked as he raised his hands and backed away.

Kara stepped in. "Okay, let's assume a couple of things. Worst case, Guzman has gotten there first and convinced the people in the village that he's the One True Cacique, sent by Atabey to reunite them and restore their civilization. What then?" She looked toward her sister.

"Well, most of the people living in that remote area are Taíno. If they think the prophesy is coming true and the Taíno are rising again, then they'll be excited to follow him. If that happens, we'll somehow have to expose him as a fraud. Quickly."

"And if he hasn't gotten there first?"

"Then we get ahead of it." Kate scooped a pile of ceviche onto a chip, then continued. "We have to gain their trust and convince them a false prophet is coming, one who's killing innocent people in the name of Atabey. Tell them we need their help to stop him.

That'll be the easier sell, I think, as long as we have some of the news footage of the missing kids along with the details of our own story." She shoved the chip into her mouth.

William set his laptop back on the table. "So, we come prepared for either of those things, and we bring solar panels and water filters. That gets us through the village."

Lucia leaned forward, bouncing in her chair, her eyes bright. "It might be easier than that. I think Noni's nephew's wife comes from that area. I'll call around. Find out if Guzman has been there yet, and see if I can arrange for a guide to help us." She began tapping on her phone before she finished speaking.

Kate grinned. "Great! Then it's the hike to the peak. I think we'll need better gear than our friend Anthony came up with in Jamaica. Hiking boots and extra water for everyone. Actual climbing harnesses and rappel devices, good rope. I'll get a caddy harness for Whiskey, too."

William pinched in on the satellite image. "It looks like we should be able to make the hike in a couple hours if we push."

"We'd better go get packed up, then." Kara pushed her chair back — directly into Chuck.

When Chuck stumbled and fought to keep his balance, Lucia dropped her phone.

Kara bent to pick it up as Lucia caught him by the elbow. "Nice save, *hermana*!"

Lucia snatched her phone back from Kara and stuffed it in her pocket. Then she turned to Chuck. "I think we're leaving, so I'd like to thank you again for all your help and for your hospitality." She gave him a kiss on each cheek, grabbed her sister's hand, then walked back to the car.

Kate turned back to William. "I think we need to be ready for the last zemí to be better protected than the rest, too. The others were kept safe because they were hidden and their locations were secret. This one wouldn't have been kept at nearly the same level of secrecy. It's in what the Taíno of the time believed to be the Cave of Origin. Even though its location has been obscured over time, they would all have known where it was then, so whoever was securing the zemí there would definitely have put some protections in place to keep it out of the hands of the unworthy."

"So how would they have decided who was worthy and who was not?" Chuck wondered.

"That, my friend, is the question we have to answer." William scratched the stubble on his jaw. "Our lives are going to depend on it."

"He's right." Kate said. "I hate to suggest it, but I think we need to be armed up like a small militia. That might pose a little problem if we clear into the country through normal channels. And we know Guzman has at least some of the officials in his pocket. I propose we file a flight plan the same as all our past routes through Santiago, but then as we get close, you declare some kind of emergency. We set down on that little airstrip and buy ourselves a little privacy to quickly and quietly offload our little army. Kara and I can hire a Jeep to make our way up the back of the mountain from there, and then William, you and Lucia can proceed to Santiago to clear in."

William leaned back, his brow furrowed. "I don't like that at all. Running afoul of immigration could risk everything. If we get caught, we'll be detained, they'll impound my plane, and the U.S authorities won't be much help, especially if we've got a small arsenal aboard."

"Well, the weapons won't be anywhere near the plane by the time they manage to catch up with us. I think if we're prepared, it's one of those times when it's easier to beg forgiveness than ask permission."

"It's not your plane and freedom you're risking, Kate."

"Aren't you the one who said we have an obligation to do everything we can?'

"I'm not sure I meant extending that to weapons smuggling."

Kate's phone buzzed. A text message from Kara contained a link to a Dominican news site. Kate clicked the URL and an article loaded on her phone. Three more homeless teens were reported missing from youth shelters in Santiago and Santo Domingo. All three were believed to have recently attended a rally for a radical indigenous rights group but never returned to their shelters. Kate pinched in on the photos. One of the boys was the kid from the van who had set them free, then disappeared into the jungle.

"William, look at this. We need to move. We've already smuggled weapons into three countries in the last two weeks. And if we don't do this right? If we're not prepared? Guzman is going to get that last zemí. He's going to kill these boys. He'll enslave helpless people. He's got to be stopped."

"Two wrongs don't—" He stopped, then started again. "Look, I get what you're trying to do. I agree he needs to be stopped, and I agree we're the best people to stop him. But we can't lose ourselves doing it. We only take the minimum we need, and we clear in. Period."

Kate jumped when a loud strum burst from the amp behind them as Branson started his set. Over the next hour, William and Kate reviewed all the details. Everything that could go wrong. Every way they could prevent disaster.

Finally, when every risk had been discussed twice, William pushed back from the table. "If we want to land around first light, we need to be wheels up at three. So I need to go kiss my wife and get some sleep. I think you'd be good to do the same."

"Kiss your wife? I love her and all, but ... not that way." She winked at William then trotted back to *Serenity*.

CHAPTER FORTY-SEVEN

Even with her polarized wraparound sunglasses, the setting sun blinded Kate as she ran west along the Overseas Highway. Across from the entrance to Shark Key, she stopped, her hands rested against her knees. She checked her pulse while she waited for a break in the traffic. Another two weeks and she'd need to cross at the light further to the west. Tourist season would be in full steam, causing impossible traffic along Highway 1.

As soon as she found a break, she trotted across the highway and walked up the narrow, winding lane that led to the marina on the point, nearly a mile north. The glossy leaves of the seagrape bushes glowed, reflecting the deep orange of sunset. Kate imagined the same orange sunset pouring into the mouth of the cave where they'd be setting up to ambush a murderer. She felt confident in herself and her friends.

But even so, a deep unease stirred in her stomach.

She and William had reviewed the plan. They had imagined everything that could go wrong and planned a way to either prevent or respond. They had the equipment and the people they needed to get to the cave, circumvent any traps still protecting the zemí, and catch and contain Guzman when he arrived. But something still nagged at her.

She was walking along the southern lagoon when headlights appeared around the bend ahead. The vehicle was moving slowly, weaving down the gravel road. When it narrowly missed a thick campsite post, Kate sprinted toward the driver's door.

"Steve!"

The truck jerked to a stop in the middle of the lane, and he leaned out the open window. "Wha... Whassaprolem?"

Kate heard the thunk of the transmission and the clink of beer bottles rolling on the truck's floor. "C'mon man, get out of the truck." Her heart thumped as her friend opened the door and stumbled out onto the grass. "You can't drive like this."

"Gotta home. Dogs." He leaned slowly to the right. His foot shifted out, his body swayed in a wide circle. Then he fell flat on his face.

"Steve, you're not going anywhere but back up to your boat to sleep this off." She heaved him back to his feet and started to lead him around to the passenger's side. He pushed her arm away then stumbled across the lane.

"No. No boat. Sharks're in the water. Sharks..." He fell to his knees and rocked side to side.

Kate felt a familiar ache in her chest. She crouched beside Steve and wrapped her arm around his shoulder. "Okay. You don't have to go to the *Hopper*, but you need to be somewhere safe, okay? I know ..." She scanned the campground until she spotted a familiar blue and white fifth-wheel camper with tidy white skirting and potted flowers that were bright even in the dim solar lights around the lot.

Babette's house.

"Hey, buddy. We're gonna just walk across the way to Babette's place. Can you do that with me?" Kate slowly rose to her feet, pulling Steve with her. She struggled to help him balance as they stumbled up the lane and into Babette's living room. After helping Steve onto the couch, Kate tucked a light blanket around him, then knelt beside him.

When she spoke, her voice was so soft, she could hardly hear it herself.

"I know how much you miss Susan. I know better than anybody. But this isn't gonna bring her back, man. You gotta pull yourself together. If you need help, we can help you. But for tonight, stay here and sleep it off, okay? I'll take your truck to get the dogs, then I'll get Babette, and we'll check on you in a little bit. Just stay here—"

Steve's deep snore cut her off, and she quietly stepped back out into the dusk.

She walked back down the lane toward Steve's truck, past the campsites around the little lagoon. Chuck kept a few sites open for temporary visitors, but most of them were snowbirds who arrived in late fall and stayed through the spring. A few new motorhomes and trailers had set up for the season. Kate waved at an elderly couple sitting beneath their awning adorned with little plastic lights shaped like owls. She glanced at Steve's idling truck, then jogged over to the couple. The husband started to rise from his lawn chair.

"No, no, don't get up on my account. Please." She extended her hand first to the wife and then to the husband. "I'm Kate. I live in the houseboat on the end of the west dock. I've been meaning to stop by and welcome you. Will you two be joining us for Thanksgiving up on the deck?"

The woman leaned toward her husband. "We saw a notice in the laundry room, but we weren't sure if we should."

Kate beamed. "Oh, please come. Chuck really goes all-out. Turkey, all the traditional sides, plus a few less conventional ones, too. It'd be a shame to miss it."

Kate chatted for a moment longer, then excused herself to go let Steve's dogs out. As she walked back to the truck, her neighborly smile began to fade. She came to the Keys for solitude. She stayed at Shark Key for the family she'd found here. But now she was planning an operation to catch a murderer before he kills again. It seemed like trouble always managed to find her.

Her heart rate had finally slowed back down as she climbed into Steve's truck. She fastened her seatbelt and threw the vehicle in gear. Before she pulled down the lane toward the highway, she tapped Babette's name on her phone and waited for her friend to answer.

CHAPTER FORTY-EIGHT

"I DID NOT EXPECT this much cloud cover."

Kate's stomach tightened as William muttered to himself, tapping the live radar screen on the instrument panel and looking back and forth between his instruments and his tablet. The plane floated just above a thick, fluffy bed of clouds. The morning sun was at their tail. Near the horizon to the north, the lush green tip of Mount Duarte peeked through the cottony floor of the sky.

"William, I don't want to sound freaked out or anything, but if that's a mountain sticking out of the clouds over there, what's to say we're not going to drop into these clouds and—"

"Yeah, Kate. Let's just not go there right now, okay? I need to concentrate."

William confirmed his altitude with air traffic control, double-checked his instruments, and talked through his landing checklist, then he muttered a prayer as he gently eased the yoke forward. The little plane slid down into a blanket of white.

The light through the windshield gradually darkened as they descended through the clouds. Water streaked in horizontal lines across the plane's windows. Kate could see about three feet of the wings before they faded into the mist. Then, as William began to bank the plane to starboard, they broke through the bottom of the cloud layer. Looming in the windshield was a wall of trees and rock.

"Terrain. Terrain. Terrain." A wide screen in the instrument panel flashed red. Kate's breath caught in her throat as she looked to her right. Instead of sky, she saw more trees. In the back of the cabin, Kara shrieked. She clutched Whiskey and began reciting the Hail Mary in Spanish.

Kate squeezed her eyes tight. As the plane continued to bank, she felt her stomach lurch and her body pressed hard into the seat. She dared to open her eyes a crack and saw individual leaves on the trees out her side window. She fought to turn her head to the left and outside William's window, she saw black, roiling clouds.

Suddenly, the plane rolled to the left, and the rain pounded the window at her ear. The aircraft slipped through a gap between mountain peaks, then leveled off with the tiny runway just ahead of them.

William blew his lungs empty. "That was—"

The plane dropped as if the fist of God had pounded on the top of the fuselage. William's headset flew off and hit the ceiling of the little cabin with a thud. He shoved the throttle forward while pulling back hard on the yoke. The nose rose, and after a moment, they stabilized. William pulled the throttle back, then the plane began to descend.

"What was that?" Kate shrieked.

William ignored her, his eyes on the instrument panel and his lips moving as he talked himself through the landing. Kate tried to match his steady breaths. Through the gloomy drizzle, she watched the small strip rise to meet their wheels. It was barely paved, and the plane skidded on the poorly cleared runway. They slowed and pulled off into an abandoned tarmac.

William took three deep breaths, and his posture softened. "Wind shear." He aimed at a worn set of tie downs and stopped the plane close to them. "Well, folks, it seems like Lucia's welcoming party thought a little rain might scare us away. Let's get everything organized, then we'll see if we can scare up a little transportation."

Kara released her grip on Whiskey. "The guy that was supposed to meet us is named Jose. Hopefully, he just got held up by the storm."

The three of them unstrapped their seat belts, and, one by one, they climbed from the small plane and onto solid ground. Kara turned her phone on and held it up in the air.

"You know that won't really help, right? Either there's a signal here, or there's not." Kate raised her eyebrows as her friend's phone chimed with a new message.

Kara pulled the phone down, wiped the rain away, and tapped the screen. "Lucia's in place at the cafe. She says she got word to Guzman's crew, so she expects him to show up soon. Right now, we have about a two-hour head start, but with this rain if we don't get moving, our window is gonna shrink."

"Look, over by the barn, there's a scooter. I feel terrible, but we need to move fast. Do you think anyone would mind if I borrowed it? Ride into the village and find Jose while you guys start getting the gear unloaded?" Before the others could respond, Kate jogged over to the scooter and found its key tucked in the little glove compartment and a helmet dangling on the handlebar. She slipped the helmet on then fired the engine up.

Just a couple miles down the lane, the thick jungle on either side of the lane opened up into a small village. Kate pulled the scooter beside a small building that appeared to be a gas station, cafe, and grocery stand all in one. Its stucco walls were painted a bright orange, and thick bars covered both front windows.

Kate stepped through the front door and waved at the old, toothless man behind the counter.

"Excuse me, we just landed at the airstrip. We

called ahead to hire a truck and a guide to take us up into the mountains? Can you help us?"

"*Sí, sí. Señora Alvaro, no?* We hear the plane land. My grandson went to get the truck. How did you get here so fast?"

Kate face flushed. "There was a scooter..."

The man glared at her.

"I'm sorry. I know it was wrong to take it. Can I fill it with gas? I'll pay and return it..."

The old man burst out laughing. "I mess with you, little *gringa*. This is why the scooter is there. No one steals anything up here, and the only people who use that airstrip are the missionaries. We all share everything, and we've got no crime. I just ask that you help us keep it that way."

Kate relaxed. "Thank you. Of course! Now, did you say your grandson—"

A four-wheel-drive truck skidded to a stop in front of the building and a young, dark-skinned man bounded through the door. "*Abuelo*, I'm — Oh, hello." He held his hand out to Kate. "I'm Jose. Sorry I'm a little late. With the rain, I didn't think you'd land this quickly. Help me load the scooter. I'll drive you back up to the airstrip." He started toward the door, then spun back around. "Oh, grandpa. Where are the cooler bags?"

The old man pointed. Jose reached behind the counter and pulled out a heavy canvas contraption that looked like saddlebags, heaved it over his shoulder, then opened the door for Kate. He tossed the bags into the back of the truck, where she discovered a donkey tethered to the truck bed between two bales of hay. As Jose hefted the scooter behind the hay bales, Kate shrugged and climbed into the truck.

CHAPTER FORTY-NINE

KATE MARCHED through the cold drizzle behind the sturdy little donkey. She pulled her jacket tight and tucked her head deeper into her hood like a turtle retreating into its shell. Behind her, Whiskey carefully dodged stones and inched up the trail, occasionally stopping to bite at the mud collecting between the pads of his feet.

Jose led the group up the overgrown trail, hacking away with a sharp machete at brush obscuring the way. "I grew up on this mountain," he told Kate when they stopped for water. "When we were kids, we used to sneak up here and, well..." The faraway look in his eye betrayed his nostalgia for things teenagers did when they snuck out of the house.

"I guess teenagers are the same everywhere." Kate picked a clump of mud from the tread of her boots and heaved her tired body up from the rock. "I thought I was in pretty good shape. I run nearly every day, but the land I run on is pretty flat. These steep slopes are killing my shins."

Kara swung at a branch with a second machete, then took another long pull from her water bottle. "I'm grateful for your help, Kate. All of you. And my sister is, too. This whole thing has given us a chance to get to know each other as grownups. As people. It's been hard for her, losing Bob like she did, and she told me last night how much it means to her that we've helped her complete his work, especially considering what you've all risked to return the zemís to their home."

Kate shook the rain from her hair and patted Kara on the shoulder. "Of course."

From a few steps lower on the trail, William called up to the group. "I hate to break up the little love fest, but we don't have much of a head start, and we're not moving up this mountain very quickly. If we don't get moving, we might not be able to get set in time."

Kate pushed past Jose and the donkey and started up the trail, shoving the vegetation out of her way. She spotted a switchback ahead and stopped. She looked up the slope at the spot where the trail passed them about six feet above her head. She shook the water off, grabbed a small tree trunk and began to pull herself up the steep incline.

"What are you doing?" Jose stopped below her as the donkey continued up the trail and Whiskey followed it.

"Shortcut."

"Please, no. It's slippery and—" Jose jumped forward and caught Kate as her footing slipped and she lost her grip around the wet, smooth tree bark. They both fell in a heap on the muddy path. Whiskey came barreling back down the trail, barking until he reached her. He positioned himself in between Kate and Jose and growled at anyone who took a step toward her.

"Whiskey, buddy. It's okay. Sit— wait, no, don't sit in all this mud. Just, stop. It's..."

William stepped up and reached his hand toward Whiskey. The dog growled, and William backed down the hill. Kate sat up and brushed the fur on his back down. "He's sorry."

William raised an eyebrow.

Kate splashed her hand in a puddle. "I'm sorry, too. This whole thing just feels off." She grabbed a tree and pulled herself to her feet. She tried to brush the mud off, but only managed to smear it down the leg of her cargo pants. Shaking her head, she turned and followed the donkey toward the switchback.

The group hiked on in silence. Jose and his machete resumed the lead, followed by the donkey, then Kate and Whiskey. William and Kara fell further and further behind until Jose and Kate stopped dead in their tracks at the sound of a high-pitched shriek.

"Kara!" Kate sprinted back the way she had come, her feet slipping and sliding down the path. William's jaw hung wide, his eyes glued to Kara, who sat in the middle of the path, legs splayed in front of her, one arm high in the air holding the back half of a snake, the other on the ground clutching the handle of a machete.

"I thought— I grabbed— Snake. It's a damned snake." Kara stared, glassy-eyed, until Jose gently pried the snake's long body from her fingers and flung it into the jungle. "I thought it was a vine, so I grabbed it and swung the knife..."

"That was no vine, *señorita.* That was a boa constrictor. You are lucky you got it before it got you. But now it's dead, and you are not. We need to keep moving, so if we can help you up, please? We're almost there."

The two men pulled Kara up, and together they all started back up the mountain.

"Kate." She felt William's hand on her shoulder and turned. "Look, I know you had good reasons to want to come in here more heavily armed and to skip the stop in Santiago. I'm not sure you weren't right. But I still believe that whatever we do, we need to do it right. If we start taking shortcuts and doing wrong, then we're no better than Diego Guzman. I know he's a monster. I know he's not bound by the law. But we still are. We need to stay true to that."

Kate reached up and squeezed William's hand. Then she wiped the rain from her face and trudged up the path into the mist.

Not long after, the trees thinned, and the group found themselves standing on a narrow ridge, surrounded by clouds. She heard a loud whistle, but in the damp mist, she couldn't tell what direction it came from.

"*Venga!* Come, come. Keep walking 'til you get to me, then we'll move on together."

One by one, the friends crept up the path, the distance between them growing with each step. Kate carefully watched the path at her feet. She could only see a few feet in any direction, so she moved slowly, taking each step only when she could see where she was going. About fifteen paces later, she came upon the group, clustered together around the animals on a small, flat clearing.

"We're almost there. Hear the waterfall? That's where we're going. Be careful from here, the path drops back down off the ridge. It'll be slippery, with loose rock and gravel, but we'll be out of the clouds before you know it."

The group stayed closer together, every stray sound bouncing through the mist and spooking them.

"Jose, have you ever been diving?" Kate shivered in the cool, damp air. "This mist is almost like being underwater. Even the noises are like tank bangs or clanging under water. You hear the muffled sound, but you can't tell what direction it's coming from."

"It's the water droplets in the mist. It disperses the sound waves and they bounce around instead of traveling in a straight line."

"Still creepy."

A cold breeze picked up as they descended down the trail, dropping below the bottom of the mass of clouds. Outside the blanket of cloud cover, the wind picked up from behind them, whipping Kate's curls across her face.

The group finally reached a flat mesa with the forest continuing to rise behind them. Below, a wide stream fed a pool then spilled in a crush of whitewater rapids through a short ravine and then a narrow gap to pour over the cliff. Kate crouched near the center of the rock and cautiously peered across the small wooden bridge that spanned the narrow canyon.

"That's a lot of water."

Jose had tied the donkey just inside the tree line and was emptying its packs. "*Sí*. Right now, it's our rainy season. And this year has been much more rain than normal. But in February and March, when it is dry, this stream slows to just a trickle. That is a much better time to visit." He shrugged and continued pulling out climbing harnesses and handed them out to each of the friends. Then he drew them together into a tight circle. "We are going down the falls for two reasons today. Both of them are important, but neither is as important as all of us coming back alive. That means you listen to me, you do what I say, and you don't do anything stupid. Can I count on you for that?"

Kara and William nodded, then all three of them looked at Kate.

"What?"

"Well, if any of the three of us is more likely to go off-script..." Kara trailed off.

Kate rolled her eyes. "I suppose you're right, but it's not like I have a death wish. Especially since I have to carry him." She hiked her thumb at Whiskey.

"Good point. I sometimes think you value that dog's life more than your own. But he's almost as big as you. Maybe it'd be easier if he rode down with me?"

Kate smiled. "William, he almost bit your hand off like ten minutes ago."

"Aw, he was just watching out for his person. But he's my bud. He'll be fine."

"Actually," Jose hesitated. "I think even though it'll throw her balance off a little more, it'll be less total weight if he rides down with Kate."

As Jose began to strap a harness around Whiskey's chest, he looked up at Kara. "How about we send the two of you down first while I help her get the dog attached so he doesn't get in the way of her belay. You guys can help pull her in. Then I can pull the rope off and just free-climb down.

Kates eyes grew big. "Free climb?"

"Yeah, I've done it hundreds of times. All this gear is for gringos." He laughed and clipped Kara's harness onto the rope. He showed her how to keep tension on the belay and within minutes, she disappeared over the edge of the rock face.

CHAPTER FIFTY

Kate's heart thumped behind her rib cage louder than the water that pounded on the rocks below them. The wide stone apron in front of the cave's mouth stretched the full width of the falls, completely concealed by the wall of water crashing down in front of it. The front edge of the stone was slippery, but as they moved through the wide mouth of the cave into the shelter of its ceiling, the rock at their feet became drier. The space smelled of musty, stagnant air.

Jose's boots dropped to the stone. He slung a heavy bag off his back onto the floor at the back of the cave then pushed the bag's contents to one end. They all slipped out of their harnesses then stuffed them in the bag for safe-keeping.

"Do all of you know how—" Jose's sentence was cut short as Kara pulled a handgun from the bag, checked the magazine, and racked it in one fluid motion.

"I grew up in the slums of Santo Domingo." She shrugged and stuffed the gun in her belt.

Jose held the bag open for Kate and William, as well. He chose a high capacity Glock. Kate picked up a smaller gun and a telescoping baton then tucked both into her pocket. Next she picked up a small knife in a sheath. She sat back against the wall of the cave and called Whiskey.

"Hey, bud, c'mere." She held the sheath up near his nose. He investigated it, sniffing from one end to another, and pausing for Kate to scratch his nose. "Good boy. See, it's okay. It's just me. Now, stay. It's okay, buddy. I'm just gonna pull this out ..." Kate pulled away from the dog and began to slowly remove the knife from its case. His shoulders tightened. His eyes widened. She slipped the knife back into the sheath and the dog relaxed a little. "It's okay, Whiskey. I'm not gonna hurt you. This won't hurt you." She pulled it out again and the dog froze.

Jose's head tilted to the side as he watched.

"Don't bring a dog to a knife fight—at least not this dog," William joked.

Kate hopped to her feet. "He's got PTSD. His handler was killed, and he was stabbed. It's why he was retired. I've been working with him on it, but he's still got issues."

"Poor guy. I hope we won't need any of this."

"That's a nice hope, but the guy coming after us is a piece of work. He'll put up a fight, and we need to be prepared." William slipped a wad of cash into Jose's pocket. "Your fee. Just in case we get separated."

"My job is to get you to this place and back out."

"Your first job is to stay alive."

"Thank you, *señor*. You're too kind, but you don't have anything to worry about. I will, how do you Americans say it? Got your back?"

The two men laughed as Jose picked up two remaining pistols and stashed them in his cargo pockets, then he handed them each a flashlight and pointed his own down a narrow passageway leading deep into the mountain.

"The passage starts out wide and straight, but then it starts to wind as it drops deeper into the mountain. We used to come up here when we were kids. When we were young, we played explorer in many of the caves around here, but not this one. And when we got older, we partied in many of them, too. But this one? No. The old ways may have died generations ago, but this place ... If it really is what they said, it is not a place to mess with. Every couple of generations, there's a story of someone ignoring the warnings and never coming back. I do not know if the stories were true, but it's been many years since someone has disappeared. I do not want to be the cautionary tale."

"So now you tell us?"

Jose shuffled his feet. "I don't really believe in curses or gods. I know the elders told us those stories to make us behave. But this place feels different. I'll stand watch for you in the first bend, but I cannot go further."

Kate stood near the mouth of the tunnel. She held up her flashlight and traced her fingers along the stone wall. Shallow, faded petroglyphs worn by centuries of wind and water surrounded the opening to the passage. She slowly followed the drawings into the passage where, in the protection of the tunnel, the images grew clearer, etched deeper into the stone.

"Guys. These are everywhere. Look."

Jose nodded. "This was a holy place. Whether it's truly the Cave of Origin or just a place the ancients believed was the place where the first man appeared, they worshipped here since the very beginning until they were wiped out. A thousand years or more. It's another reason we didn't mess around with this. Kids are kids, but we were taught to respect the old ways, even if we didn't believe in them."

"We respect them, too." Kate glanced back at Jose, who had guided the others into the tunnel. "And we want to protect them from being used to abuse people now. I think we want the same thing, Jose." She turned and led the group into the passage.

The tunnel was wider at the top than its bottom, with the walls angling gently away from the center. Even as the tunnel narrowed, it felt spacious and safe.

They slowly moved down the dark passage, admiring the stories told by the petroglyphs. Some of the symbols were impossible to understand, but many of the images carved deep into the stone showed stories of the ancient Taíno life. One scene showed a village, its round structures with conical roofs a clear precursor to the tiki huts that dotted the Caribbean resorts today. The scenes showed a squared off building a bit larger than the other huts. Beside the building, the village's shaman stood in front of a group of kneeling tribesmen, holding a tall staff with a loop at the top. In each image where the shaman's staff appeared, a thin drizzle of glittering gold filled the space where the loop had been carved out of the rock.

"Gold was plentiful here before the Spanish arrived." Jose's voice startled Kate in the darkness.

She pulled her fingers from the wall and faced him.

"The people here found it beautiful and used it on jewelry and holy items like that one. But they never thought it had value—not like food or utility items like cooking baskets or canoes. So when the Spanish arrived, the people offered them the beautiful jewelry as a gesture of friendship, thinking them simply trinkets and symbols. They had no idea their trinkets would hold more value than anything else the Spaniards saw. No idea these bracelets and necklaces would lead to their enslavement and the destruction of their culture."

"What one man holds dear..." Kara's fingers flitted to a gold chain around her neck. "What is it about gold that makes men so crazy? It's hardly anything more than a soft rock, anyway."

Kate said, "It may be soft, but I can certainly attest to the fact that it's heavy as hell. It's impractical as a currency. If you ask me, the Spanish and all the Europeans who raped the Caribbean for its gold were idiots, willing to sink whole flotillas of ships for sparkly metal. That said, the gold we recovered for Chuck has certainly helped us secure our home, so I guess we should be thankful that some good can come of it."

"Can't you say that about anything, really?" William asked. "It's not the thing, it's the person behind it. Their intention. Inanimate things have no inherent good or evil. It's the people and how they choose to use the object."

Kate dropped her voice in a deep imitation. "'Hello class, my name is William Jenkins. Welcome to Philosophy 101.'"

They all laughed, their voices echoing off the walls of the tunnel.

CHAPTER FIFTY-ONE

As they rounded a bend in the passage, the space opened up then narrowed again on its journey deeper into the mountain. Kate shined her light up toward the ceiling. The chamber was quite wide at the top, and a high, narrow shelf encircled the perimeter of the room.

"This is as far as I can go." Jose stopped at the bend in the tunnel and set the bag along the far wall. "I don't know how much farther the chamber is." He climbed up onto a large stone, grabbed the lip of the high shelf, then pulled himself up easily, his triceps bulging as he dangled. He swung a leg up and within seconds, he was lying flat on his belly on the ledge. "Pass me that bag?"

Kara hefted the bag and shoved it up the wall. Jose caught the handle on the end and pulled it up. He pushed himself up and sat hunched over to avoid hitting his head on the low rock ceiling above him. He removed a small black cylinder with two rows of small holes from a side pocket of the bag and screwed it onto the end of his pistol.

"So much for the quiet villager cover. Jose, you're a badass."

He shook his head. "Not really. I just did a couple years in the military before coming back to the village to help *Abuelo* with the shop. And I have no plans to go deaf defending you all." He grinned and lay back down on the shelf looking down the pistol's sights at the entrance tunnel. "I'll keep watch here. What's the phrase? Fish in a barrel? I'll make sure your sister and the leader go on through, but if he's got anyone else with him, they won't get past me." He lay the long canvas bag along the edge of the ledge to guard his body. "Be careful, and good luck."

Kate raised her flashlight then stepped into the dark tunnel. "Stay close together, move slowly, and let's look before we leap, okay? I don't believe any of the superstitions, but I bet the Taíno didn't leave this place's protection to their gods, either. I'm sure they'll have—" She stopped short. Stretching her arm out to her side to block the way forward, she trained her flashlight beam at a pile of bones lying to the side of the tunnel a few yards ahead.

"Traps?" Kara finished Kate's sentence, her voice shaky.

"Traps." Kate shined her light up the wall and across to the other side. Above them, the tunnel's ceiling was hollowed out, and a huge boulder mounted to a thick post hung in the cavity. "Stay back..." She flashed her light along the floor and stopped on a thin, straight crack spanning the width of the tunnel. "It's gotta be a pressure trigger. Step on it, and the pendulum drops, smashes into you, and boom."

"It's the full width of the tunnel. How do we get past it?"

They examined the walls and ceiling. The tunnel was too wide to suspend their bodies by pressing against the walls. There were no ledges to creep along. There was just no clear way past the pendulum.

"The shamans had to have a way to get by."

"Maybe they were into sacrifices. Do you think they'd trigger it, then run past behind it?"

Kate picked up a skull lying on the hard stone floor.

"Kate, that used to be a person. You can't—"

A massive whoosh cut Kara off as the boulder swung down through the center of the tunnel just feet in front of them. It swung up into the deep hollow in the ceiling opposite them, paused, then swung back toward them. They leapt back, and the pendulum swung back up into the tunnel's ceiling and caught above them, latching back into place with a thick snap.

"Impressive." William's low whistle echoed off the stone walls. "Look at this. The stone doesn't go all the way to the floor. It's measured to hit an average-height man in the torso. We can get through by crawling under it."

"Under it? I'm not going anywhere near that thing."

"William, that's brilliant. Of course. The shaman would know exactly how low the rock would hit, and he'd easily be able to crawl below it! And until battery-operated flashlights got strong enough, no one coming in here would have been able to see it in time to avoid getting hit. Whiskey, stay!" Before anyone could react, Kate dropped onto her belly and shimmied like a lizard across the floor. She kept her head down and the pendulum swung above her, clearing the top of her back by two feet.

"Dammit, Kate!"

"I'm fine. Someone had to test it out. You guys will get past it fine. The only challenge will be getting Whiskey to crawl low enough to stay under the stone. Kara, hold onto his harness while I try to give him directions, okay? William, keep your light pointed at me?"

Kate watched from across the span of the trap as Kara and Whiskey looked at each other. "Whiskey, lie down."

The dog dropped down to his belly. Kate dropped to her belly to match him, she looked into his eyes across the length of tunnel.

"Whiskey, stay low. Now, crawl. Come to me, boy." Kate pulled herself closer with her arms, staying low to the floor and hoping the dog would do the same. He started to stand, but Kara pushed him back down at the shoulders.

"I'm not sure this is going to work. If he freaks out in the middle and stands up, he's done for. I'm gonna go across with him." Kara dropped to her belly with one arm draped across Whiskey's shoulders. She held the dog low, and began to inch toward the trigger. They developed a rhythm, but Whiskey froze when they hit the trigger. The floor of the tunnel slipped down a few inches, and the boulder whizzed above them. Kara started forward, and their full weight was over the trigger as it flew back and latched back into place in the ceiling.

"Look, it's finished. It's not coming down again. William, get on the ground and try to come across. I bet if we keep this trigger pushed down, we can pass back and forth without any problem."

William lowered himself down and shimmied onto the trigger plate. The boulder stayed safely tucked away in the ceiling even with the additional weight on the trigger. As soon as they knew it was safe, Kara released Whiskey and the dog jumped up and ran to Kate.

Kara and William carefully crawled forward, gradually rising up, then stepping off the trigger plate on the other side of the trap. She heard a short grinding noise as the trigger released and the stone rose back into place.

"That's amazing. The shaman who knew how this

worked wouldn't even have to crawl. He could just throw something onto the pressure plate heavy enough to trigger the boulder, let it swing back into place, and then just walk across. It's brilliant."

"We need to disarm this for good in case Lucia tries to come through here." Kara's voice was filled with concern for her sister. Kate crouched down close to the floor and pressed the trigger plate. The huge stone swooped toward them and then back into place as Kate knelt to hold the trigger down.

"Throw me all the stones you can find. We can stack them up on here so it can't release." William and Kara collected stones and rolled them over to Kate. When she had a heavy pile of them stacked along the side of the passage, she carefully crept off the trigger plate and sat on the floor of the tunnel beside it. They waited a moment, then Kate stepped back onto the plate. The stones held firmly in place. The trap was disarmed.

They trained their lights forward and continued on down the tunnel.

"Do you think that's it?"

"I doubt it. I know if I was trying to protect the place where I believed all life originated, the resting place of the holy spirits that represented that life, I'd have backups to my backups, wouldn't you?" Kate waved her light around the circumference of the tunnel as she slowly proceeded down the passageway. Up ahead in the distance, she noticed the tunnel widening. They cautiously approached, and gasped as the tunnel gave way to a massive chamber.

"I can't even see the other side."

"Hang on. There's a torch mounted on either side of the passage." Kate smelled the sulfur as Kara struck a match. With a loud whoosh, the torch behind her burst into a bright flame. Then the fire followed a thin channel in the wall, and in sequence, a series of torches lit up at even intervals along the wall to their left, stopping at the opposite side of the huge cavern.

Kara lit the torch on the opposite side and within moments, the entire space was lit in flickering torchlight.

"It's beautiful," Kate whispered as she slowly stepped forward. The lower six feet of the walls were smooth and covered with faded painted scenes depicting every imaginable aspect of Taíno life. Village scenes, crops, canoes on the ocean, mountains. Kate spun around to admire the rich history contained on these walls, but the sudden motion made her slip.

"Kate, watch out!" Kara screamed.

As she fell, she noticed the deep chasm widening behind her.

CHAPTER FIFTY-TWO

"WE KNEW there'd be more traps."

Kate crouched at the edge of the chasm, still working to catch her breath. She'd nearly fallen into the pit, its false floor falling away behind her when she'd backed onto a trigger stone. She'd barely managed to shift her weight and jump away in time. They peered into it with their flashlights. Bones littered the bottom ten feet below.

Kara's voice shook. "Okay, so no walking anywhere without testing the stone ahead before you step on it. And just to be safe, let's post Whiskey at the entrance so he doesn't accidentally set something off."

Kate pushed herself to her feet and called Whiskey over to the dark arch between the torches. "Whiskey, sit. Guard."

His ears pivoted forward and he stared back down the dark passageway.

Kate turned back toward the cavern. "Y'all, look." She pointed at the smooth stone tiles paving the floor of the cavern. "The one I stepped on that triggered the trap? It's a different color than the rest. It's subtle, but you can see a few of them from here." She pulled the baton from her belt loop and snapped it out with a flick of her wrist.

"Damn! Remind me not to get on your bad side, girl!" Kara muttered as Kate whipped the long weapon in front of her.

Kate approached a slightly darker floor tile. She stood on the tile beside it and gently pressed the tip of the baton to the stone. She felt the stone give, but it wasn't until she put more pressure on it that the trigger engaged. Kate screamed as the stone beneath her feet gave way.

"Kate!"

Kate clung to the edge of the pit by her fingers. William and Kara raced to the edge, grabbed a wrist each, and pulled her back out.

"Looks like we need to watch a little more closely."

Kate raised an eyebrow at William. "Hey, can you guys lower me down there? I dropped my baton."

"Are you kidding?" William flashed his light into the pit. Only a few bones were scattered on the bottom, and a skull that looked like it was from a large rodent.

Kate peered down into the pit. "It's not as deep as the last one. I probably wouldn't have even broken my leg if I fell all the way down."

"Still not going to risk falling in any more of them. But—" William sighed as Kate scrambled over the edge and dropped into the bottom of the pit. She tucked the weapon back into her belt loop, reached her hands high over her head, and jumped up. She caught the lip of stone with the tips of her fingers. William clasped her by the wrists and pulled her back up.

Kate stepped over to the next trigger stone. This time, she straddled two adjacent stones as she pushed the trigger. When the stone beneath her left foot started to shift, she bounced to safety on the right. She continued around the room and tripped three more pit traps before she declared the floor safe.

The three friends came together in the center of the big room and finally paused to take it all in. They were encircled by the entire story of a Taíno people they'd thought was completely lost to history.

And set on a wide altar on the opposite wall stood a large golden statue that could only be the Taíno god Yúcahu.

CHAPTER FIFTY-THREE

Diego Guzman shoved past a thick palm bush onto the open stone. The crash of the waterfall below him obscured the sound of the followers crashing through the brush behind him. More than once during this whole ordeal, he had wished he could collect the zemís by himself. People sometimes proved useful, whether as sacrifices to keep the rest of them in line, or to fight their way through the series of defenses the elders had certainly put in place to protect the Origin. But even as he'd been able to follow the clumsy trail the abomination and the rest of them had hacked through his precious jungle, the idiots who followed behind him were far more hassle than he thought they might be worth.

When he spotted the little donkey tied to a tree a few meters away from the mesa, he knew they were close. He was surprised to discover no ropes led down the cliff face, though. He snapped his fingers at one of the boys in the group behind him.

"Here, *señor*." The boy ducked out of a coil of rope and began to tie the end off around a thick tree near the edge.

One by one the men dropped over the rock's face and lowered themselves to the flat rock behind the water. Then the lone woman with the group clutched the rope.

"You have them?"

Guzman seethed. How dare this woman question him. But it was not yet time. He still needed her, so he patted the small satchel slung across his chest, then followed her down the mountain.

He saw fresh scuff marks all over the stone leading from the edge near the water to the mouth of the tunnel. Scattered among the muddy boot prints and streaks where they'd dragged their gear, he also spotted the thick paw prints of the damned dog. He racked his gun and jammed it into its holster, fired up his high-powered lantern, then stormed into the tunnel.

Footsteps echoed as the group clamored in behind him, the woman in the lead.

He hurried down the tunnel as it narrowed slightly, then opened into a wider, more open space around a bend. He stomped through the little chamber and continued on down the passage as it tightened. He heard the woman's heavy breathing behind him. The rest of the group, carrying the gear and weapons, had fallen farther behind, but Guzman paid them no mind. They'd eventually catch up and serve their purpose.

A faint, sharp crack echoed behind him in the tunnel, and Guzman spun, slamming into the small woman who followed him. The two fumbled, then Guzman pushed her out of the way. He pulled his gun out and nearly shot his own man as he sprinted toward Guzman from the small bend.

"They're down! Two men down!" Guzman shoved past the man and flashed his light around the little chamber where two bodies lay crumpled in the center of the tunnel. He ran back the way he'd come but found no sign of an assailant. Whoever took out his men must have already run outside to safety, and chasing him would just slow him down. He stomped back down the tunnel, pausing to strip any useful gear from the two bodies, then kicking them to the side.

"Here. Carry this." He shoved an armload of gear at the panting man, then stormed deeper into the mountain.

He swooped past a string of skulls and bones, heathens clearly struck down in their misbegotten attempt to desecrate the temple of Atabey. He nearly tripped on a stack of rocks piled near the bones, then he stumbled on an odd spot of the tunnel floor that was practically as abrupt as if a step had been deliberately cut from the stone. He finally whipped around another bend in the passage and saw a light up ahead.

Guzman stopped short and held his hand up for

the remaining woman and man to hold in place. A low growl echoed in the tunnel. He slipped back around the bend.

"It's just ahead, and that dog is standing in the way." He pushed Lucia around the bend. "It knows you, so you go first."

Lucia crept up the tunnel, her hand stretched out in front of her. "Hey, Whiskey. You know me. It's okay." The dog's tail thumped slowly on the stone, then beat faster as Lucia drew closer. When she reached him and he licked her hand, Guzman and the other man drew up the tunnel and slipped around the sides of the chamber to flank the three people staring up at the altar on the back wall.

Guzman noted the holes scattered across the floor. Then, without a sound, he darted across the chamber and jumped on the back of the person closest to him. He held a gun to the side of the drag queen's head and screamed. "Everyone get down!"

CHAPTER FIFTY-FOUR

KATE SPUN around to see Diego Guzman clinging to Kara's back, a gun held to the side of her head.

Lucia's screams filled the chamber. "Nooooooo!"

"Shut up, woman."

"You said—"

"I said what I needed to say for your cooperation."

"But that's my—"

"Your what? Your brother? Your sister? I don't know what it is, but it's an abomination that will be my pleasure to kill."

William's attention was on Kara and Guzman, but Kate spotted movement and whirled. Creeping toward William was the sheriff from Constanza — the man who had refused to investigate their claim against Guzman — a gun in his hand. Kate charged, tackling him with a shoulder to his gut. The gun bounced from his hand and clattered across the tile then down into a nearby pit trap.

William spun around. "What—" He ran toward Kate, but stopped as Lucia screamed.

"Everyone freeze, or I'll blow this thing to bits!" Lucia stood between the altar and a deep pit. She held the heavy golden zemí of Yúcahu over her head in one hand, and a small revolver in the other. "I'll do it."

Guzman dropped to the floor and stepped back, his aim still on Kara's head. The sheriff glanced over at Lucia, distracted long enough for Kate to pound his temple with the handle of her baton. His body flopped to the stone floor.

She straddled his limp form, pointed her gun across the room at Guzman, and looked up at Lucia. "Lucia, set the zemí down, we've—"

"You've got nothing. You think you know everything, don't you? You people always think your way is best. Helpless Lucia needs to finish Bob's work." She spit into the deep pit in front of her feet. "For centuries, white European pigs have desecrated the memory of my people. Declared us extinct. Studied us like animals. I've had enough." She gently stepped around the pit and slipped an arm around Guzman.

"I met Bob for the first time not long after my Diego was ripped from my arms."

Kara gasped and fell to her knees.

"Yes, *sister*. This man is like a son to me. His father

was my first love. My only love. He lived up in the mountains, in a village not far from here. He taught me everything about our heritage. About how the Spanish raped our women and enslaved our men, taking our people to the point of extinction. He told me how the spirit of Atabey would one day return, gathering her children from the four horizons to avenge our people." She held her hand out, and Guzman passed her the heavy canvas bag.

"Diego was just a boy when his father was taken home to Atabey. Then his whore mother pulled herself out of the brothel and took him from me."

She returned the figure of Yúcahu to the altar. "I swore that day I'd get him back and together we would restore the Taíno people. I hid an ancient tribal staff in his grandmother's things. I knew that woman would latch onto any heritage that would make her boy more than just the son of a whore.

"For my part, I found an ambitious American professor and began to fill his imagination with stories of the lost zemís. He took far longer than I expected to track them down. You all were much more efficient." As she spoke, she removed each zemí, one by one, caressing them gently and placing them in the niche to either side of Yúcahu.

When she was finished, the line of zemís formed a triangle, with two tiny zemís on the ends, slightly taller ones standing beside them, pointing to the largest one in the center. Guzman joined her at the altar and took her hand. As they both turned to face the room, his gaze remained fixed on the golden idols.

"Now that the gods have returned to their home, we can bring our people back and rule them together."

Guzman's cheeks tightened, and his head began to slowly shake back and forth. "No. No, mother. No woman has ever ruled the Taíno people, and no woman ever will. I am grateful to Atabey for your provision. For restoring my life, giving me purpose. For teaching me my rightful place as Cacique of the true Taíno people. But no woman will ever challenge her for her place as the queen of our people. I return you to Atabey." He stepped back, raised his gun, and fired.

Kara's scream filled the chamber. Lucia's body tumbled into the pit while her sister fell blindly to her knees at its sharp edge.

Time slowed to a crawl as Kate watched Guzman lower his gun toward Kara. The muscles in his hand tightened as he began to squeeze the trigger. Then his body flew backward, his blood splattering against the painting of a woman planting corn.

Kate turned to see William lowering his gun and falling to his knees. She hurried to him then rested her hand on his back. "Are you okay?"

He nodded and waved her toward Kara. "I'll be fine. She won't."

Kate knelt beside Kara, who wailed into the deep,

wide pit. It was deeper than the light from the torches could reach, and for that, Kate said a word of thanks. To God. To Atabey. To whoever had dug the traps in the first place. Kate was grateful Kara couldn't see the broken body of the sister she'd so recently reconciled with and who had ultimately betrayed her.

William caught his breath, then pulled Kate off to the side. He nodded toward the sheriff, a weak groan rising from the man's motionless form on the other side of the room.

Kate followed his glance. "What are we gonna do with him?"

William shrugged. "Well, we can't take him with us, but we can't very well leave him here, either."

"I guess we could drag him past the pendulum and leave him to find his way out? By the time he gets down the mountain, we'll be long gone, and there's no way he's gonna tell anyone about all this. But we need to deal with this first." She nodded toward Guzman's body.

William agreed, and together, they carried Guzman's body across the room then dropped it into the deepest pit trap.

"Hey, you might wanna keep the noise down in here. The neighbors might start complaining." Jose's voice bounced from the tunnel as he bounded into the chamber, then froze. "Look out!"

William and Kate both spun around as Jose

whipped his gun up and fired. The sheriff's body dropped over the edge of a pit just a few feet from them. Kate fell to her knees. Whiskey bounded up and sat beside her, his heavy body leaning into her. Tears streamed down her cheeks, and she buried her face in his fur and cried.

CHAPTER FIFTY-FIVE

The four of them stood in front of the altar, all five zemís lined up side by side.

Kate broke the silence. "I know we had planned to turn them over to the authorities, but that was before. It feels like they really belong here, don't you think?"

"Seems right." William squeezed her hand and turned back toward the tunnel.

Jose turned to Kara. "Our villagers will block this chamber off and stand as guardians over this holy place. You have my word – no one will ever know what lies here or what happened today. Your sister's grave will never be desecrated." Kara bowed her head to him. She stepped over to the pit and whispered a few words, kissed her fingers, then blew the kiss into the bottom of the pit.

Kate and Jose walked to the arched exit, and all four of them paused to take in both the beauty and the horror of the ancient chamber, a place that gives life and brings death.

She whistled to Whiskey, and the ragged group made their way through the tunnel, carefully resetting the pendulum after dragging the bodies of Guzman's two assistants into a pile with the other, older remains.

It took nearly two hours for the return trip to Jose's truck, but the rain had passed. The sun was shining, the air was cool, and a soft breeze rustled through the leaves. Jose dropped the three friends at the airstrip and within minutes, William's small plane was in the air, pointed back to their home in the Conch Republic.

Three days later, the afternoon sun sparkled on the rippling water as Kate dipped her paddle from one side to the other. The kayak cut quietly through the clear surface. Schools of tiny fish darted back and forth above the sandy bottom as the shadow of her little boat passed over them.

When she drew close to the dock, the breeze shifted, blowing the delicious scent of turkey and nutmeg and butter across the salty cove. She climbed onto the faded boards, pulled the kayak up onto the dock, then leaned it against the piling to dry out.

She bounded up the steps to the deck. Everyone – even the couple she'd met across the lane from Babette's – was gathered around tables, chattering and carrying platters and trays from the kitchen to where

Patti had covered two long tables with butcher paper and set up a massive Thanksgiving buffet.

Chuck tapped his glass with a knife, but the low drone of voices continued. Kate bounced up beside him, winked, and grabbed a conch shell from the bar. She pressed it to her lips. The low wail caught everyone's attention and silence fell quickly over the crowd.

Chuck cleared his throat. "Everyone, I'd like to welcome you Shark Key Campground and Marina's annual Thanksgiving Feast. For those of you who are new this year, this is my way of welcoming you to the Keys, of showing hospitality to anyone in our community who doesn't have a place to go or who can't afford a holiday dinner, and of saying thanks for all the blessings I've been given.

"I was born and raised in this place, and never more than this year have I realized just how special it is. I'm grateful for each and every one of you who have helped me keep it in the family, and who give your everything for the family we've built here. I know we're not blood, but I think we've all learned the family we choose can sometimes be stronger than the one we're born into.

"For those of you who are new, welcome. For those of you returning, we're thankful you made it home safely. And for those of you who've given that extra little bit for someone else this year, know your gift is accepted gratefully and with love.

"Now, grab a plate and eat up everyone! Feast's on me!"

The crowd cheered, and a line formed at the top of the long buffet table. Kara pulled Kate over to a table where William and Michelle sat waiting for the line to die down. She wrapped Kate in a hug, then rested her massive hand on William's shoulder.

"There's nothing I can ever say or do to repay you."

William shook his head. "There's nothing you have to say or do. And we would do it all again without even thinking about it. We're family."

Kara's eyes misted over. "You're better than family." She pulled them all together into a group hug. "Now let's get some turkey."

THE END

THANK YOU

Thank you for reading LOST RELICS. I hope you enjoyed joining Kate and the Shark Key family on this adventure.

If you'd like another quick adventure, check out the prequel, *Lost Palm*. It takes place the summer before *Lost Key* and *Lost Relics*, and finds Kate and Chuck in the Keys backcountry where they run into just a little more trouble than they bargained for.

Lost Palm is exclusively available (totally free) for my VIP Reader Group.

To start reading, just join my VIP Readers at chrisnilesbooks.com/vip.

AUTHOR'S NOTE

When Mark and I traveled to the Dominican Republic for our anniversary last year, I knew I wanted to set a book there. The people we met, the food we ate, and the beautiful landscape stuck with me. So when I came across an article about how DNA mapping was helping to reconnect the indigenous people on Hispaniola with their Taíno heritage, I dove headlong into the most interesting parts of the Internet (a welcome change from most of it, right?).

While the golden zemís scattered around the Caribbean are all fiction, the stories of Atabey, Yucahu and Guacar, and the lesser gods they created are all part of the Taíno belief system. As I approached the daunting task of weaving the legends and history of these proud people into a fictional adventure thriller, I knew I was running the risk of stepping on some toes. I hope that I've lightly danced through the challenge and presented the Taíno people and the other indigenous cultures Kate and her crew encountered with respect and in the favorable light they deserve.

My thanks go out to everyone who helped me take this novel from a grain of an idea in my imagination to a full-fledged story available to adventure lovers everywhere. Any errors or disrespect are unintentional and are wholly my responsibility.

ABOUT THE AUTHOR

Chris(tine) Niles has been telling stories since she was a lying kid. Now she's figuring out how to make a career of it. Because she likes to eat, she tried for about fifteen minutes to write romance. But her characters kept killing each other, so she switched to thrillers.

Her heart is buried deep in the hammock north of Sugarloaf Key, and you can only find it from a kayak. Despite that, her body lives in northeastern Indiana with her husband, two adult daughters, and a hungry four-legged sack of fur named Franklin.

You can find out more at chrisnilesbooks.com.

ALSO BY CHRIS NILES

The Shark Key Adventures

LOST PALM

An extraordinary prize lies hidden in the remote Florida Keys backcountry.

When Kate Kingsbury finds a map tucked in the pages of a rare Hemingway novel, she sets off to discover a little more about the islands around her new home.

But in an instant, her sunny adventure becomes a dangerous fight for her life.

Can Kate survive the threat lurking among the mangroves?

LOST PALM is exclusively available to members of my VIP Reader Group. Join today for free at chrisnilesbooks.com/VIP

BOOK 1: LOST KEY

It only takes a moment to lose everything.

When a corrupt real-estate developer sets his sights on Kate Kingsbury's marina in the Florida Keys, Kate and her neighbors must band together to save Shark Key. Their only hope is a lost treasure stolen from the infamous Al Capone. Can they find what's been hidden for almost a century before time runs out?

BOOK 2: LOST RELICS

In the aftermath of a devastating hurricane, five long lost indigenous idols are linked to a series of missing teenagers in the Dominican Republic. And when Kate Kingsbury joins the search for the ancient zemís, the killer sets his sights on her.

Can Kate find the ancient idols before he kills again?

BOOK 3: LOST FLEET

A shocking secret lies at the bottom of the Caribbean Sea.

When her journalism mentor is killed in a horrific plane crash off the coast of Key West, Kate Kingsbury travels to New York to lay him to rest.

At his funeral, she learns he might have found proof that a Chinese fleet arrived in the Caribbean nearly a hundred years before the Europeans. As she follows his leads, she meets the charming Brian Yim, whose uncle — a powerful Chinese oil magnate — is searching for the fleet, too.

Is Brian searching for the truth, or is he a mole for his uncle? And will Kate live long enough to find out?

BOOK 4: LOST GEMS

The hunt is on.

When a young mother disappears from Shark Key without a trace, Kate and her friends must answer one question: what's she running from?

But after a Columbian cartel targets her six-year-old son, her dark secrets come tumbling down around him, and Kate must risk everything to protect the boy and unravel the woman's web of lies.

This edge-of-your-seat adventure will lead Kate from Boca to Bogota, dragging her deep into an underbelly of the Caribbean few visitors ever see. And she'll have to call on some unexpected allies in order to make it out alive.

The Anna Mitchell International Thriller Series:

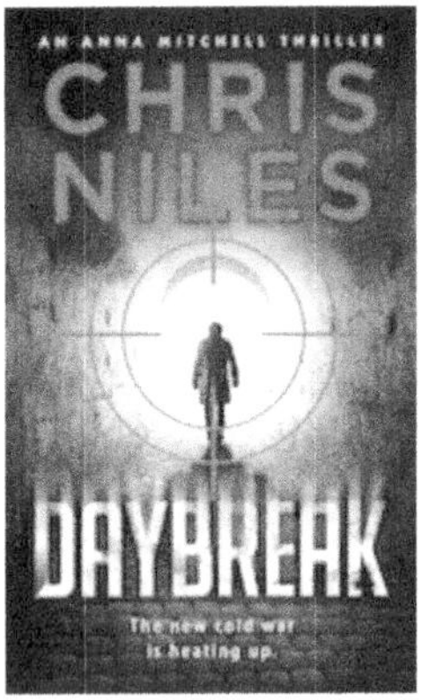

DAYBREAK

The new cold war is heating up.

Russian-backed terrorist Sasha Volkov plans to launch a series of attacks on American soil that will plunge the world into chaos. And only former CIA operative Anna Mitchell can stop him.

But when Anna uncovers a secret about her own past that ties her to Volkov, she must make an impossible choice: learn the truth about herself, or save innocent American lives.

Learn more at chrisnilesbooks.com

Made in the USA
Las Vegas, NV
30 November 2022

60782574R00215